MIRROR, MIRROR

MIRROR, MIRROR

Stella Whitelaw

Severn House Large Print
London & New York

This first large print edition published in Great Britain 2007 by
SEVERN HOUSE LARGE PRINT BOOKS LTD of
9-15 High Street, Sutton, Surrey, SM1 1DF.
First world regular print edition published 2006 by
Severn House Publishers, London and New York.
This first large print edition published in the USA 2007 by
SEVERN HOUSE PUBLISHERS INC., of
595 Madison Avenue, New York, NY 10022.

British Library Cataloguing in Publication Data

Whitelaw, Stella
  Mirror mirror. - Large print ed.
  1. Life change events - Fiction 2. Breach of promise -
Fiction 3. Psychological fiction 4. Large type books
  I. Title
  823.9'14[F]

  ISBN-13: 978-0-7278-7618-8

All Severn House titles are printed on acid-free paper.

Printed and bound in Great Britain by
MPG Books Ltd, Bodmin, Cornwall.

One

The November afternoon that Aunt Stasi took Gina and Lindsie for a walk along the Embankment and over Westminster Bridge shaped the rest of their lives.

Gina walked demurely at first, lost in a corridor of misty coldness, her thoughts peering into a crystal ball that mirrored hazy promises of wealth and power. They said she would be rich one day. There was a tension in the biting air that she was too young to grasp or understand.

Big Ben loomed like a giant finger pointing to the sky, its gilded spire glinting in the weak sunlight. Gina broke into a skip alongside her older cousin, making the most of the unexpected excursion and all the excitement and noise of the busy river traffic ploughing the muddy water.

Aunt Stasi stopped in the middle of Westminster Bridge and took off her red velvet hat, letting her fair hair blow out of its careful Knightsbridge bouffant. She had an unconnected look to her face as if she'd left herself somewhere else, her eyes quite blank.

'Take Gina home now,' she said to Lindsie. 'You'll find money for a taxi in my handbag.' She handed the burgundy suede pouch to her bewildered daughter. Lindsie was eleven, going on twelve.

'Are you going somewhere different?' Lindsie asked, frowning. 'Can't we come?'

'Pick a driver with a nice face,' said Aunt Stasi. She turned to Gina and touched her hair. 'Sweet girl,' she said distantly.

Aunt Stasi climbed over the parapet of the bridge and sat for a few moments with her legs dangling into space. Gina watched without comprehension. It seemed an odd thing to do.

Almost silently, with no more than a wounded sigh, Aunt Stasi let herself go and fell into the swiftly running ebb tide of the grey river below, right into the path of a string of coal-laden barges.

Arms and silken legs thrashed for a moment in the churning wash, then disappeared.

Gina blinked, biting her nail through her gloves.

'Mummy! Mummy...' Lindsie cried.

Gina would never forget the sound of her cousin screaming and screaming or the sight of Aunt Stasi's hat bobbing on the water like a crushed strawberry.

6

Gina stared into the water, as she was to stare into a stagnant lake many years later.

A crowd gathered in seconds, devouring the scene. Gina leaned further over the parapet, expecting to see Aunt Stasi swimming to the bank. The siren of a police launch began to wail from a distance.

'Careful now, lassie. We don't want you falling in, too.'

A kindly policewoman took them home to the house in Cranbourne Square. Lindsie was crying, her face blotched and red. It was such a shock. No one could talk about it. No one tried to explain to the two children. Grandfather Jordan came and went with an ashen face. Lindsie quietened down when Betsy served them tea in the dining room and was calmed with her favourite jam and home-made scones, making little gulping noises between each hesitant mouthful.

'There, there,' said Betsy to each girl in turn. 'Eat your tea now. You'll need your strength.'

Gina could not eat. She let her ice cream melt on the plate and then chopped up the mound of raspberry jelly till the pieces floated like crimson icebergs on a pool of white. The bits of jelly looked like Aunt Stasi's hat, and she stirred them till they too disappeared.

Aunt Stasi had done this dying thing, which meant they would not see her again.

How could she be there one day, so happy and laughing in her lovely sweet-smelling dresses, flying around London, doing things with Lindsie in tow, then without warning, she was not there at all? Did it mean that she too, Gina thought, would one day do this dying thing? And Grandfather Jordan? Oh no, not Grandfather Jordan. That would be unbearable. A clammy coldness crept along her skin.

'I think I'm going to be sick,' she said quite clearly to Betsy.

That night, Gina walked. It was the first time ever. She rose from her bed and, in her bare feet and rose-embroidered nightgown, walked along the nursery landing and down the stairs to the main bedrooms.

She opened the door to her grandfather's bedroom, then after a few moments, closed it. She moved silently towards her cousin's bedroom from which there was the sound of sobbing, but Gina did not really hear it.

The night world was empty and her traumatized mind found refuge in this dislocation. She drifted like a moth without light, flitting soundlessly.

They found her in the early hours of the morning, curled up on the stairs, cold and stiff. No one told her that she had walked. Nor did she find out that sleep held a different music until many years later when her existence was again collapsing around her.

★ ★ ★

Jordan Conway had told Gina many times that he was born at the turn of the century, just before the old Queen died. There was electric light in the house in Cranbourne Square by then and flowered porcelain water closets had been installed on every floor. There was even a lumbersome system of central heating with huge cast iron radiators. But Jordan was born in a big brass-knobbed bed in the first-floor bedroom with a fire burning in an open fireplace, the bed warmed with a stone bottle filled with hot water.

There was still a washstand with a large porcelain jug and basin in the corner of the room. Young Master Jordan had the debris of his first journey washed off in that bowl. Years later the same bowl and jug were used for flower arrangements at Gina's wedding.

Gina had always lived in the imposing late-Georgian house standing in a quiet, tree-lined square in Belgravia. The bay windows either side of the classically proportioned porch extended to the first floor, with two more floors above. A flight of marble steps led to the white stone architraves and columns of the carved porch, and another flight led downwards to the basement area behind ironwork railings.

The interior of the house stayed the same for decades with dark and heavy Victorian furniture in mahogany and oak, all through

Gina's childhood and adolescence. The centrepiece of the basement kitchen was a huge black range with baking and roasting ovens and a hot closet to warm plates. A kitchen dresser was loaded with an elegant dinner service. Gina loved the copper pans and jelly moulds that hung, well polished and gleaming, on the walls. The staff scuttled up and down the stairs all day with coal and meals.

The Conways were a shipping family, following Brunel's *Great Britain*, the first steamship to cross the Atlantic Ocean, with a fleet of their own ships. At first it was freighters, then medium-tonnage passenger ships. The huge oil tankers were to come much later. Jordan was immensely proud of Conway Lines.

'We're among the first, Cunard then Conway,' he often told Gina. 'Two great shipping lines. Be proud of your name and your heritage.'

Grandfather Jordan found time to talk to her, brought gifts from foreign places, told her tales of his travels. She had known no other home than this big house. Her mother, Aveline, was not a homemaker, nor did she marry Gina's father, Royce Quentin, the famous explorer. Aveline and Royce spent the years chasing personal dreams deep in Africa and Mexico, leaving their small daughter to live with her grandfather in

Cranbourne Square. She often wondered if her parents ever remembered her at all. They seemed surprised to see her when they returned, both tall, suntanned and handsome, slightly bemused that this small winsome creature was something to do with them.

Gina loved the house and her grandfather, and Betsy, her mother's personal maid, and the two parlourmaids and scullery maid, even the stiff-necked butler, the cook and the chauffeur. They were her family, caring for the little girl in that big house. She went to a small private school, taken every day by car, brought home early each afternoon. Sometimes Betsy took her to the park, but it was going out with Aunt Stasi that she liked best. Aunt Stasi was fun and flighty, they said. Now Aunt Stasi was in a cedar box. They had found her, wet and bedraggled, washed up on a sandbank.

Lindsie came to live at number nineteen Cranbourne Square after the death of her mother. Her father, Oscar Morgan, had turned up after the funeral, thin and long-haired, tapping the belt of his black leather jacket with restless fingers. He barely noticed his daughter, forlornly standing like a stone effigy in a corner of the drawing room.

'So you're all right here, aren't you?' he said.

11

Perhaps he had been thinking of happier times when he and Stasi had eloped against Jordan's wishes; when his jazz band had been a success and they toured the world. He certainly hadn't been thinking of Lindsie and she knew it.

'You weren't there,' said Lindsie mutinously. 'And you never wrote. Not never once.'

'Letters,' he grumbled. 'I don't write letters.'

'Best that she comes and lives with us,' Gina heard Betsy telling Cook. 'She'll be properly looked after. Go to a proper school and all. That father of hers is jazz mad.'

Gina hardly knew her Uncle Oscar. He was more of a sound than a person. There were records of his band around in the house but no one played them any more.

Perhaps it would be good having Lindsie to live with them, even though she was older and different. Lindsie was lumpy and not as much fun as Aunt Stasi. She got upset about things easily, like wanting to stay in the guest bedroom on the first floor next to Grandfather and not move up to the nursery floor.

'I'm not a baby,' she protested.

Gina pressed her nose against the front bay window to watch the road for the moment when the dark Daimler would turn into Cranbourne Square and proceed towards the house.

'Grandfather, Grandfather,' she called, reaching the front door before the butler. He stood back, folding away his dignity, allowing her to struggle with the heavy doorknob.

Jordan swept the little girl up into his arms and hugged her. 'Darling girl,' he said, giving her a whiskery kiss, dreading the thought that one day he would lose her too, to some stranger, some man.

His wife had died in the process of giving birth to the second of his daughters, Stasi. He did not think the exchange had been fair. Stasi had been a difficult child to bring up, wayward and unstable, crying for hours on end till her little face was indelibly puckered and nurses left in despair. She had not improved with adolescence, chasing a wild life, then leaping into an unstable marriage with an unsuitable spouse. Now, she too had gone, of her own accord and no one knew why. Oscar was only waiting around for the pickings of what was left of Stasi's money.

'Tell me about your ships today,' Gina said, tugging him into the formal drawing room. Nothing in it had been changed. Glass covered Victorian ornaments cluttered the mantelpiece; classical overstuffed sofas strewn with richly patterned tapestry cushions were pulled up before the open grate. Flames flickered. 'Where did they go?'

'Our ships, you mean,' said Jordan, 'Conway Shipping Line is going to be yours one

13

day. I've no son and Aveline and that explorer of hers are too busy gallivanting around the world to ever produce one, so you'll inherit it all. You're going to be a very rich young woman.'

Jordan loved this little girl more than his two striking daughters. Aveline and Stasi had always been remote from him, growing up at young ladies' boarding schools, being finished expensively in Europe while he worked all hours modernizing and expanding the shipping line.

Gina was not listening. She did not understand what rich meant. She knew more about oceans and currents and tonnage. 'I want to know where they have been,' she said eagerly. 'Did any of them cross the Atlantic Ocean today?'

'Many oceans, all over the world, Gina. Australia, Barbados, Bermuda. Let's get the globe and I'll show you the routes. Now this is the route of the banana boats. Imagine all those bananas coming to England for your tea.'

They pored over maps, spun the globe, ate an evening meal together in the panelled dining room where the butler still measured the place settings and served Gina with as much dignity as if she were a grown up young lady. Gina was allowed to stay up and keep her grandfather company. Jordan liked it that way and saw no harm as long as she was in bed by eight o'clock and had an after-noon rest.

A place was laid for Lindsie at the table now and she was pleased. She liked being treated as a grown up and wore her best dress. But Grandfather Jordan was less pleased. Lindsie prattled on and on about school. She seemed to have forgotten her mother already.

'My new school is super,' she said, tucking into asparagus soup as if she were starving. 'We did geometry and algebra and French and Latin today. But my homework is horrible. I hate it. Much harder work than at your school, Gina. You just do baby lessons.'

'They are not baby lessons,' said Gina indignantly. 'We do jomtry and ajibra too, all the time. Sometimes twice a day.'

Jordan choked. Lindsie was not amused. She launched into more school talk. 'But I like art the best. My teacher says I'm good. I'm really into still life, fruit and flowers. I'm going to be a painter one day and have exhibitions in London,' she said. She was still chattering a long time later when Gina was fighting back sleep over a dish of whipped apricot dessert.

'I love you bestess in the world,' Gina said, twining her arms round her grandfather's neck as she kissed him goodnight.

'And I love you bestess in the world, too,' he whispered, ruffling her hair. 'And tomorrow I have a treat for you.'

'A treat? For Lindsie and me?'

Jordan shook his head. 'No. Just for you. Lindsie is too old to miss her schooling. Geometry is very important for young ladies.'

Gina hopped on one foot, barely containing her excitement. 'What is it? What is it?'

'We'll go for a drive...'

'A long drive?'

'A very long drive, all the way to Southampton.'

'Are we going to see one of your ships, Grandfather?' Gina was ecstatic.

'No, chicken. Not one of mine. But I promise you, she's the biggest liner ever built.'

They drove down to Southampton in Grandfather's Daimler, his chauffeur at the wheel. It was a grey, wet day and the clouds looked like geese chasing each other across the sky. Gina hugged her thoughts to herself. She was going to see a huge new liner, the biggest in the world, leave on her maiden voyage.

'Maiden voyage,' Gina repeated the words to herself quietly. They had a special magic to them. This was her maiden voyage too; her first trip to Southampton. 'I'm going to go on a maiden voyage one day.'

'It's important that you understand the

amazing new developments in shipping,' said Jordan as if she were twenty-six, not six years old. 'This new passenger liner is the start of a whole new era in transportation. A transformation.'

'Why isn't it one of yours?' Gina asked, content to be sitting beside his familiar grey bulk, hardly looking at the Surrey and Hampshire countryside flashing by.

'Conway isn't ready to build this size yet. It's Cunard's new crown. But that doesn't mean that I'm not proud of her. She's a real beauty.'

'Is the Queen going to voyage on her?'

'No, but she came down to see the liner yesterday. You know, a private visit without the crowds. Today is the first time she'll put to sea with a full passenger list.'

Gina's eyes widened with amazement when she saw the throbbing scene. The docks at Southampton were in a festive mood with bunting and banners aflame with messages of goodwill, sirens blaring and a military brass band playing their hardest against all the noise.

The great black-hulled liner with its livery of red and white was swarming with activity, strapped to the dockside by heavy chains, passengers and luggage going through the formalities before boarding. She was huge, majestic, awesome. Gina drank in every line with yearning. She wanted a ship like her. A ship of her own.

'Where's all their food?' Gina asked, being practical.

'That was loaded on yesterday. Imagine how much food they need for 1,500 passengers and the crew.'

'Mountains of cauliflowers,' said Gina, who loved cauliflower au gratin more than anything, cheese glistening like molten gold on the crumbly top. 'Mmnn...'

'Mountains,' Jordan laughed. 'Conway will build a liner like this one day, you'll see. Soon,' he added, thinking privately that soon meant when he had raised the capital.

They got out of the car and Gina walked beside him trying to be sedate and well-behaved when she really wanted to skip and jump. Grandfather was tall and upright in his dark wool overcoat and cashmere scarf against the chill of the day.

'Will you call your liner Queen Something?' Gina asked.

He shook his head. 'No, Cunard have the Queens. My liners will each be a Countess. *Countess Aveline* first, after your mother. Then *Countess Stasi* after her sister.' He swallowed uncomfortably. 'I want to entwine Countess with the Conway emblem.'

'And then will there be a *Countess Georgina*, after me? Will I be a 'blem, too?' said Gina, starting to hop at his side, tugging his hand, her long tawny hair flying in the sea breeze. She had untameable hair. It spun a wild life of its own.

'Hold on, young lady. Liners don't get built as easily as that. It takes time and money, an enormous amount of money.'

Money, thought Gina disdainfully. Grandfather talked an awful lot about money. She didn't care. All that mattered was this magnificent white liner, soaring aloft like a fairytale castle on the glistening water, and that one day she would have her own liner. But it would be at a price, she thought, with sudden maturity.

Two

The brass band swung into a classic jazz number, braving the drizzle, and the stirring sounds were cheerful and uplifting. The sea was grey and choppy, slapping the hull of the liner as if to remind the flagship that she had the sea to master. Flags and bunting fluttered in the wind, adding to the noise and bustle of the dockside scene.

One day, thought Gina, the *Countess Aveline* will be making her maiden voyage and we will be on the deck and everyone will be waving at us and cheering and throwing streamers. My mother will be here with us, wearing the feathered hat that I bought her with my pocket money. She longed to have her mother at her side, waving, slim and lovely in some pale dress, the wind lightly lifting the gleaming peacock feathers that clasped her head.

'When will you start building your liner?' said Gina, who simply couldn't wait for the great day.

'Soon, chicken, very soon.'

'Lindsie wanted to come today, you know. She was very annoyed that you made her go to school.'

'Yes, I know,' said Grandfather, his eyes twinkling. 'But Lindsie can't have her own way all the time.'

The VIP passengers were arriving on the special Sail-Rail train from Waterloo, porters trundling cabin trunks and expensive cases, press photographers popping bulbs at famous faces. It was all very exciting. So many important people wanted to be passengers on this historic maiden voyage, film stars and politicians and titled aristocracy.

Gina watched the luggage being taken aboard by two conveyor belts, stern and aft, while passengers went through brief formalities in the reception hall. The women were beautifully dressed, with furs and jewels, as if they were going to a party.

'Can we go on board, Grandfather?' Gina urged, clinging tightly to his hand now the crush of people was growing. She had never seen so many people.

'Not this time. But I promise I'll take you on a trip,' he said, his eyes glowing darkly under his brows. 'You'd like to see New York, wouldn't you?'

'Oh yes,' she said, but she wasn't even sure where New York was. It was the enormous power of the liner that drew her with its glossy dark hull and dramatic single funnel, the cabin windows like rows of tiny jewels, the little lifeboats hung along every deck. 'But we'll have our own liner one day, won't we, Grandfather? I would rather go on our ship.'

'Oh yes, Gina. We'll have a liner even more beautiful,' he said, his heart warmed by the enthusiasm of his small granddaughter. This delicate fawn-like creature. He stroked her silky hair, wishing his wife was alive to share this special moment. 'She will be a white lady, pure elegance.'

They waited until the liner slipped her moorings at the terminal and the tugs took her down the narrow channel to the sea. It was very late. Ten o'clock at night and Gina was nearly asleep on her feet, struggling to stay awake. She only vaguely heard the cheers and the sirens as the brightly-lit liner was swallowed into the darkness.

Gina slept all the way home in the back of the Daimler, her head cradled in her grandfather's arm. She had seen the *Queen Elizabeth II* embark on her maiden voyage and Grandfather had promised to take her on a voyage in that floating city. She knew he would keep his promise. Her very own maiden voyage. With no Lindsie.

Gina watched a taxi draw up at the pavement and a woman got out. She was wrapped in furs, a small hat pulled down low over her incredible eyes. She was laughing and helping a man out of the taxi, though her efforts were muted so as not to disturb her immaculate appearance.

He was on crutches, awkwardly manoeuvring the wide gap to the pavement. The man was tall and very handsome, hair thick and vigorous, his face tanned to bronze by the African sun, pain carved into the lines that ran from nose to full mouth.

The taxi driver was piling luggage on the pavement. They seemed to have an awful lot of it. Leather cases, covered in sea and airline labels, tumbled all over the place. Pedestrians had to move out of the way.

Gina saw the butler opening the front door and instructing someone to help with the cases. Her heart lurched with doubt. The woman paid the taxi driver, taking a note from her bag and waving away the change, the man negotiating the steps with difficulty.

'I can manage, Aveline. Don't fuss so,' he said. 'I'm not an invalid.'

'But I love looking after you, darling,' she said, flinging her furs across a chair in the hall. They fell on to the polished floor and Betsy retrieved them, stroking the pelts as if to soothe their nerves.

'Thank you, Betsy,' Aveline said, her voice floating into the drawing room. Gina kept very still behind the curtains. 'It's lovely to see you again. Lovely to be home. Look what Royce has done! Broken his leg, can you believe it? Such a silly accident.'

'I don't call a rampaging elephant charging at me a silly accident,' said Royce, hobbling to the same chair. He sat down with a groan. 'A bloody big elephant.'

'But he thought you were going to kill him, not just take his photograph,' Aveline went on. 'So, it was silly. Is our room ready, Betsy? It's been a very long journey, very tiring. The flight was ghastly with Royce's leg. Could we have a tray of tea, Earl Grey, lemon. Run a bath for me.'

'Yes, Miss Aveline.' Betsy shot a glance towards the front room but Aveline did not recognize its meaning.

Gina climbed down from the window seat and tidied her hair and smoothed down her dress. She hesitated in the doorway, thrown as always by the beauty and attractiveness of

23

the two adults who had arrived. She felt their togetherness, their passionate and exclusive love, a feeling that generated a wall between her and them.

'Mummy?' said Gina, as if she was not sure.

Aveline flung her arms round her and Gina was smothered in perfume. 'Darling, darling, my darling little girl! But not my little girl any more. My, how you've grown! Sweetheart, everytime we come home, you've grown.'

'I'll try not to grow so much,' said Gina.

'My goodness, darling. There's a sharp little tongue. Where does that come from? And what does that expensive school teach you? Certainly not how to say hello properly to your mummy and daddy who haven't seen you for months. Aren't you pleased to see us?'

'Yes, I'm pleased to see you. Hello, Mummy.' She kissed the proffered cheek, smelling the dusting of powder that clung to the fine down. 'Lindsie lives here now, Mummy,' said Gina, full of her news. 'She came after Aunt Stasi fell in the river. She has the bedroom next to mine. Sometimes she cries in the night.' But Aveline was already going upstairs, taking off her hat and fingering through her curls.

Royce pulled Gina against him. Gina stood stiffly, aware of the shock of flaxen hair so

24

close to her chin, the deep brown eyes that dared her not to cry.

'Aunt Stasi died,' she said, determined to get her news in. 'She jumped into the river. We saw her jump. Lindsie and I were there. She took her hat off first.'

'I know, I know,' he said softly. 'Poor Stasi. Poor beautiful Stasi. She never knew what she really wanted, nor whom. Always striving for what she couldn't have.'

'Have you really broken your leg?' Gina asked.

He stuck out the leg and pulled at the trouser material so that she could see the plaster. 'Very broken,' he said. 'This elephant didn't want his photo taken.'

Gina giggled. This was the father she liked. The one who made her laugh.

'Aunt Stasi had a funeral,' Gina went on. 'I went with Grandfather, but I had to sit in the car at the cemetery. Grandfather bought me a comic to read. Afterwards everyone came back here and we had tea and cakes.'

'Quite right, too.' He was not looking at her. He was staring out of the window.

'Lindsie went to the funeral.'

'Well, she's five years older than you and it was her mother.'

'Why didn't you come?'

He held her tighter. 'We were miles from anywhere. It was a week before we got the telegram. By then it was all over. Besides, you know how your mother doesn't like anything unpleasant. Funerals are very unpleasant. We've really only come home now to make sure those idiots have put this plaster on properly. I don't want one leg shorter than the other.'

So even this visit was going to be short. Gina's heart fell. She felt rationed to his time, saddened that the lovely couple would be gone as soon as Royce's leg had healed. But there would still be Grandfather and now there was her cousin, Lindsie. She would not be quite so lonely.

But something was wrong in the house. Gina could hear her parents arguing behind a closed door, their voices raised. It was such a rare occurrence that Gina stopped and listened, alarmed and frightened.

'Don't you feel any remorse, any guilt, you bastard?' Aveline was shouting. 'She was my sister.'

'You talk as if it was my fault.' Royce was also clearly angry. 'I wasn't even here.'

'Always the blameless, golden-haired angel. So boyish, so charming. As long as everyone thinks you're wonderful and adores you, you're happy. If people could only see your face now. Look in the mirror, Royce, and see yourself as you really are.'

'Aveline, you're a fool. I love you and you only. You know that, my darling. She was nothing to me. A mere frolic. Come here, woman ... this bit's not in plaster...'

'Don't touch me! Don't you dare touch me ... What have you done with those letters?'

'I've thrown them away.'

Gina heard a groan and the voices stopped. There were silken noises and then a sharp cry.

The house went still, bricks breathing on their own. Gina crept upstairs, shaking. Rows were like strangers at number nineteen. She could not tell Grandfather. Nor Lindsie. Lindsie was preoccupied with school and art and growing up. Gina wrapped the heated words and knotted them into her heart.

That night when she sleepwalked the dimly-lit corridors, she was strangely not alone. And her name was breathed on to the air from some unknown source.

They departed on the same wave of laughter and drama and perfume. They were going to some volcanic island to take photographs. Gina wondered if her mother suffered hardships on these trips, or did she use her money from Grandfather to get supplies of hot water, food and drink and a comfortable bed. Nature couldn't be bought. Money couldn't banish the flies, heat and dust, surely?

She did it because of Royce, of course, thought Gina suddenly knowing. She would follow him anywhere like an adoring slave, never letting him out of her sight.

Gina wondered if she would ever feel like that about a man. She doubted it. Unless he was like Grandfather Jordan.

Aveline hugged the two girls. 'Take care, my darlings,' she said. 'Look after each other till we return.'

'And I can have special art coaching at my school,' Lindsie reminded her aunt of her promise. 'Like you said?'

'Of course, of course. Anything you want. I'll send a cheque. And what do you want, Gina darling?'

Gina drank in her mother's luminous face, framed with tawny hair, her lashes fanned on the sculptured cheekbones. She had tried telling her mother about hearing her name spoken in the air, but Aveline had dismissed the story with a laugh. 'I want you to stay at home,' Gina said, trembling.

Aveline threw back her head and laughed again. 'Isn't she a poppet!'

Royce lifted Gina into the air and swung her round, her legs flying out like a doll. 'We'll be home again soon, sweetheart. Be a good girl.'

Then they were gone and only Aveline's perfume hung in the air. Lindsie sniffed and fingered her sketch book.

'They don't love you much, do they?' she said.

'They do. They do,' said Gina fiercely.

Soon after their departure Gina went up to the fourth-floor attics to rummage through her mother's unwanted dresses. Aveline said there were trunks full of clothes and Gina could have anything she wanted for dressing up.

The door closed on her. She did not hear it close as she pulled open the first heavily lidded trunk. It had grown dark before she decided to leave, her arms full of creased chiffon and taffeta and silk. But the door wouldn't open. It was stuck fast. She tugged and tugged and then called out, banging and shouting. But no one heard her at the top of the house. She began to feel afraid.

Downstairs they searched everywhere for her, in the walled garden, in the park square. When Jordan arrived home, he insisted that the police alert Heathrow Airport in case Gina had gone in the taxi with her parents and was lost in the crowds. He made the staff search the house again.

Eventually Betsy found Gina asleep among all the crumpled clothes in the attic, tear stains on her face. The door opened quite normally and there was no explanation.

Three

1999

'Listen, Gina. Look at me. I'm speaking to you.' She couldn't look. She wouldn't listen. She ignored the faint voice in her head as she always did.

The last of the guests had gone. Gina ran up the wide mahogany staircase, her ivory satin skirt rustling and billowing like ocean sails against a crimson sunset. The heel of her slipper caught in the hem, almost tripping her up and an embroidered spray of crystal beads broke loose, scattering down the stairs in a cascade of tears.

Her breath came in angry, despairing rasps as she flung open the door to her room and slammed it behind her. She was alone for the first time in a day that had become a nightmare. She had been humiliated in front of all her friends. It was not the whole world, but it was her world. She howled in rage, thumping her pillow, wishing it was his face.

All afternoon Gina had kept a smile fixed to her face. It became set in concrete. She knew that if she relaxed, even for a moment, desolation would crack her features. She sent desperate thoughts through the airwaves, believing that they had some special means of communication. It was nonsense, of course; there was no answer. The air was as barren as her bed. Timothy, her young, burning bridegroom, had disappeared.

'Timothy Trenchard,' she moaned. 'Tell me, tell me why. I want to know why and I will try to understand.'

Howard had done all the right telephoning, discreetly and immediately: Tim's flat, the hospital, police stations. There were no admissions, no reported accidents, no messages; the enquiries were fruitless. Dr Trenchard had completely vanished.

They were very kind at the church. After all, she was Gina Conway, owner of Conway Lines and a wealthy woman in her own right. The wedding was a glitzy affair at St George's, Hanover Square, the classical-style church for the fashionable. Gina had invited everyone she knew. The press were there in full, cameras at the ready, waiting for a quick routine shot for the gossip columns. It was a true romance story of an heiress marrying an overworked junior doctor. Instead they got front page drama: the groom had not turned up; the radiant bride had been left stranded, her emerald engagement ring flashing distress signals in the watery sun.

But Gina had strength. She did not panic, standing in the porch of the church in her fabulous wedding dress, the slanting light from the sixteenth-century Flemish windows bathing her in patchwork colours. Dew formed on her flawless skin as something died inside her. She straightened her back, ramrod stiff, drawing on hidden reserves, finding a composure that she did not feel. There must be some reason. She and Tim were so much in love and had planned this wedding with enthusiasm. Damn him, there must be a reason.

'I'm sorry,' she said to the red-faced, embarrassed vicar. He was waving his arms about as if attempting some last minute black magic. 'Something must have happened to my fiancé. He works these ridiculously long hours at the hospital. He's probably overslept. We'll postpone the wedding, but there's no need to cancel the reception. After all, people have travelled a long way to be here.'

She had the guts to make such an announcement and the vicar admired her for it. He had seen jilted brides before; they usually had to be fortified with brandy in the vestry. Gina was different, as if a mesh of steel enclosed her spine.

Nothing had changed at home; it was exactly as she had left it an hour ago, happy and excited, a beautiful bride. The old elegant house in Cranbourne Square closed round her with comfortable arms. The high carved ceilings, the inlaid wood floors polished to the patina of satin, the sparkling crystal chandeliers and long windows leading out on to the garden did not seem real. Gina had made many changes, bringing number nineteen up to date. But she had been ready to swap stylish living for married life in a modern, custom-built flat near the hospital.

Her friends thought she was mad. She had lusted for love, wanting to relive her parents' devotion to each other. Now she wrapped the house space around her like invisible armour. At least there were no gawping hotel staff and curious management. The caterers hardly knew that there was no groom. They circulated with tulip-shaped glasses of champagne while Betsy and Howard formed a human barrier to shield Gina from the more malicious guests. The overflow filtered from the drawing room on to the garden patio. It was a benevolent spring day, moist with overhanging rain clouds, and although the walled garden was small, the hanging flowers and statuary were reminiscent of Italy; their perfume full of Mediterranean promise.

'Well, where has this lucky young man got to?' asked a tactless neighbour, her button eyes glinting. 'How have you managed to lose him on such an important day? You must be shattered, my dear.'

'Not at all,' said Gina, holding her head high. She had quickly dispensed with the coronet of pearls and misty veil. Her tawny hair was piled high into an elaborate arrangement of curls. 'He's been kept late at the hospital. Some awful emergency. A transplant or something. He's such a dedicated doctor. Even I come second to his work.'

'But on his own wedding day, my dear! It does seem a little extreme...'

'More champagne, madam,' said Betsy, steering her tray between the well-corseted woman and Gina.

'Tim will be here soon, I'm sure,' said Gina, still smiling. 'Why don't you enjoy yourself? I'm going to.'

She drank nothing, only sipped some mineral water. She glanced at her gold watch. Was it only two o'clock in the afternoon? How much longer must this charade go on? Half of her was crying out for news, the other half did not even know what was happening. She was in a trance, acting out a role.

'Of course, we were absolutely amazed when we got your invitation. You kept it very quiet, didn't you? Was it all very sudden, Gina darling?'

'Sudden? I don't know,' said Gina. 'What is sudden? We've known each other six

34

months. Is that sudden?'

She was feeling faint, faces weaving out of focus like blobs. She put down her glass, hands moist and slippery. Getting married had been the most important decision of her life. Timothy Trenchard had swept into orbit when work had been grinding her into the ground.

He brought reality to each day, refreshing and alive, made her see the endless routine of work, decisions, directors' meetings, parties and social engagements as soul-destroying, dehydrating her skin as well as her body fluids. Living together would have a purpose, a pattern, something for them to build upon. She began to think that at last she had a chance for a genuine relationship, marriage, a real family life, children. She had been alone for too long.

'You should have something to eat, Miss Gina,' said Betsy, appearing again with a plate of smoked salmon canapés. 'You hardly touched your breakfast.'

'I can't stand this farce for much longer,' said Gina. 'No one believes that I actually want to be a doctor's wife. Tim's working hours and the low pay ... they aren't that important to me.'

They're important to him though, thought Betsy, keeping her thoughts to herself as any good servant would. Perhaps the prospect of having a rich, powerful wife had turned sour or scared him off. She liked the good-looking, fair-haired doctor, a few years younger than Miss Gina, but that didn't matter these days. She had seen and approved of the happiness growing in Gina's eyes as Timothy became a frequent visitor to the house in Cranbourne Square.

The drawing room was packed. Gina felt herself being pressed against the sharp edge of the grand piano as more guests surged towards her, curious to see her face, hoping to find some outward change in her immaculate appearance.

She was being watched, not only by her guests but by someone in particular. It was as if she was being taken apart, feature by feature, evaluated, found wanting and then discarded. Her eyes were drawn to a man who stood across the room. His expression was cold and distant, like a scientist who has just discovered something revolting.

He was not only taller than most of the men in the room, but he was holding himself apart, refusing to become another guest at the gathering. No glass in his hand. There was an impact to his look which alarmed Gina, sending a chilled shiver down her spine.

Gina tried to break the mesmeric stare, but he was holding her to it. It was uncanny, as if she had no control over what was happening. These people were devouring her. A cramping pain clutched her stomach as she forced herself to turn and greet her cousin, Lindsie.

'Gina, what a terrible ordeal for you. You're being wonderful about it all, I must say. I don't know what I would have done if Barry hadn't turned up at our wedding. You will come and spend a weekend with us, won't you? It'll do you good to get away. Come down to Plas Glwydan. You must visit us now we've moved. It's a real Welsh castle! Sounds fantastic, doesn't it, but it's pretty rundown really.'

Gina focussed on her cousin's amicable but anxious face. Lindsie had worn this expression since childhood, as if she was perpetually wondering if she had left something simmering to a cinder on the stove. Gina supposed it also came from being married to Barry Wykeham. He was a meticulous man, fanatical about his ancestry and his inheritance of a crumbling pile of battlements in Wales, uncertain what eccentricity he was up to next. Even his glasses were always askew.

'It's so kind of you, Lindsie, but I don't think...'

'Oh, you won't have to sleep in a dungeon!' Lindsie attempted a joke. Her flower-covered hat nodded, the matching dress flowed. 'We're more civilized than that. A decent guest room for our friends is top of the list of renovations.'

'I'll let you know,' said Gina. Her cousin was only trying to help but a weekend of the Wykehams was more than she could cope with at the moment. Barry had been going to give her away at the wedding, but his role had been cut. Gina never knew what he was thinking and it unnerved her. 'Thank you, Lindsie. Would you like another drink?'

The tall man moved from across the room. He was muscular but lean-hipped, broad shoulders sitting easily in an expensive suit. His blunt-cut silver streaked hair was striking, making his angular face look more tanned than it really was. He faced her. He did not look curious or amused. He was controlling anger, piercing blue eyes aiming lethal shots in her direction.

'What have you done to Timothy?' The cold voice was sliced hostility, faintly transatlantic. 'I want to know what you have done.'

Gina felt the room swimming round her. 'I'm sorry ... I don't understand what you mean. Done? I haven't *done* anything. Timothy didn't turn up to our wedding.'

'You needn't try to deny it. Timothy is not the kind of man to run out on a commitment without a damned good reason. There's something you are not admitting and I'm determined to find out what it is. Don't think you're going to get away with this, Miss Conway. I'll make damned sure you won't.'

'I don't know who you are or what you are doing at my wedding,' Gina returned with spirit. 'You're being quite insufferably rude and I won't tolerate bad manners in my own home. Howard will show you out.'

'Hardly a wedding,' he snapped back.

'My reception, if not my wedding,' Gina corrected herself, taking a deep breath. 'Maybe you should leave if you are going to continue to be so unpleasant.'

'Don't worry. I was just going. I've seen enough of you and your friends. Perhaps Timothy had a lucky escape.'

The man turned abruptly and pushed his way through the crowd. She had no time to ask him who he was or what he meant. Nor did she care. She was too shattered to absorb any more hurt. All her energy was concentrated on staying upright and being some kind of hostess to her guests; most were being considerate, aware of the drama being enacted before them. Some were actively enjoying it. Normal weddings could be so boring.

Howard appeared, coughing discreetly. 'There's a telephone call, Miss Gina. One of the tabloid newspapers. I did try to put them off.'

'I'm not talking to the press,' she said.

'If I may suggest, it might be helpful if one newspaper carried a story that was not a complete fabrication. You know what they are like. If you don't tell them something, they'll make it up.'

'I suppose you're right, Howard. I'll take the call in Grandfather's study.'

She did not want the usual gamut of wild stories and pointless exaggerations. They had printed enough ridiculous photographs and false stories about her in the past; always hoping to catch her with her mouth open or her skirt riding up her thighs.

'Gina Conway,' she said, putting the receiver close to her jewelled ear to shut out the noise from the reception. She listened to the journalist's stream of leading questions, quietly marshalling her thoughts.

'Let's get this straight,' she said. 'Firstly, I have not been jilted. Our engagement is still very much on, only the wedding is postponed. Dr Trenchard was delayed at the hospital, an emergency ... No, I don't know the details. Life before love, you could say,' she added, feeding them a sound bite. 'Yes, we carried on with the reception. Why waste all that lovely champagne! Besides, my guests have travelled miles – I couldn't suggest they went home.'

She dabbed at the perspiration on her upper lip. There was definitely going to be a storm. She was feeling desperately tired. Every bone in her face aching from all the smiling and endless pretence.

'Yes, I'll let you know the date of my next wedding.' She managed a light laugh. 'Of course, I shall wear the same dress – this one isn't worn out.'

She was not going to let them invent a new extravagance. They had written columns on her clothes, the racks of unworn dresses and shoes, the huge store bills. Not true, of course. If they were short of news, they sent the wealthy Miss Conway on a shopping trip.

She took a deep breath and plunged back into the crowd. The champagne had loosened tongues and overcome initial embarrassment and the noise level was rising. Howard had opened the tall, elegant windows that led to the gardens and a slight breeze stirred the blades of the crystal chandelier to faint music. Even the cooler inner hall was crowded, and the younger guests sat on the wide, curving staircase, sipping champagne and eating everything in sight.

Betsy was shadowing her with a tall goblet of Buck's Fizz. 'You must have something, Miss Gina,' she said firmly. 'You've had nothing since your breakfast and that wasn't much.'

Gina smiled at her diminutive maid. She was lucky to have Howard and his wife to run the house and Betsy to look after her. A much smaller staff now. What would she have done without them today? They were marvellous. She must remember to say so, do something special for them as a thank you.

There was another discreet cough at her side. Howard was standing there, his lined face a mask. Gina recognized the look. She had known him a long time and it was his 'bad news' face. More bad news? Surely she'd had her fill for today?

'Miss Gina, a letter has arrived by special delivery. I have put it on your grandfather's desk in the study. Perhaps you would care to read it alone.'

His message was clear as if he had X-ray eyes or had steamed open the letter. Gina caught hold of a Regency china cabinet to steady herself; the collection of priceless porcelain rattled as if unseen hands moved it.

'Thank you, Howard.'

Gina went back to the study and shut the door. It was Grandfather Jordan's study. She had changed nothing since his death. There were his books, his walnut desk, his deep armchair, the Savarron carpet, the carved fireplace and the globe they had spun together, but now there was this letter. The handwriting was not immediately recognizable.

Timothy had never written to her during their brief courtship, but she had seen him scribbling things occasionally, a date, an

42

address, a phone number. She could hardly bring herself to open it. Every nerve in her body was tingling, distress rising inside like a single scream. It was a fear that had been there, waiting in the shadows, all afternoon.

She stood and read the letter. The writing blurred into a meaningless web of lines. She was stunned by the violence in the message.

'...slut ... whore ... bitch...'

Lightning flashed across the room but she did not see it. A few moments later, a roll of thunder cracked overhead and a fall of heavy raindrops sent her guests scurrying indoors. A spring storm was set to bring down the curtain on the day. But Gina heard nothing, saw nothing. Her feelings slowly turned to stone.

They had all gone. Her staff and the hired caterers were clearing up the mess. Gina took refuge in her bedroom, not wanting any more kindness or sympathy from Howard and Betsy, and refusing all help. She had to face this on her own.

The wedding dress came off and she stepped out of it, leaving the gown on the floor, a pile of crumpled satin and crystal embroidery, hours of painstaking work. Despite her brave words, she would not wear it again. It could go to a charity shop.

She kicked off the matching slippers and left them abandoned like Cinderella's. But she did not feel like Cinderella. What Prince? No one had danced with her. She felt as if she had been punched in the stomach. It was a physical, knife-twisting pain.

She stood in the bathroom, creaming make-up off her face, wondering whether she really liked what she saw. Apparently Timothy did not like it. She saw a vulnerable, heart-shaped face with good skin, high cheekbones and velvety brown eyes and long lashes that hardly needed their daily coating of mascara. Her father's eyes. The mouth was sad, curving lips drawn into a tremulous line.

'Apparently you're a selfish bitch,' she told herself, quoting the letter.

For a second the brown eyes lightened, gleamed, then grew dark again. She felt the oddest, fluttering sensation as she stared at herself in the mirror. That expression of malicious amusement had not been true to her feelings. Where had it come from? It was completely alien to the way she felt at that moment. The face still moved in unison to her hands as Gina took a tissue to wipe off the cleanser, but suddenly she did not trust it.

Perhaps she was two-faced. A two-faced selfish bitch, Timothy had written. She was bewildered by his vitriolic letter. She knew she had flaws ... she was a workaholic, obsessed with keeping the Conway Line afloat, creating profit, dividends ... but Timothy said she was rotten to the core, devious and scheming, a despicable woman. She did not understand why and shivered at the ashen taste of his words. How could he hate her so much?

Her glance slipped down to her bare brown shoulders, still tanned from a winter break in Cannes. The silky slip was edged with real lace, creamy and hand-washed by Betsy. Behind her gleamed the fitments of her bathroom: gold taps, the oval contoured bath in the palest pink with jacuzzi jets, the ceramic wall tiles a garden of hand-painted roses.

It had once been her parents' bedroom. Nothing was the same. The bathroom was like a background to a painting and she felt no more than a marble statue in that garden.

Gina turned away from the mirror, unable to face herself. What had she done to generate such hatred in Timothy? She wanted to share her wealth with him. She had told him that, drawn up a pre-nuptial agreement, giving him half of her fortune.

Jordan Conway had built up the fleet of ships with the distinctive wavy-blue Conway Line. *Countess Aveline* and *Countess Stasi* cruised the Mediterranean with holiday-makers, the Atlantic, the Caribbean. Every penny was honestly earned; why should any-one worry how she spent it? She was more than a decorative figurehead on the board. She ran the shipping line with a firm but feminine hand.

The eyes in the mirror followed her. Gina bowed her head and started to weep. But the eyes in the mirror were not crying.

Four

The despair was still with her when Gina awoke the next morning. She drank the tea Betsy brought, then showered and washed out the artificial curls of yesterday. It had been an artificial day. Redundant bride. Her face looked wavy and unfocused in the mirror. Maybe she needed an eye test.

The house would save her sanity. She loved every brick, every stone, and especially the kaleidoscopic views of the London skyline from the top windows. She knew the different sounds made by the narrow stairs, creaking like old knees, that led from the main bedrooms up into the attics which housed the dust-wrapped possessions of past Conways.

Look at me, Gina. I'm waiting.

Gina turned to see who had spoken but there was no one there. She thought of the attics though she had not remembered the incident for years. The door had closed behind her, a small girl intent on exploring, and she had been locked in at the top of the house for hours. Betsy, downstairs in the kitchen, didn't hear her cries. Lindsie, who lived with them, was at an extra art class. It grew dark in the attic and she had been terrified. Betsy had found her.

Grandfather's influence was everywhere in the house. If only he was around now to help her regain her confidence. She would find solace in her work, carrying on the famous wavy-line, make good decisions at directors' meetings. Top woman administrator using swing doors. She used his office, feet on or under his desk, clocked in for work at nine thirty at the Piccadilly head office, not always sure of what she was doing. She was on a steep learning slope. Slippery. Pass the grip tape.

Suddenly she was scared. Events had shaken her carefully contoured life like an earthquake. Nothing had ever gone so catastrophically wrong before. She was not clear about anything. That hateful man yesterday hated her. Pox on him.

Her bruised mind refused to absorb any further shocks. She wanted to disappear. There was no Timothy, only dreams to haunt. This should have been her honeymoon. Some honeymoon. No strong arms holding her, no firm limbs folding round her body, skin against skin, a demanding mouth taking the love she was longing to give. She groaned in the agony of missing him, wanting him, her body aching.

But where was he? She wanted to know why he had abandoned her. She had never known how to flirt and Timothy had shown her a different life. She freely admitted a shallowness, becoming a high-flier, a responsible member of society, learning how to run a big business, knowing that people thought she was too young and inexperienced.

'Timothy...' she groaned. 'Why did you do this to me? You rotter.'

No children, no heir ... Her confused, sleep-dazed mind rambled into egg-shell thoughts, seeing lonely stretches of life ahead like taut elastic, ready to snap. Lindsie could have the Conway fortune; rebuild castles, paint her murky watercolours, run an art gallery. Gina wanted flesh and blood children. She would probably be the last Conway.

'I'm sorry, Grandfather,' she murmured. 'I've let you down again...'

Standing naked in water was an instant replay of yesterday's ritual cleansing. Clean bride to the altar. She tried not to think how happy she had been, drenching the spray with perfume, dusting her skin with talc, slipping into delicate silk underwear. Michel did her hair before the ceremony, creating a goddess. Now she brushed out the tawny locks vigorously, wondering why on earth she had chosen such an elaborate style. A Madonna impulse.

She threw on any clothes. Indigo jeans, cream silk shirt, leather boots with gold heels, thought them old. Studs went into her ear lobes; moisturizer and mascara her only make-up. She did not look into the mirror. It seemed an alien place. She did not want to see a jilted face.

She went down the curving staircase, a hand steadying herself on the carved balustrade, catching sight of fragments of crystal missed in clearing up. Her high-heeled boots tapped hollowly as she walked across the marble tiled hall.

The scent of massed flowers on the Regency tables at the foot of the stairs brought back yesterday. No one had cleared the wedding flowers. The scent was overpowering as the greenhouse blooms came into full fragrance in the warmth of the reception. They smelt funereal, heavy with grief.

'Betsy. We can't keep all these flowers,' she cried out, her iron control going haywire. 'Give them away. I don't want to see a single petal when I come home.'

'So, you've emerged at last,' said a masculine voice. 'It's taken you long enough, Miss Conway. What a temper. Do you always treat beautiful things so carelessly?'

Gina swung round. She was not used to being spoken to so crudely. But she remembered echoes of that voice.

'Oh, so it's you again.' Her heart plummeted. 'What are you doing in my house?' she snapped. 'I said I wasn't seeing anyone. I don't want visitors.'

'I'm not a visitor.'

'Please go. I don't want to see you.'

'You'll see me,' said the man, coming out of the drawing room into the hall. 'I've been waiting all morning and I don't intend to go until you've answered questions.'

Gina's heart sank deeper despite her air of composure. It was the man with the silver crew cut. The man at the reception. Those stern features, the strong, flared nose, faintly shadowed square chin, amazing cerulean eyes. Her tired mind was playing tricks. He looked familiar.

'I don't know who you are and I don't care. Somehow you gatecrashed the reception yesterday, were extremely rude to me and now you've forced your way into my home. If you don't go immediately I shall call the police.'

'I've already called the police.'

'What do you mean?' Gina asked. 'The police? Is this some kind of sick joke?'

'No joke,' said the stranger, those compelling eyes darkening to navy. 'Sit down and listen to me.'

Gina found herself being manhandled into her own drawing room. She was too astounded to protest and he was too big for argument. He slammed the door behind them, leaning against it. He was looking at her in that uncomfortable, dissecting manner as if she were a nasty insect. He was not a man to mess with. She glared back, her temper rising. Here cometh the mini sermon.

'We haven't met before but I know a lot about you, Miss Conway. I was at your wedding yesterday, officially invited. I was Timothy's best man and arrived in the UK just in time. I'm still jet-lagged. So, what happened, or didn't happen, was a shock to me too. I want to find out what you've done to him, Miss Conway.'

'I'm not listening to this,' said Gina.

'Oh yes, you are and I'll tell you why. I'm Mark Trenchard. Timothy is my younger brother.'

Gina caught back a breath, holding on to a chair. The resemblance, of course. 'Timothy's brother? Timothy? I didn't know you were coming. He never told me. He hardly ever mentioned you.'

'We drifted apart, lost touch. We had different interests and different careers. None of it matters now. I want to know where my brother is and how you got rid of him.'

Gina stared at the stranger and savoured

the likeness, but whereas Timothy's face was young, unmoulded clay, this older one was as hard as granite. She recovered her composure quickly, straightened her shirt. 'I presume you have brought me an explanation from your brother, Timothy.'

'The hell I have, Miss Conway. I am here to find out exactly what's been going on between you and Timothy. You went through a charade yesterday. I know my brother. He didn't walk out on you. It's not in his nature.'

Gina lifted her head, tossing back her hair. 'The wedding was arranged and Timothy didn't turn up. How do you think I felt, standing there in the church, waiting, looking a fool? Was I flower arranging? There's nothing I have to explain to you and if you've nothing to tell me, then you'd better go.'

'We should both talk to the police.'

'The police? Whatever for? I'm not going to the police.'

'It's a police matter,' said Mark Trenchard. 'My brother has disappeared. He fell in love with you, dazzled by your looks and money. You played him along like many another poor fish. I suppose you ditched him suddenly, realizing that being the wife of an impoverished doctor would not be easy, but it served you better to go through a wedding and then play the tearful, jilted bride.'

'That's not true,' said Gina with a bubble

of irritation. She could cope with a verbal battle. It was the unknown that frightened her. She walked over to a gilt-framed Chippendale mirror above the Robert Adam fireplace and smoothed her rumpled hair. She noticed a minute discrepancy breaking the clearness of the mirror, but knew nothing about the liquid property of glass slowly dragging itself downwards.

She caught a glimpse of the man standing behind her. His expression was fathomless, dark and grim. She did not understand his attitude at all. Where was the sympathy? Her nerves were jangling and she wanted him to go.

'Let's start again,' he said evenly. 'Timothy has disappeared. It must mean something to you. You're supposed to love him, aren't you? He's disappeared and has taken nothing with him. No passport, chequebook, money, clothes, nothing from his flat ... not even a razor. I've looked everywhere. Nothing has gone. He's simply vanished.'

'Vanished? I don't understand.' She tried to take in walking out with nothing, moneyless into the world. 'I thought he was working at the hospital on some emergency. If you are right, something is wrong.' The phrases were short, static, as her mind wrestled with this new information. 'I got a letter from him, afterwards. A very angry, hurtful letter. But it didn't sound like him, not at all. Perhaps he's been taken ill. This isn't making a lot of sense.'

'It makes sense to me, Miss Conway. Whatever you did to Timothy must have been so dreadful, so obscene, so painful that Timothy fled. So what was it? I want to know.'

'I did nothing. Everything was perfectly normal. Timothy was as keen on this marriage as I was. We had fun making the arrangements. Perhaps the whole affair became larger, grander than he would have wanted, but he did understand that I have a lot of friends and people on the Conway board that I wanted to be there.'

Her voice faltered and for the first time tears pricked her eyes. 'We both wanted this marriage.'

The tall man was trying to contain his bitterness. His eyes narrowed to sapphire slits, disbelief lurking in their depths. 'You're a cool one. You remember only what you want to remember. Perhaps you also remember that he spent a great deal of money on you, most of the money he inherited from his grandfather.'

'I don't know about any grandfather,' said Gina with spirit. 'That's news to me. If Timothy has an inheritance, then he's old enough to spend his money exactly as he pleases.'

'Spend, yes, but not throw it away. Nine

hundred pounds at Lingfield races? Six hundred pounds at a nightclub? He paid four thousand pounds for a diamond bracelet from Garrods. On a junior doctor's pay?'

Gina concealed the shock she felt. She had no idea that Timothy had been dipping into a nest egg. He always seemed to have money, a full wallet that he spent freely.

'I didn't realize,' she stammered. 'The bracelet was a wedding present, lovely, but I gave it back to him, straightaway. I knew he was being far too generous. I told him to return it to Garrods. He lent me money at the races. It was a loan and I was going to pay him back. I don't remember the nightclub. He paid for all of us, one night. I suppose he felt he had to take his turn.'

Mark glared at her. They were almost at eye level. Gina knew that her high heels gave her an extra advantage but he was still a tall man and able to make her feel small. He was uncomfortably aware of her allure. All that sweet-smelling hair tumbling to her shoulders, some strands still crimped in ringlets from yesterday's church performance. The velvety brown eyes were flashing with annoyance and the porcelain skin faintly flushed as she breathed more quickly.

For one wild and crazy moment Mark Trenchard wanted to feel that shapely body under his hands, to tame that spirit. His brother's intended wife. He stamped on the feeling. He was going out of his mind.

'I shall find out what's happened to my brother,' he said flatly, fighting the stupid desire which threatened his resolve. Her wayward charm curled round him like smoke from a candle. 'Aren't you at all concerned?'

'Of course I'm concerned,' she said. How many times did she have to tell him? 'I thought Timothy was working late at the hospital, an emergency and that he'd call me to explain. But if you say he's disappeared, then I want to know what's happened to him.' She steeled herself. 'I hadn't realized you were coming to the wedding. Timothy didn't tell me.'

'We've been out of touch. I was surprised when he called to say he was getting married and it was a last minute decision to fly back from America. There's our grandmother's farm in Wales to get into shape. Erddig farm has been empty for months and is neglected. Timothy invited me to the wedding so I flew back, but too late to stop this fiasco. Or to stop Timothy taking off to wherever.'

'He went of his own accord. It was his decision. I had nothing to do with it.'

'So you'll come to the police with me?'

Gina went over to an ornate Louis XV desk and opened one of the drawers. She hunted for her chequebook and wrote out the amount in her large angular writing.

'Here you are,' she said, containing her scorn. 'A cheque for six thousand pounds, made out to Timothy. It should take care of any bets Timothy placed for me and the bills he ran up. Does that satisfy you? Now, if you'll excuse me, Mr Mark Trenchard, I have a busy morning ahead.'

She thrust the cheque into Mark's hand, refusing any eye contact. Gina had no wish to see him ever again.

She turned on her heel and strode through the hall, downstairs to the kitchen basement. Her heart was racing, out of control, fluttering like a hunted bird's. She hated losing her composure and hated the man who made her lose it.

Gina was no stranger to the kitchen. She was as much at home here as she was in the rooms above. Mrs Howard ran the household efficiently with the help of a daily woman. The Howards had a self-contained flat in the basement. Betsy had a bedroom on the third floor with a wonderful view of the distant park. Recently Gina had persuaded her to take over an adjoining room and fit it up as a sitting room.

'Can I have some coffee please, Mrs Howard. Strong and black,' said Gina, throwing herself in a chair. 'I've just had a most unpleasant interview with a dreadful man and I'd like to get the bad taste out of my mouth.'

'Of course, Miss Gina. Would you like it

here or in the drawing room?'

'Here, please. I'm going to sit in your rocking chair and pretend I'm a little girl again. Don't look so worried, we Conways survive. Centuries of inherited guts.' Gina sat back, pushing against the floor with her heels, listening to the tapping of the wooden rockers. Rock-a-bye lady.

Mrs Howard took a brandy bottle out of a cupboard and put it beside the cup of freshly made coffee. 'A few drops, Miss Gina? Purely medicinal?'

'Purely medicinal,' Gina agreed with a grin. Could become an alcoholic. No problem. Dry out at a clinic.

Gina sipped the hot coffee and the fire of both made a path down her throat, settling the turmoil in her stomach. To let another man, another of the Trenchard breed upset her was ridiculous. Hadn't she gone through enough yesterday?

Her breathing quietened. She wanted to know what had happened to Timothy. She was deeply concerned. Perhaps he was ill, had an accident, but a sick person would not have sent that vitriolic letter. She had not told Mark Trenchard the vile contents of the letter. She dabbed moisture from her upper lip. The lace handkerchief once belonged to her mother. It was a fragile square of lawn edged with lace, coffee-coloured with age. Using it made Gina feel close to the woman whose lovely face was blurred and faded.

The kitchen mirror reflected light from the window. It looked cracked. The distortion fractured the image of the plane tree outside, making it a caricature of nature, its trunk bent into forked servility.

'Your mirror is cracked,' said Gina. 'You'd better get a new one.'

Mrs Howard and Betsy exchanged glances and raised eyebrows. Gina was certainly not herself this morning. There was nothing wrong with the mirror. It was perfect.

Five

Mark's temper cooled in the open air, pacing the pavement. He felt a primeval urge to punish her, to make her feel some of the pain Timothy must have endured. She should not be allowed to get away with whatever it was that she had done.

But how did one punish a woman like that? A woman who had everything in life, money, looks, position and now synthetic sympathy. Poor soul. How could he dent that confident image so that her world went through the office shredder?

The police did not show much interest in

Timothy's disappearance on his wedding day. It was not that unique, the sergeant said, straight-faced. Many a bridegroom took off for last-chance freedom. Cases of wedding-day cold feet littered the missing persons book like trampled confetti.

'Can't you look up some list or something?' Mark insisted. 'This is the age of technology.'

They ran a quick search on the Police National Computer but nothing came up that matched Timothy's description.

'Often happens, sir,' said the officer. 'Changed his mind and couldn't face the young lady. Nipped off to Paris to sow a few more wild oats.'

'My brother does not nip off,' Mark said. 'Besides, he's taken nothing: no passport, money, personal belongings.'

'We can only make routine enquiries.'

'But he took nothing. How can he exist?'

'He might have other funds or friends. Would you fill in a form and drop in a recent photograph? He'll probably turn up in a couple of days. Perhaps the young lady could shed some light. Maybe they had a row.'

'I've no idea. No one seems to know anything.'

Mark left the police station. He was staying on at Timothy's flat while arranging his move to Erddig, his grandmother's farm. She had been unable to farm for years now and had let the land out to tenants. Mark wanted the land back and in good shape. He wanted to find his brother. He wanted to find his roots again. He wanted revenge. A pyramid of wants.

'Damn her,' he said, gritting his teeth, wanting the London gloom to clear too. 'Damn Miss Gina Conway.'

Mark Trenchard's visit disturbed Gina. He thought she was unfeeling about Timothy. They had been head over heels in love, as the saying goes, and their marriage seemed a perfect match. She had been proud of Timothy's profession. He was everything she admired: industrious, dedicated, outgoing.

True, she had made use of him at first. He appeared, vertical, when she was between escorts and she hated going anywhere without a dancing partner. Timothy fitted the role. He danced well in a loose-limbed style and had the energy to dance into the early hours of the morning. How he organized dating Gina with his long shifts at the hospital was a miracle. He fitted in sleep at odd hours. She dazzled him, showed him a different world, banished the misery of blood and gore in A & E for a few enchanted hours.

Gina had not expected the romance to become serious. But it did, slowly, without them noticing. She felt a sudden need to belong to someone, to cement a real relationship, and Timothy felt the same way. But what had she done to make him so bitter, to have made him write that cruel letter? She could understand him backing out of the wedding at the last moment; nerves were funny things. Timothy was unprepared for commitment. But the hurt was desperately painful. The humiliation in front of all her friends, a public scalping.

Betsy came into the drawing room. She was concerned. 'You've eaten nothing all day, Miss Gina.'

'I'm not hungry, thank you, Betsy. Oh well, more coffee perhaps, and fruit. I'll have it on a tray in here.'

She tried to read, flicked through a newspaper, but the print did not register. She should have been on her honeymoon in the sunshine, enjoying the white sandy beaches and clear blue seas of Stocking Island, and the warmth at night of Timothy's long-limbed body. Her legs curled in anguish, aching, sliding, twisting awkwardly, a sort of cramp.

Coffee and fruit conjured by Mrs Howard was not a cup of instant and an apple. Betsy came into the drawing room carrying a silver tray with a Georgian coffee pot and cream in a silver jug, fine bone china cup and saucer, a linen hand-stitched napkin, a crystal dish of raspberries and slices of honeydew melon dipped in port.

'That looks lovely,' said Gina, still not hungry. 'Please thank Mrs Howard.' She knew she was being spoilt.

The phone rang. It was an invitation. The Parkinsons who owned a merchant bank. They wanted to take Gina out that evening. Dinner somewhere, quite informal, then a nightclub. It would take her out of herself, they said.

'You're being kind,' she said. 'It's a super idea, but I'm still in mourning weeds ... I'd rather stay at home.'

'Come on, Gina. It's what you need. You can't stay at home moping, really you can't.'

'I know, but not yet. Give me a few weeks in purdah. I need some time to get my public face straight. But don't worry, I'll be in circuit again soon.'

'Two weeks, Gina. You're allowed two weeks to get over this creep. Then we want to see you out and about.'

'I promise,' said Gina. She wanted to say that Timothy was not a creep. But that letter ... it was so unlike him. What had she done? She could think of nothing except managing Conway Lines and being successful. Her generous salary made his National Health pay look like pocket money. He hadn't seemed to mind, teased her, made fun of it. Miss Moneybags.

She switched on the television. The

announcer was reading a newsflash. A tanker had gone down in the Gulf. Gina prayed it was not one of the Conway line. Cargo, cruise liners, tankers. Conway Lines was well diversified, but tankers were expensive shipware. She must phone the office.

'Miss Gina. Some flowers have come for you.'

'How nice,' said Gina. Flowers were arriving from her friends as if it was a death in the family. She felt bereaved. 'Will you put them in a vase, please.'

'I think you ought to see them.'

'I'll see them in a vase.'

Betsy allowed herself the merest smile. 'I don't know whether we'll have enough vases.'

Gina got up reluctantly, stretching her slim legs. She had taken off the boots and walked in bare feet across the carpet, but before she even reached the hall a wave of rose perfume met her.

The hall was full of roses, yellow roses. It was like a moist cavern of velvet sunshine, overpowering, heady. The delivery man was grinning, enjoying her surprise. A single rose is beautiful, a dozen an elegant expression of feeling, but this ... there must have been several hundred blooms.

'Looks like he bought the shop,' said the man.

'There's a card, Miss Gina,' said Betsy.

Gina tore open the tiny envelope, her heart beating wildly. Timothy, they must be from Timothy. The barricades were down. Now she would know. He would put it all right. The plain piece of card in her hand was her lifeline, more important than the roses filling the hall with their sweet perfume and velvety beauty.

The wording on the card was cryptic: 'Every rose has a thorn. You are going to get scratched. A thorn in the eye can blind.'

There was no signature.

Six

Gina drove westwards on a Friday afternoon. She could not face another weekend in London. It was a month since her aborted wedding and if she went on another goose chase, she would scream. She needed a second wind somewhere in the country, and on impulse she decided to visit her cousin, Lindsie and husband, Barry, in their inherited castle in Wales.

It was not often, even in Gina's circle, that a couple inherited a castle. Money frequently, but historic stones, that was an inheritance of a different kind.

'Come any time,' Lindsie had said at the farewell party in their St John's Wood flat. 'We've hundreds of rooms if you don't mind sharing one with a ghost.'

'As long as he keeps his head on,' said Gina.

'Have some coffee before you leave,' said Barry. 'I've a fresh pot in the kitchen.'

Gina drove her lapis blue Mercedes fast along the M4 motorway to Wales. She had not phoned that she was coming, which was not fair on Lindsie, but she could not bear the thought of being told that they already had visitors or were going away themselves. Gina wanted space around her, cooling and temperate. There had been no word from Timothy, despite all the trail searching. The hospital were baffled, knew nothing of his whereabouts. Gina was desperate to get out of London and not find the drawbridge up.

The pain of Timothy's disappearance was receding. People were tactful, quiet, as if she was recuperating from an illness. Pass the paracetamol.

The police had been round, asking questions, but nothing she said was of any help. She did not show them the letter. Timothy's name was put on file with the thousands of other people who, every year, disappeared, deciding to give themselves new lives and new identities.

She had roamed the hospital, talking to colleagues. No one could help. Timothy had not shown any sign of wedding nerves.

Gina huddled deeper into the fur collar of her Canadian fox jacket. She did not buy fur but this was her mother's and there was no point in a dustbin grave. The cavemen knew what they were doing when they wore fur. She listened to music on the car radio. She was driving mindlessly. She could have driven for ever, to go on and on till she fell off the end of the world.

The fast car ate up the miles and soon the Severn Bridge was ahead. She liked the comfort of a big car; it could carry a lot of people and Howard drove it for her in London traffic. After one party she went to with Lindsie, it had carried eleven people piled in, lap-sitting and hugging. They had gone back to Cranbourne Square for coffee and wine. That was the night that a pair of nineteenth-century hand-painted bronze birds disappeared from the escritoire in the drawing room. Someone took the kingfisher and the wren, both small enough to slip into a pocket. She often wondered if she might come across them in an antique shop.

She saw little of the rolling countryside as she sped along the motorway. Newly planted trees loomed gaunt and bleak on the embankments; a suicidal bird flew across her bonnet. Misted villages were shuttered from the noise of thundering traffic that cut a swathe through their farmland.

It was slightly ridiculous to be driving all this way even though there would be a welcome the other end. She swept over the Severn Bridge and past the straggling town of Chepstow, aware that it was once a historic gateway settlement which controlled a strategic river crossing into Wales.

'Romans,' said Gina, dismissing centuries of history with one word.

Plas Glwydan Castle had a signpost to itself. Gina turned off the main road and slowed down as the road twisted and narrowed. Overhanging branches hid the castle from view until the last moment, then with a dramatic gesture they yielded sight of the ancient fortification.

The castle crouched like a watchful animal on a rocky rise, its aspect sturdy, menacing. A small castle by feudal standards but it had survived chaos, changes and ravaging time. It was built of pale red sandstone from the banks of the Severn, interlaced with thin slabs of grey pumice stone. It rose two storeys, the battlements and eleventh-century three-storey tower had disappeared from the main walls, demolished and cannibalized for the stone. Some of the remaining walls were nine feet thick, seeped in conflict, drenched in blood from old battles.

The keep had been pulled down and what

was left of the castle had been transformed by successive owners into a manor house. Stone turrets stood sentinel at the corners of the castle; groups of twisted Elizabethan chimneys pointed tall to the sky. The grim walls were softened by a spreading growth of Virginia creeper whose little green suckers clung to crevice and crack like colonies of long-legged frogs.

Gina turned into the driveway and swept round the courtyard facing the castle, spitting gravel. The porch was a massive stone entrance with walls thick enough to shield a visitor from the bitterest Atlantic wind. The heavy door was blackened oak studded with brass, old and forbidding, left over from a gothic nightmare. Gina almost ran away. She made herself pull the long brass bell, suppressing a wild desire to flee. Plas Glwydan was something out of a Hammer Horror film. She expected a sinister, fanged butler to open the door.

The door creaked open and a light from the hall flooded the porch. There was a crash as someone knocked over the stand for umbrellas and walking sticks. The contents clattered over a stone floor.

'Hell!'

'Lindsie,' said Gina, amused. 'It's me, Gina.'

'Darling!' There was a cry of joy and amazement. 'What a lovely surprise. Come in, come in.'

The lady of the castle welcomed Gina in the most unladylike manner, her bright copper curls bouncing unrestrained in all directions. She did not look the part, dressed in muddy jeans and a baggy knitted top. She had sneakers on her feet, no make-up on her round, shining face.

'This is absolutely marvellous,' grinned Lindsie. 'And you look terrific, even after all you've been through. Any news of...? No, well, come in and tell us everything that's been happening. We're absolutely buried out here, up to our necks in swine. Of course, you're staying. We've masses of bedrooms. Let me take your jacket.' Lindsie held the fur against her cheek and sighed. 'Barry won't let me wear fur.'

'You've got a castle instead.'

'Big deal.' She tucked Gina's arm into hers and took her across the hall. It was dark and gloomy with panelled walls and a heavy oak staircase that turned twice before reaching the first floor, its balustrade intricately carved with oak leaves and vines. But the room they went into was warm and comfortable with a roaring log fire in a deep stone fireplace, innumerable lamps everywhere throwing pools of light on to worn furniture. Two large black Labradors got up from their places in front of the fire and sniffed at Gina's expensive boots. They approved.

'Barry, look who's here,' Lindsie babbled on. 'Don't be afraid of Jake and Jasper. They only look big. They won't hurt you – just inspecting.'

Barry got up from one of the deep armchairs and held out his hand. He was a thin blade of a man with sparse brown hair and thick pebble glasses. Lindsie was ten years his junior but their marriage seemed compatible, her lively, effervescent personality matching his quieter, more intense nature.

He shook Gina's hand and gave her a chaste kiss somewhere near an ear. 'It's good to see you. We've been hoping you'd come and inspect our ancestral home.'

'I hope you don't mind. London was getting me down. I throw myself on your hospitality. But, if it's inconvenient, I'll take myself off to a hotel in Chepstow.'

'Nonsense,' said Barry. 'We won't hear of it. We've plenty of room, if you don't mind things being a bit primitive. We're delighted to see you.'

'Now, get yourself warm and I'll see about some supper,' said Lindsie. 'Sherry first. We must have some sherry to celebrate our first visitor.'

'I don't want to put your staff to any bother,' said Gina.

'Staff? Oh, you won't,' said Lindsie cheerfully as she went out. 'We haven't got any staff.'

Gina sat down near the fire and surveyed the room. It was a long room with tall windows either end, an oak-blocked floor covered with rugs. The stone inglenook fireplace had corner seats where one could roast in comfort. Bookshelves were lined with yards of books, oil paintings of landscapes and horses hung on the walls. Under the windows facing the Atlantic were window seats covered with faded velvet cushions. The room had a lived-in look but Gina could tell it needed money spending on it. There was no central heating and it was only warm being toasted by the roaring fire.

'A place this size must need an army of staff. However do you manage?'

'Unfortunately we've no one yet. It's hard to get domestic staff and the young women of Clwyd can get better jobs in town. We have to make do with Dai, the gardener. He keeps the grounds in some order.'

'But that's terrible,' said Gina. 'No one to help? Lindsie can't do everything.' She saw herself washing-up in a damp, dungeon-like kitchen.

'We manage,' said Barry. 'Please stay. Lindsie is lonely. She misses London company. We'll eat out tomorrow for lunch, if that will salve your conscience.'

'My treat,' said Gina quickly.

'We'll argue about that tomorrow,' said

Barry.

Lindsie came bustling back bearing a heavy brass tray. Barry fetched a three-legged contraption on which the tray would rest. The tray was laid with an assortment of food: paté, tomatoes, toast, butter, Swiss roll, chocolate biscuits and a dish of dusty pink Turkish Delight.

'Lovely,' said Gina. Lunch out tomorrow was a must; Lindsie's culinary arts were being stretched.

'I hope you haven't been telling Gina our troubles,' said Lindsie, practically sitting on top of the fire. 'She doesn't want to hear them. We prefer to eat in here, Gina. The dining room is like a parade ground and freezing. We can't light a fire in there yet as the chimney needs sweeping. There must be a thousand birds' nests in it.'

'Don't worry. This is lovely,' said Gina, spreading paté on a slice of toast.

'I'll make some coffee when you're ready,' said Lindsie happily. 'Oh, it is nice to have you here.'

'I'm longing to see round your castle,' said Gina, chewing on the cold toast. How could anyone go wrong with toast? Perhaps the kitchen was a mile away. 'I'm curious.'

'We'll go on a guided tour.'

'The north wing should be left until morning,' said Barry. 'It has no electricity, only oil lamps. The wiring doesn't reach everywhere yet. And some of the floors are rotten. I would hate you to fall down a hole in the dark.'

'Don't scare Gina,' said Lindsie laughing. 'She might think she's getting a sleeping bag on a floor. There's a sweet room in the south turret, waiting for our first visitor. I've switched on the electric fire and an electric blanket in the bed. We haven't been up to London since...'

'Since my wedding,' said Gina. 'You can say it. It doesn't hurt so much any more, though I'd still like to know where Timothy is and why. There's been no word. I've made countless enquiries. He's completely covered his tracks.'

'Oh Gina, how awful. We are both so dreadfully sorry ... How is he surviving without any money?'

How did they know he didn't have any money? Odd.

Gina shrugged. 'I've no idea. Perhaps he has another heiress tucked away.'

The cake was stale and the biscuits soft. Even the tomato skin had a spot of mould. Perhaps everything in the castle was mouldy.

'How about this tour?' said Gina, feeding her biscuit to one of the dogs. 'I want to see everything.'

'If you've had enough? Come along, then.'

Plas Glwydan castle needed a lottery win spent on it. It had once been a magnificent fortification, at its height in the sixteenth century, sumptuously furnished, a family of servants, nearby farms supplying food. The upkeep had overwhelmed the ensuing generations. It had been partially modernized with modern plumbing and electrification by Barry's uncle.

They went into the lofty panelled dining room overlooking panoramic views of the distant Atlantic. Another enormous stone fireplace flanked with rampant lions. The fireplace was unlit and choked with dropped leaves and straw, flattened like the bedding of wild animals. Gina shivered.

'I told you everything was awful,' said Lindsie. 'But Barry loves it. This is the original baronial hall, twelfth century, I think. The upper windows have gone, bricked up. There's the gallery where ladies used to sit and look down on the knights at their feasts. Talk about sexual discrimination. Barry's planning to banish me up there.'

Lindsie and Barry had deserted the big bedrooms for a smaller, cosier room with windows that faced inland. Gina's octagonal turret bedroom had three narrow windows facing the sea. It was comfortably furnished with a blue carpet and poppy-patterned duvet thrown over a single divan.

'You've your own bathroom,' said Lindsie, opening what Gina thought was a wall panel and switching on a light. It was the smallest bathroom Gina had ever seen, converted from an original closet, with a corner wash-basin and plastic shower unit. But nothing could be done to disguise the cold stone walls and Gina knew she would not linger within its icy cell.

Gina lay in bed that night remembering when she and Lindsie had been as close as sisters in those gingerbread days. The welcome at the castle had been warm, but it was a far cry from number nineteen, and she longed to be in her own room. How she loved the graceful old house.

Her cousins were obviously short of money, she thought, as she drifted into sleep. There had been no money with the inherit-ance from Uncle Owain. It couldn't be easy living with Barry, a man obsessed with Plas Glwydan.

As Gina slept, she dreamed vividly of a young girl laughing and out of breath. She sounded happy. She was running through the grounds of Plas Glwydan, her skirts and hair flying.

1472

She ran down the ill-lit oak newel staircase clutching her shift. It was the morning of her fourteenth birthday and she knew her father had a special present for her. Perhaps it would be a horse of her very own. She longed for a horse.

Her father was out riding in the park. She heard the chime of hounds. He hunted red or fallow deer every morning with his stewards, but would be back soon to break his fast.

The great red-bricked manor house, paid for by money made in the Courts of Law, was bustling with activity even at that early hour. The maids, the servants, the gardeners, the stable boys and grooms were bringing the house and outbuildings to life. She saw Will Brigges, the gardener's boy, trundling a barrow up a pathway. He was bringing freshly picked strawberries to the kitchens for her birthday.

Will was nearly seventeen, dark and broad-shouldered, but not tall. He was like a stunted tree, waiting to grow. He seemed to know she was watching and flashed a white-teethed smile at the oriel window where she stood.

'M'lady will be vexed with you, young madam, at the window in your shift. Be gone now and put decent clothes on.'

'Oh Moll, you are such a fusspot!'

Georgina gathered her skirts again and ran up the staircase, hopping and skipping on the polished floor of the long gallery, a new innovation. Will had seen her and last week her night shift had been stained with blood. She was glad Will had smiled at her. She stretched her arms and remembered his smile all day.

Seven

Lindsie woke her with a breakfast tray. Gina saw the envy on her cousin's face as her wispy straps and tanned shoulders emerged from the duvet.

'I wake with creases like a road map on my face,' said Lindsie, putting down the tray. 'I can't even surface without two cups of tea to fortify me.'

'This is lovely,' said Gina at a loss how to be conciliatory. 'You're spoiling me.'

'We eat ours in the butler's pantry which is hardly your style. That kitchen gives me the creeps. I'm sure there are cockroaches. How they managed to cook vast meals on those blackleaded ranges, I'll never know. I burn everything including my fingers.'

She held up two bits of sticking-plaster on her knuckles with a wry smile.

Gina nibbled at the breakfast despite a gnawing hunger. More soggy toast. The scrambled eggs were rubbery and the orange juice was long-life. She drank some juice and coffee and threw the rest of the breakfast out of the window. She peered down at a yellow blob on the path below, hoping the birds would quickly remove all trace of her hasty action. A robin hopped down from a chestnut tree and perched on a triangle of toast. He cocked his head sideways, listening, waiting for orders.

'Tuck in, baby,' she said.

After a fast, tepid shower, Gina dressed in whipcord trousers, a plaid wool shirt, leather jerkin and buckled boots. She pinned her hair back with a tortoiseshell clip, pulling strands round her face. The mirror was poorly lit and she didn't bother with it.

Plas Glwydan was even more imposing in daylight, the stone passages greyer and gloomier. The fire had gone out in the long sitting room, though there was residual heat from a pile of log ash. The black Labradors came over to greet her as she crossed to the windows and passed her as friend. It was a magnificent view over rolling green hills, swept with soft mauve valleys and distant mountains and scattered swathes of forest like a brush of watercolour. The far horizon had a sparkle that could only be a reflection of cold sea.

Gina folded her arms against the chill of the room, kneeling on the window seat. She had not realized that Wales was so beautiful. To live within reach of both sea and mountains. She had a longing to walk the shore, to feel cold sand between her toes, to listen to the pounding waves and to let a filtering wind lighten her headache.

She had a vague headache, not enough to resort to paracetamol but it was there. She felt unreal, as if nothing solid was around her. It was hunger and too much coffee.

Timothy had told her about staying with his grandparents on their farm in Wales, and playing on long stretches of golden beaches. It was easy to imagine a young, floppy-haired Timothy absorbed in building sand-castles or trying to dam the oncoming waves. But not the older brother. Gina felt that Mark's boyhood had been brief, that he had been grey before his time, burdened with responsibility.

'No sense of humour,' she said aloud. The dogs lolloped over at the sound of her voice. She looked at them sideways. They were big dogs with powerful shoulders. She could be afraid of them if she had not seen how docile they were with Lindsie and Barry.

For a second she saw a reflection of herself in the lemony orbs of their eyes and a prickle touched her neck. It was like the stab of a sharp, cold needle into her spinal cord. She rubbed the spot vigorously to dispel the feeling and tremor of apprehension.

She swung away from the coldness of the room and a dog growled. She crossed the hall quickly, went through a creaking baize door and followed a stone-flagged corridor that led to the kitchens. She was momentarily touched by the sight of hollows in the stone that had been worn by centuries of feet. How many hundreds of servants had walked that passageway to the bidding of their lords and masters, laden with serving platters of food? Dishes of stuffed swan, quails' eggs, roast suckling pig ... The images reminded Gina that she hadn't returned the breakfast tray. No Betsy to clear up after her here.

The massive kitchen was not a place to linger, its stone vaulted ceilings dingy and grimed with soot. The high windows allowed only glimmers of light to filter through, shafts that fell on to ugliness and hidden dirt. The red tiled floor was chipped and uneven. Gina turned up her nose at the ancient equipment, the monstrous old range, deep earthenware sinks and wooden draining boards. A large table in the centre of the kitchen was deeply scored by the knives of countless cooks. Lindsie was busy scouring the top bone white with a scrubbing brush and a tin of abrasive powder.

'Honestly, Lindsie,' said Gina. 'This is medieval. I don't know how you put up with it. How could you leave that nice flat in St

John's Wood for this monumental ruin?'

Lindsie looked up from her labours, cheeks unbecomingly flushed. She pushed curls out of her eyes.

'We're mad, absolutely mad,' she agreed. 'We didn't think it was going to be as bad as this, although we knew that nothing had been done for years. Barry's Uncle Owain was childless and left the most complicated will. The castle and the income from a trust fund come to Barry solely on the condition that he lives here. If we don't, then we lose both. Plas Glwydan goes out of the family. No one gets anything.'

'Sounds as if Uncle Owain was off his rocker. I should say no thank you and good riddance, and let it pass out of the family,' said Gina, perching herself on a dry corner of the table. 'What will you gain from staying on here? You can't spend your life scrubbing tables and trying to prop this place up. Be sensible.'

'It's Barry,' said Lindsie, her shoulders drooping. 'He's crazy about the place. He's always dreamed of owning it. You see, the castle did once belong to his line of the family. He feels he has a right, a heritage. It's an obsession, putting Plas Glwydan on the map and having a historic castle to pass on to his children.'

'But you haven't got any children.'

'IVF's the second item on his list of priori-

82

ties.'

'Tell him you want someone else to do the scrubbing if you get pregnant. I'll probably tell him too.'

Lindsie put her hand swiftly on Gina's arm. 'No, please, don't say anything to Barry. It does mean so much to him. You can't destroy a man's dream.'

'What about your dreams? What about central heating and a decent cooker? I'm getting you a microwave for that butler's pantry for a start.'

Gina left the kitchen before she said anymore to upset her cousin. She was fond of Lindsie and could never understand why she had married Barry. He had always seemed an odd fish, a quiet, colourless man, without any of the bubbly fun that was Lindsie's main attraction.

She went outside followed by Jake and Jasper who thought she was going for a brisk walk, then lost interest when they found out that she wasn't. They invented a game of their own, chasing and leaping with gleaming flashes of jet black fur like panthers hunting prey in a jungle.

The grounds were equally neglected. There were paths, shrubs and the remains of a formal garden. It was long since overgrown with tangled blackberries and weeds. Great rhododendron bushes swept the grass with heavy heads of buds soon to burst into flower. As she hunted for flowers, she found promises of spring: yellow celandine, dog's-tooth violet and the globe white of blood-root. She scooped up a broken head, its crown tipped with the red of hidden petals that would open to palest pink. She picked daffodils, primroses, forsythia and a cluster of snowdrops that grew close to a stagnant lake.

The lake was turgid, swamped with weed and debris, like vegetable soup that has gone bad, edged with a froth, a scum that eddied uncertainly. Gina walked carefully around the muddy path, keeping her eyes from the unpleasant lake, searching for flowers, hoping she was not lost.

She was unaware of an opening in the wall behind her, or that Dai was standing there, watching. It was the entrance to an underground tunnel that led from the grounds, right under the nine-foot-thick wall and into part of the castle. Dai stood silent, worried. Gina went back to the cold kitchen and searched the dusty cupboards till she found a vase. She slopped in some water and arranged the flowers. Not quite Constance Spry, but close. She put the vase on the blackened sideboard that stood in the slant of sunlight from the stained glass windows over the stairs.

'Very nice,' said Barry.

Gina jumped. 'Heavens, I didn't see you.'

'Soft shoes,' he said. There was mud on his trainers. She knew who would be sweeping that up.

He did not look particularly pleased. Maybe he was planning to sell flowers from a roadside bucket.

'Was it all right to pick the flowers?'

'Of course. You are our guest, but flowers are best left where they grow.'

'Sorry.' Gina accepted the criticism. She added spring bulbs to her gift list. 'Lunch time soon.'

They went out in Barry's battered estate car, Lindsie huddled up in a duffel coat, a knitted woolly hat jammed on her curls. She did not look dressed for a formal meal and Gina resigned herself to a pub lunch.

'If you were staying longer we could take you to the Brecon Beacons. It's breathtaking up in the Black Mountains. Ystradfellte is a wonderful walk with spectacular waterfalls,' said Barry. 'But there won't be time if we're going to stop for lunch.' He made eating sound like an extravagance. 'I have to see a man this afternoon about selling some wood.'

'You're going to chop down trees?' said Gina, wishing they had gone in her car. She was feeling sick, sitting in the back with a strong smell of dogs.

'Yes, it's a necessity both for the money and to create some space for the other wood to grow. It should have been thinned out years ago.'

'You're serious about living at Plas Glwydan,' said Gina, forgetting her promise to Lindsie not to interfere.

'Naturally. It's what I've dreamed about for years. It's my right, my heritage. I'm restoring the castle and the land to its former glory. Plas Glwydan is going to be the showpiece of South Wales.' His voice rang with enthusiasm.

'Be realistic, Barry,' said Gina, refusing to meet the pleading look in Lindsie's eyes. 'This ruin hasn't seen any former glory for centuries. And who'll want it when you and Lindsie have worked yourselves into early graves? Certainly not The National Trust. They are not interested in castles that have been tampered with to any extent.'

'Tampered ... Plas Glwydan hasn't been tampered with.' Barry bridled at the insinuation.

'It's true. There's been alterations and changes to the castle and little of the original fortification is left. That awful stinking lake,' Gina went on. There was no stopping her. She was in a mood to argue. 'You'll have to get it dredged. It must be a breeding place for mosquitoes. God knows what else you'll find there.'

'Please, Gina,' said Lindsie, distressed.

'Sorry,' said Gina quickly.

She caught a glimpse of Barry's stony face in the rear view mirror. She had nothing in common with Lindsie's husband. She did not even like him.

Gina knew little about Barry's background, only that he had worked abroad for many years, fund raising. He saw Plas Glwydan as his chance to put down roots and achieve an ambition to be a respected landowner. Short men often had big ambitions instead of inches.

Gina glimpsed lovely limestone escarpments, woodlands covering the gorges and running rivers dotted with red boulders, little streams tumbling over smooth rocks and down shallow falls. It was so leafy, patchworks of fields in the valleys, the smooth green Brecon Beacons forming a huge, unbroken horizon.

'You're both crazy, but the scenery is worth it. This is gorgeous and right on your doorstep. I'll be a tour guide when you open Plas Glwydan to the public.'

'Takes training,' Barry grunted, still annoyed.

'You're booked!' said Lindsie. 'We'll make a terrific team.'

They stopped at a black and white timbered post inn in the centre of a small town, once a busy highway with a demand for hostelries.

'This inn has a priest's chamber and

several secret passages,' said Barry grudg-
ingly as he parked in the cobbled courtyard.
'It also does passable food.'

The inn radiated hospitality with a roaring
fire and beams hung with gleaming
copperware. The heat came at her like a tidal
wave and Gina felt warm for the first time in
two days. They settled at an inglenook table
with glasses of wine before ordering.

'This looks wonderful,' said Gina, almost
devouring the menu. She chose tender Welsh
lamb with apricot sauce followed by almond
mousse. It was a pleasant meal. Gina relaxed
and enjoyed the chatter, the surroundings
and home-made food. After a second cup of
black coffee to counteract the sweetness of
the dessert, she began to think kindly of Plas
Glwydan Castle.

Someone, big, bulky, hemmed in at a table
in a far corner, was trying to leave. There was
a general movement of scraping chairs to
make way for the marooned luncher and a
sudden overzealous thrust jolted Gina's arm.
Her coffee spilled. She mopped at the brown
stain spreading up her wet sleeve with a
napkin, annoyed at the man's clumsiness.

'So sorry. It was an accident ... Miss Conway? Ah, this is unexpected. A little rural
slumming?'

Mark Trenchard stood by their table,
genuine surprise on his craggy face. Gina
Conway was the last person he expected to

find in this ancient inn far from the bright lights of London. She shone like a diamond in a haystack with her immaculate clothes, tawny hair and flawless skin.

'You,' said Gina with a flash of anger. She remembered the heat of their last meeting, his accusations, his cruel taunts. He was the last person she wanted to see. 'What are you doing here?' she snapped, still mopping up.

'I live here,' he said, cool. 'Erddig is not far from this town.'

Lindsie coughed, reminding Gina to introduce them. She said smoothly, 'This is my cousin, Lindsie, and her husband, Barry Wykeham. They've inherited Plas Glwydan Castle. This is Mark Trenchard, Timothy's brother.'

Lindsie paled, embarrassed. 'Oh dear,' she said. 'That Timothy? The one who...?'

'That Timothy,' said Gina, keeping her voice even. 'The one I didn't get to marry. The one that ran off and left me in the lurch, at the church, like the song.'

She felt Mark stiffen. 'I don't believe we met at the wedding,' he said to Lindsie. 'It was pretty crowded.'

'Very crowded,' said Lindsie.

She didn't want to talk about the wedding, but Gina was not going to lose the opportunity to ram home a few blunt remarks. 'Has my wandering fiancé turned up yet?' she asked icily. She unlocked her anger.

'Could he give me a call? To apologize or something. It would be a sign of good manners. I know good manners don't run easily in your family.'

'No, I've no news. I remember hunting in the woods around Plas Glwydan as a child, quite unofficially, of course,' said Mark. 'It was a gloomy old ruin, even then.' He turned to Gina, blue eyes glinting with hostility. 'I don't know what's happened to my brother, but it must have been devastating. The police are baffled. It might help them if you came clean about what really happened.'

'Come clean?' Gina exploded. 'What the hell do you mean? If anyone was up to something shady, it was Timothy. He didn't turn up. I was there, waiting.'

She blinked, smarting. Her eyes hurt. Perhaps her mascara had smudged. She took out a pocket mirror and peered into it. The eyes that stared back were malevolent, not quite her own.

Eight

Sitting only inches away from Mark Trenchard brought a swift sense of desolation to Gina, a dreadful loneliness. He reminded her of Timothy even though the resemblance was not that strong. This man had a steeliness in his eyes and a stubborn jaw, whereas Timothy's face had boyish charm.

'Are you drying out?' he asked. 'Shall I be getting a bill for a new shirt?'

She was watching his face, seeing the way expressions flitted across the plane of strong features. This was volcano country. A clamouring pulse throbbed in her body as if he had touched her wantonly.

She ignored his barbed remark, was on her guard. Mark Trenchard was not a friend and this shift of axis was not natural. His eyes travelled over her face, making a close inspection.

He sat down, his arm brushing her sleeve. It was electric. She started back, nerves tingling.

'I intend to settle here,' said Mark, helping himself to some of the fresh coffee that had arrived. 'Sheep and cattle. It's true sheep country. I'm going to stock hardy breeds, Brecknock Hill Cheviots or Beulah Speckle Face.'

'Best to stock several breeds. Source of milk, meat and manure, skins and wool. The Roman invaders brought in the white-faced Welsh Mountain, the beginning of the small sheep. Best for these harsh mountains,' Barry added.

The two men began to talk soil contents and land reclamation and Gina's mind drifted free. The country was beginning to lose its novelty. She wondered how soon she could go home. First she had to buy a thank-you present for Lindsie.

What else did people do in the country? Dawn was nice. She had seen a few pink-tinged dawns after parties, but here she felt like a prisoner.

'This afternoon we're seeing someone about selling some wood,' said Barry.

'Miss Conway, I was wondering if you would like to have a look round my farm instead?' said Mark, offering a lifeline. He did not look enthusiastic.

'I didn't bring my green wellies,' she retorted. It was the last thing Gina wanted to do, wandering round muddy fields or watching smelly cows in sheds, but she might be able to shop instead. 'Would you mind, Lindsie? I'm sure Barry could conduct his negotiations more smoothly if your uninvited guest was not hovering in the background.'

'Of course, Gina,' said Lindsie, forever amiable. 'Go and see Timothy's farm – oops, sorry, Mark's farm. We'll see you back at the castle around supper time.'

'I shan't need any supper,' said Gina. 'Such a lovely lunch. I'll settle the bill on my way out.' Which she did, with plastic.

'Erddig is interesting,' said Mark. 'Come along.'

Gina flicked translucent powder on her nose while she waited for Mark to pay his bill. Each feature was perfectly reflected in her compact mirror. Grey shadow accentuating the deep brown, long-lashed eyes; eyebrows a dark sweeping arc. Her mouth was rosy and glossy; tawny, russet hair.

The image in the mirror stirred, like liquid, a visual disturbance as if a migraine was starting. Gina snapped down the lid. Perhaps it was her new lenses. Tricky things.

Gina climbed into Mark's Range Rover and sat silently as he drove out of the courtyard. She wondered why he had asked her. Had he forgotten their tooth and claw parting?

'Did you send the roses?' she said, breaking the silence. 'They were unexpected.'

'Yes. I was angry. I still am. As angry as Timothy must have been to walk out.'

Gina swallowed hard. The look on his face was enigmatic.

'Contrary to what you think, I'm upset. I am still upset. I had nothing to do with Timothy's disappearance and I still don't know why he went. Do you? Have you any news?'

'No. He's simply vanished, Gina. He's never turned up at the hospital. No money has been drawn from his bank. His car is still in the garage. The police have checked airports, ferries with no clues.'

'I don't understand. What on earth can have happened to him? It's not like Timothy.' The concern raking her voice was genuine and Mark shot a surprised look at her. 'I can understand him changing his mind about marrying me, after all, I'm probably not the easiest person in the world to get along with...' she trailed off, staring out of the rain-spattered window. 'But disappearing. It's not like him at all.'

'So your cousins have inherited Plas Glwydan,' said Mark, changing subject and gear as the Range Rover tackled a steep gradient. 'I should think that's a headache.'

'The place needs a fortune spent on it. They have more enthusiasm than money. They're more or less camping out in a couple of rooms. I had no idea before I came down.'

'Or you might not have come?'

'That's true,' said Gina, admitting it. 'And

94

I might as well confess that I don't want to look at your farm. I came yesterday without bringing a gift for Lindsie and I want to go shopping. It would ease my conscience. Do you mind?'

Mark chuckled. Now she could see why he'd got those laughter lines at the corner of his eyes. For the first time she tried to imagine him in America, driving a dusty trucker or on horseback, the heat beating down savagely.

'So, Miss Conway has a conscience. I'll drop you at some shops but don't expect Harrods.'

'I'll get a taxi back to Plas Glwydan.'

'A taxi here? You're joking. Up in these hills? I'll see you safely back to your cousins. It's no trouble.'

He dropped her at a market town three miles from his farm. It was a picturesque place with a cobbled main street and an ancient Celtic cross dominating the green. A stream ran alongside and children were fishing with home-made nets.

The town was full of timbered cottages with quaint windows and low, irregular roofs, miniature gardens already spilling with spring flowers. Gina had a sudden longing for such a tiny uncomplicated place, to play at housekeeping with a doll's house to look after. But she knew it was only a fantasy and she would not be able to stand it for long, that its smallness would suffocate her.

Finding a suitable gift was not easy. A cheap china souvenir was out of the question; a decent gun cabinet in an antique shop seemed too serious. The grocers had a good dry sherry and Gina ordered a case to be delivered to the castle.

An unoffending ginger cat was curled up in the shop window among the packets of detergent and tins of beans. He blinked sleepily at her and she smiled, wishing she was a cat in a window. He curled himself into a more comfortable position, tucking his nose deeply into his own furry duvet.

If her blue Mercedes had been parked close by, Gina knew she would have driven straight home at that moment. But she was stranded in this Godforsaken spot in the middle of the country, waiting for a lift from a man who had other things on his mind. Then there was the prospect of another chilly evening at Plas Glwydan with oddities on a tray.

Her gaze went back to the comfortable cat; his fur zig-zagged for a second most disconcertingly, a flaw in the window glass accentuating the diamond-bright strangeness. She blinked rapidly, the cottages no longer quaint and doll-like. By the time Mark arrived, she was almost insensible with gloom.

'I thought you'd forgotten me,' she said,

climbing into the seat beside him.

'There was a hold-up at some road works.'

'I've been here at least a century. What a place to live in.'

'A lot of people like it.'

'Not me. I can't imagine a worse fate.'

'I take it your shopping was not successful.'

'I had to settle for a case of sherry.'

'Sounds good. My farm is ten minutes' drive from here. A short detour.'

Gina could hardly believe her ears. It served her right. He was getting his own back for being treated as a chauffeur. She shrank back on to the seat.

'It's a Grade II listed house,' Mark went on, ignoring the chilly silence. 'You'll find it interesting. We've a few antiques. My grandmother was a collector.'

Gina froze. She did not care if it was Buckingham Palace. She was stuck; she would have to see out the whole day. Her need to return home was now desperate. The fates were conspiring to turn it into an ordeal of patience.

She cast a sideways look at her driver. Yes, he was attractive in a mature way. She liked the sternness of his profile, the jutting chin, the firm nose. The silver strands merging with his fair hair gave it a steely glint, but his eyebrows were darker, a faintly quizzical look.

He reminded her, not necessarily of Timothy, but of the companionship she had lost. To feel wanted, to be part of a relationship, a genuine friendship. She felt bitter towards Timothy for denying her this long-held dream.

'Here we are,' said Mark, turning off into a tree-clad drive. The low branches dripped the morning's rain on to the vehicle and splashed the windscreen like an erratic carwash. 'This is Erddig Manor Farm.'

'Earwig?'

'Erddig – an old Welsh name, but don't ask me what it means.'

The gravelled drive stopped in front of the house, a low shadowy building nestling among the trees like someone too shy to be seen. It was a two-storeyed house without any clear uniformity of style, a knitting together of different architecture that worked, time erasing the joins.

'Strange looking place, isn't it?' said Mark, switching off the engine and leaning back, the pride in his voice unmissable. 'The central part is the oldest, the diagonal brick and stone walls with the tall twisted chimney.'

'Elizabethan?'

'It used to be a hunting lodge, they say. Makes you think, doesn't it? An Elizabethan hunting lodge. I'd like to know who did the hunting. The right-hand wing with the brick and timber dates from the early seventeenth century. We don't know much about that time though there's mention of smuggling.'

'There was a lot of it about.'

'About the 1860s, some ancestor built on a hideous early Victorian extension, pulling down a lot of the original outhouses. This was a dreadful mistake and my grandparents demolished the Victorian rooms and added on that rather elegant white weatherboard end. My grandfather managed to get some old slates for the roof and tied it in with the original roof. There's a modern kitchen, utility room, extra bathrooms.'

Gina sat in the Range Rover, looking through the rain-smudged windscreen, feeling quite ill. She did not know what it was; a feeling of faintness and nausea with a hard, contracting knot in the wall of her chest muscles which threatened the rhythm of her breathing. She tried to concentrate on breathing normally, listening to the expulsion of air as if her life depended on it.

She tried to push away a mesh of cobwebby thoughts, to look at Timothy's family farmhouse. He would have brought her here one day. Instead she was with Mark, hardly listening to a word. Something was wrong. She ought not to have come.

The light seemed to be fading rapidly but she knew it could not be. It was still afternoon, but the air was darkening for a heavy storm. A swirling mass began to cloud her vision. There was an odd damp smell in her nostrils, like something that had been stored and untouched for years.

'Gina ... are you all right?' Mark was standing outside, bending towards her. She had not noticed him getting out. His voice was a long way off, echoing down from a tunnel.

'It's my damned driving. You're so pale. I forget I'm not on a dust track in Texas. I'll get you a drink.'

'Please...' said Gina nodding, moistening her lips, suddenly parched. Her palms were damp, forehead dewed with perspiration.

He opened the door and helped her out, supporting her as she stumbled, his hand firmly under her elbow. His sheepskin coat made him look bigger and broader; the silver-streaked hair caught in the upturned collar. Gina longed to trust him, to let him take care of her, to protect her.

To protect her ... but from what? A shudder ran through her like the gloved wash of a cold grey sea.

The rain stopped as if cut off with a knife. A patch of bruised sky peered wanly through the scurrying clouds. If it had not been for those clouds, Gina would never have gone into the farmhouse. She would have pleaded thin boots, wet hair, anything to stay in the 4 x 4.

She followed Mark shakily along a paved

path to a canopied entrance with marble surround, moulded cornice and fluted architraves.

'This Regency porch is another oddity,' he said, putting a key into the lock.

He led her into the hall. It was part of the Elizabethan hunting lodge, a cool dark place with carved oak panels and a flight of oak stairs, the treads worn and polished by many feet. The walls were hung with framed pictures and the small, mullioned windows let in arrowed light. It had a mellow beauty but cried out for flowers and light. The low, beamed ceiling was a crushing weight, tired of holding up that slate roof for so many years.

Gina felt she was walking in a dream, her legs moving by themselves, skimming the floor. Mark showed her the drawing room, part of the seventeenth-century extension. This had exposed timber framing, a brick and timber floor and fine inglenook fireplace with a royal oak fireback.

She went over to the full length windows that looked out on to the rain-hung garden, moving the long tapestry curtains to see the sweep of lawns and shrubs. What a house, charming in many ways, unique in history and design. This room was elegant with its graceful proportions and antique furniture that blended so well with the exposed timber and brick.

The bread ovens on either side of the fireplace had been turned into alcoves for a collection of china and glass. Gina stared at the pieces, two in particular, a kingfisher and a wren. They were unmistakably nineteenth-century hand-painted bronzes. Exactly like her own. The ones that had been stolen from Cranbourne Square. But how could they be?

She bit on her lip. Mark was talking, but she couldn't take in what he was saying. This visit to Erddig was turning into a strange experience. Gina longed to get away, to shake off the tangles of this confusing day.

She went over to an oval dining table of polished walnut standing in the middle of the room, the mellow rose-tinted wood reflecting years of care and elbow grease.

'I'm feeling dizzy,' she said. 'Do you mind if we go?' She gripped the top of a chair. 'Lovely t-table.'

Nine

She steadied herself, ran a finger tracing the whirls of the grain. 'Someone has looked after this,' she said.

'My grandmother. She made her own polish from beeswax. She kept her own bees.'

'Heavens,' said Gina. Made her own polish? Didn't the shops sell polish in Wales?

'The house has a special feeling about it, don't you agree?' said Mark, his pride unconcealed. 'While I was in America, which was great in every way, I forgot what an interesting place this is.'

'The hall's a bit dark and gloomy.'

'The Elizabethans didn't go in for windows and high ceilings. They were taxed on windows and had to conserve heat. Perhaps I could let in some light somewhere.'

'A few glass doors? A mirror?'

He shot her a quick look.

'This is the new kitchen, my grandmother's pride and joy. The blue ceramic tiles were specially imported from Italy, and the island counter was way ahead of its time when they fitted it.' He poured glasses of orange juice from the refrigerator.

'Thanks,' said Gina. 'Even I could boil an egg with such modern equipment.' She couldn't remember ever having boiled an egg, not even once, but it made her feel good to pretend. She knew they were put in water. Easy.

'So tell me about your work,' he said evenly.

'I run an international shipping company. My job is a cross between direct contact, quick decisions and remote policy-making. I sit with my feet in a drawer, the phone on voice mail, drinking coffee and gossiping with Mavis, my efficient secretary.'

'Sounds exhausting.'

'Extremely,' said Gina, following him upstairs on his relentless tour. The bedrooms varied enormously: the eighteenth-century rooms were gracefully proportioned with wide latticed windows; the rooms over the new extension were modern, but cramped and claustrophobic cell-like chambers crouched in the hunting lodge. They made her shudder. Gina could not get out of them fast enough. She retreated down the dark staircase, gripping the balustrade, her palms damp and sweaty.

As she turned at the foot of the stairs, slightly out of breath, her glance rested on a portrait she had not noticed before. It was in a heavy gilt frame and the dull gleam from the ornate gilt first caught her eye. It was a head and shoulders portrait of a young girl; a young girl of about thirteen or fourteen. She was dressed in an early Tudor style dress with big brocade sleeves and tight brown velvet bodice, trimmed with gold. Her frizzy, light brown hair was mostly hidden by a stiffened headdress edged with pearls.

Her face was interesting; roundly plump but with a quaint air of worldly experience and resignation. For all the opulent clothes and jewels, she was still a child. Gina wondered if beneath that rich dress, she was barefooted, toes twitching to be off from the tedium of sitting still for the portrait painter.

The girl's features were plain: a broad childish brow and pale arched eyebrows; her nose straight and a little long; full, uncoloured lips were set in a closed determined line. But her eyes ... they stared with an intensity that the painter had captured with skill. Her eyes were wide and clear; their colour a strange grey-green like mossy pools. They looked straight at Gina with an expression that was difficult to define. A knowing look of a young head on old shoulders, her thoughts veiled but uncompromising.

Gina found herself smiling. She bet that young lady had been a handful. Suddenly she shivered. The girl was dead now. The hourly passing of time chilled her momentarily. She struggled to put these thoughts out of her mind.

'Do you think we could go?' she suggested flatly. 'It's been a long day and I didn't sleep well last night.'

'Of course,' said Mark. 'Your own home in Cranbourne Square is so beautiful, no comparison to Erddig.'

'It's a fascinating farmhouse,' said Gina, making a determined exit. 'I can see why you're fond of it. But surely for a farmer the land is of more importance than a house?'

'The farm land is excellent. There's a belt of woodland with Norwegian maple, Scots fir and Dutch alder. A hundred and ninety acres of harsh but good sheep pasture for my Beulah Speckle Face and Clun Forest.'

'Your what?'

He grinned. 'They're the breeds of sheep I'm planning to stock. The Speckle Face produces wool for high quality fabrics with the coarser wool going into carpets. The Clun Forest are considered to produce the finest wool in Britain and goes into hosiery and knitting industries. Then there'll be a pig unit with farrowing pens.'

'Stockings and carpets.' Gina wrinkled her nose. 'Doesn't sound much like farming.'

She stepped awkwardly into a puddle and the rainwater splashed up her boots on to the nap of her cord trousers. It soaked through immediately. Her cuff was still damp from the spilled coffee. She began to feel grubby and bedraggled.

'Would you like to stop somewhere for a meal? I owe you for dragging you round Erddig and spoiling your shirt.'

The irritation which had been fermenting inside her suddenly swept through her. She was tired of being manipulated by other people and the last person she wanted to be with was Timothy's brother.

'No, I'm wet and tired and I'd like to get back to Plas Glwydan. I don't want another lecture about the infamous way I treated your brother. I'm sure that was on the menu. I've had enough lectures from you to last a decade.'

'I'm sorry you feel that way,' said Mark. There was a matching ice beneath his voice. 'There were no strings attached. We might have talked about Timothy in the hope of finding some clue to his whereabouts. You're not too worried.'

'It's very normal to be left at the church, looking a fool in front of friends and half of the world's press. Happens all the time. I'm the one who had to deal with the mess. Timothy is probably sunning himself in Barbados with a blonde nurse.'

'With no passport, no money? Have some sense,' he said through gritted teeth. 'Get in.'

'Haven't you heard of duplicate passports? Secret bank accounts? No, thank you. Perhaps you'll ring for a taxi. I'd prefer my own company.'

'Since I also find your company intolerable, I'll turn on the radio. I'll easily be able to pretend you aren't here.'

'Turn up the volume.' Gina rubbed away at the steam on the window to rid herself of some of her annoyance. She wanted to get home. Cranbourne Square beckoned her with comforting arms, as it had through other disasters: when her parents crashed; that bleak day when beloved Grandfather died.

Mark gripped the steering wheel as the rock band thumped discordantly into the interior. Gina clamped her jaw shut. Her nerves were stretched to breaking point, but she refused to ask him to turn it down.

The gathering night was inexpressibly menacing. Her senses were quickened to danger, but what kind of danger she did not know. Darkening branches swooped like injured birds against the windscreen, wings beating for freedom.

She was limp with exhaustion and noise by the time the Range Rover swung into the gravelled drive of the castle. Mark switched off the radio, then the engine. The stillness pounded her ears as if she had gone deaf.

'Your taste in music is as appalling as your rudeness and bad manners,' she managed to say.

'I didn't quite catch what you said. Were you thanking me for driving you back?' he enquired. 'I'm beginning to think my brother had a lucky escape. I can't imagine what he saw in you. Certainly not charm. Looks, loads of money, but nothing much else.'

Gina gasped. No one had ever been so rude to her. He hated her. It made her cringe. To her knowledge she had never acted badly towards any human. Brownie points every day. She loved Timothy and had wanted to marry him. But nothing she could say to Mark Trenchard would make him believe her.

She put out her hand to wrench open the door. He moved as swiftly, imprisoning her wrist. She could not move.

'Let me go,' she hissed. 'Caveman tactics are so boring.'

'You wouldn't know a caveman if you met one swinging a club. Time to pay for the lift.'

His mouth came down on hers with a fierceness that took her utterly by surprise. She struggled, but his body was an immovable weight. She felt she was suffocating beneath his size and flesh and there was no escape. Small sounds of anger and fear came from her as his mouth moved with a hungry insistence on her soft lips. His hands were tangled in her hair, tugging her head back. She felt the roughness of his chin burrowing into her tender flesh.

He let her go, as suddenly, and she fell back, trying to catch her balance.

'I wanted to find out what it was like. Timothy did have a lucky escape,' he added laconically.

Gina hardly heard the insult. Her senses were reeling, shattered by the passion that Mark's kiss had aroused in her. A moment longer and she might have been recklessly responding with a fervour and wanton desire that brought a blush to her cheeks. She thought cavemen were extinct. That single kiss had sent her wild.

Her breathing was ragged; kisses in the past had been clumsy, meaningless. Even Timothy's kisses had been light and youthful, a pleasant, happy show of affection, undemanding.

She was disturbed and angry but she could not deny that her traitorous body was elated. She had not known such passion existed. It was there, hidden in her soul. She had only to find the right man with the key.

As her racing pulse steadied, another feeling took over. It was anger at the cruel joke fate had played; that the object of her body's craving should be a man she thoroughly disliked and who disliked her even more.

She stormed into the stone porch of the castle. Jake and Jasper rose up from the hall floor and came over to sniff the odours from her splashed cords. They lost interest and ambled away.

'You forgot your bag,' Mark called. She was too angry to answer. He tossed her bag into the porch and immediately the dogs pounced on it, snarling, tearing at the leather straps.

Gina shrank back, astonished and frightened by their ferocity. She heard footsteps hurrying.

'Stop it! Jasper! Jake! Bad dogs!' Lindsie dragged the bag away from them and the dogs hunched down, their back legs sliding on the floor, slobbering. 'I'm so sorry, Gina. Are you all right? It must smell of pig. I've never seen them do that before. I'll make you some coffee.'

'I don't want any coffee.'

'It'll do you the world of good. I bought proper fresh coffee today. You'll like it.'

Gina gave in. She did not care any more. She felt hot and her forehead was damp. She was sickening for something. She followed Lindsie into the long sitting room, praying for strength to endure whatever was in store for her. The room was quiet and restful, the fire blazing merrily and spitting sparks in all directions, the day's newspapers scattered on the floor.

Real coffee and shop biscuits. Lindsie began to feed broken biscuits to the dogs. They made short work of the bits, woffling and growling, leaving a mess on the floor.

'I'm sorry about your bag. You won't want to use it again. It's all wet.'

'Doesn't matter,' said Gina, feeling degrees better but longing to go home. 'I'll go home tonight. I don't feel well and I've imposed on you long enough. You're both so busy.'

'Nonsense, you can't drive if you are ill. You must stay here until you feel better. You might have an accident.'

'I'm all right to drive. Mrs Howard knows how to look after me. I can't possibly give you any more trouble.'

'It's no trouble at all. Just a few trays,' said Lindsie kindly.

Gina thought of Lindsie's trays and closed her eyes with resignation.

'How old is this castle?' she asked numbly, not knowing why she asked.

'I'm not sure. Middle Ages, perhaps further back. The hall is medieval. Barry knows, of course. He knows everything about it.'

'It's not Elizabethan?'

'No, much older.'

'I'll start packing.' There was a desperation in Gina now. She would be ill if she stayed any longer. Something weird was seeping into her bones, sapping her strength, and only Cranbourne could make her feel right.

Lindsie looked hurt but then she patted Gina's arms. 'There's nowhere like your own bed. I'll make you a thermos of coffee for the drive.'

Lindsie's good nature made Gina feel guilty. She hoped the case of sherry would make up for her sudden departure. She hurried to the turret room and threw stuff into her overnight bag. She could not shake off this disorientated feeling.

'Say goodbye to Barry for me,' said Gina, stumbling through the hall, her lungs bursting for fresh air. 'You must come up to London for the weekend. We'll go to the theatre, do some shopping. You can't stay buried in the country.'

She could smell a whiff of freedom now that she was actually leaving. It dragged her like a magnet.

The cousins kissed each other on the cheek.

'Thank you again for a lovely weekend.'

'It's been lovely seeing you,' said Lindsie, a touch of wistfulness in her voice. 'Take care.'

She looked lonely, lost in the vastness of the porch, the castle looming bleakly behind her, the dogs ambling round her feet, getting in the way.

Gina drove slowly, resisting the temptation to accelerate and celebrate her escape. Once she was out of sight of the castle she put her foot down. Soon the motorway was signed ahead.

The powerful car ate up the miles. She could not remember a worse weekend. She felt restless, a kind of inner ripping apart. Then there was Mark Trenchard and his degrading kiss. She refused to be made to feel guilty about another Trenchard, especially when she did not deserve it.

Rain spotted the windscreen, slowing her down, and the wipers moved cautiously, feathering the drops into smears. She put her foot on the brake lightly while the washer spurted water on the windscreen. She could not see clearly. It was frightening. She thought these lenses were all right. A fast car approached from behind. She leaned forward to adjust the position of the rear-view mirror which was slightly off centre.

At first it did not register. She was looking into the mirror to check the view behind her. Something was not quite right.

This time she had a weird feeling, a cold shiver ran down her spine, an ominous feeling of dread. Her glance locked on to the eyes in the mirror and she could not believe what she was seeing. She saw round eyes set under arched brows ... deep green mossy pools. Strangely green with thin brows...

The eyes that stared at her from the mirror were not her own. They were alien eyes. They were hostile. They bored into her like lasers. Her skin crawled and Gina felt needles of pain burning into her skull.

Ten

Gina was an expert driver. Her feet and hands did all the right manoeuvres while her mind reeled with shock waves.

Trembling, she peered again into the mirror. The same green eyes locked on to hers with an uncanny grip. She couldn't believe it. It must be a hallucination. Perhaps she was more ill than she thought.

She tried to control her panic. There was moisture on her upper lip which she licked nervously. This was ridiculous. She stared, stunned, at the red tail lights of lorries flashing past like strings of shimmering Arabian rubies, thundering towards their suburban harems.

The sign ahead was a knife and fork, a service station. She got there without thinking. Gina parked between a Mini and a transit van, then sat with her head on the steering wheel, waiting till she felt calm enough to go in.

The cafe was busy, noisy, a lot of people buying food and drinks, playing the pinball machines. Gina stood in the queue for a coffee. She felt alien, out of place.

'Where are the spoons?' she asked a girl.

The girl, Asian, tired and starting a late shift, flicked back a long black plait. 'By the till,' she pointed.

The brown liquid was bitter and tasted of chicory. Disappointing. Her whole body was crying out for caffeine. Gina remembered the flask which Lindsie had given her. Dear, kind Lindsie. It would be better than this stuff. She got up to fetch the flask from the car.

Someone caught her arm. It was a woman in a cheap rayon overall.

'The coffee may be expensive but it doesn't include the cup,' she snapped, taking it out of Gina's hand.

Gina backed off as if the woman had slapped her. The woman thought she had been stealing a brown cup.

When she got to the Mercedes, she tied a handkerchief over the mirror. Lindsie's flask was in the glove compartment. It was good and strong, tasted of farm milk. She drank two cups and felt better. She would drive with the mirrors covered, even if it was against the law.

She drove slowly, ignoring the impatient drivers who shot past. She joined the crawling London traffic, knowing that Cranbourne Square was not far away. The square was dark and cold, the trees like black sentinels. She remembered the man she had seen walking in the darkness, knew that it had been Mark Trenchard. He'd been stoking up hatred, hatred that he was able to cover with charm when it suited him.

She left the car by the pavement for Howard to put away in the mews. A stab of grief reminded her that Timothy was still missing. Her eyes pricked with tears and she blinked hard. Damn Mark Trenchard and his accusations.

'Miss Gina, we didn't expect you home yet,' said Betsy, hurrying through from the kitchen. 'Is there anything you'd like? A hot drink?'

'No, thank you. I'm going straight to bed. But if Howard could put the car away?'

'Very well. Goodnight, Miss Gina.'

'Goodnight, Betsy.'

She switched on the lights in her bedroom. It was warm and familiar, a pink cocoon, a nest in which she could hide. Still averting her eyes, she walked over to the dressing mirror and threw her coat over it. She had no wish to be reminded of the horrifying experience in the car.

She undressed with wooden arms, leaving her clothes on the floor. Wrapped in a huge, fleecy shawl, she curled up in an armchair to watch a late movie on television. The plot was tense enough to drive fears from her mind, though afterwards she could not remember any of it.

Gina woke early the next morning, hoping the misty sunshine was a good omen. She must have imagined it all. But then Betsy told her it was Monday when she felt certain it was Sunday.

She showered and dressed in a silk shirt, grey suit and leather belt, fastened a gold bracelet that had been her mother's. She pulled her luxuriant hair into a tight knot, securing it with long granny pins.

Today was hiring and firing day. She would enjoy promoting a junior manager in cruise reservations who was ready for grooming; the other was a trusted colleague who had lost an expensive contract through carelessness. She would not enjoy asking him to go.

She thought of Lindsie working like a demented beaver in that huge, gloomy castle. It was not housework, but castlework. Lindsie had always played house, even as a little girl, dusting the doll's house with a miniature duster, making hoovering noises as she cleaned tiny carpets. A smile quickened Gina's mouth and, off-guard, she caught a reflection of herself in the mirror she had been avoiding so carefully.

The green eyes stared at her with coolness, more knowing, their paleness like water that had stood unruffled for a long time. Gina's hand shook violently and she dropped the blusher she had been using. Her gaze was held by the intruder eyes and she could not break away however hard she tried. They were molecules with intense power, a streak of lightning caught in mid-flash and frozen.

A clamp of fear seized her throat and she gasped for breath. The intake of oxygen broke the spell and she flung herself away across the room, staggering to the window, flinging it open and drawing in gulps of sharp morning air.

She leaned against the window, not seeing the square moving into quiet activity: prams pushed, dogs walked, post delivered. She saw nothing, only those insidious eyes that for a moment had replaced her own. She put her hand up to her face, half expecting to find empty sockets; her long lashes brushed against her fingers and she was surprised to find them wet.

She must see someone, get help. There was a rational explanation. Perhaps there was something wrong with her eyes. Alarm bells rang. She had never been ill in her life and the idea of some part of her body becoming diseased was frightening. She would have her spectacles checked and her contact lenses. Maybe the lenses were rogue.

'Betsy,' she called urgently. Her maid was never far away when Gina was getting ready to go out.

'Yes, Miss Gina?'

'I want you to make an appointment for

119

me with an ophthalmologist, the best in London. And I must see him this morning. Do you understand?'

'Your optician?'

'No, an eye specialist. The London Eye Hospital will tell you who is the best.'

It was not easy to get an appointment. Gina found herself facing the tape-bound administration of a big hospital. It did not matter who she was, she would have to wait for an appointment. The best ophthalmologist in London was Sir Giles Barnett and he was in America at a medical conference. One of his colleagues was Mr Benjamin Hallam and she managed to get an appointment with him in the afternoon.

She went to her office in Conway House, hoping that work would take her mind off the shock of seeing the eyes again. She had no idea what her face looked like; her make-up had been applied without a mirror. She took care not to look into anything reflective, wondering if the screen on her desk would give another shock. But the screen showed nothing but the information she keyed in. She ordered sandwiches at her desk for lunch, scared of shop windows.

'You don't look very well, Miss Conway,' said Mavis. 'Why don't you let me cancel this afternoon's appointments?'

'I've got a headache,' said Gina, with a half truth. 'I don't think my new contact lenses are quite right.'

'You ought to see an optician.'

'I am, later this afternoon. Could you get me some more coffee, please. I have an awful thirst.'

'It's the screen, Miss Conway. A lot of the girls have complained of headaches, or neck pain. Repetitive strain injury, it's called.'

'My two-finger typing is a repetitive injury?'

Mavis grinned. 'I'll get that coffee.'

'Maybe I need a new chair,' said Gina, making a mental note. She had read somewhere of an advice centre, chairs checked for height and back support. She would mention it at the next board meeting.

She left early, wrapping a wool scarf round her neck against a cold east wind. She walked streets of pleasant town houses hidden from London traffic. Small, discreet corner restaurants and ethnic shops brought colour and life to the side streets, dusty squares were an oasis of quiet. She crossed a main road, darting between lumbering red buses and cruising taxis, as if bent on her own destruction.

Gina began to feel calmer as she walked and her headache eased. She usually felt so well; she could not believe that anything was wrong with her.

Mr Hallam would probably suggest a complete rest, perhaps a cruise on one of her own ships. She might process the reservation herself.

It was a long walk and Gina was late when she reached the consultant's rooms. She craved for a drink but it was not the taste of coffee that tantalized her. It was something she could not identify ... honey and herbs and an elusive flower. There was an after-taste in her mouth. Was it ginger? But she didn't like ginger.

Mr Hallam wasted no time in examining her eyes with a thoroughness she could not fault. His examination was assisted by the latest technical equipment. A machine in a darkened room blew puffs of air into her eyes and computerized the reaction.

'There's nothing medically wrong with your eyes, Miss Conway,' he said, sitting on the edge of his desk, hands in the pockets of his white tunic. 'You've nothing nasty to worry about. Apart from being long sighted and needing glasses for everyday wear, your eyes are perfectly healthy. Perhaps allergy-free mascara might be the answer. Mascara can irritate the lash roots and tear ducts.'

'That's all right, then,' said Gina with a slight laugh. 'Nothing to worry about.'

'But you haven't explained exactly what is worrying you.' Mr Hallam was looking at her keenly. He noticed the signs of tension, clasped hands, the dry mouth.

'It must have been something I imagined,'

said Gina, gathering her coat from the back of a chair.

'Would you like to describe your imaginings?' he probed, keeping his voice casual.

'If you say there is nothing wrong with my eyes, nothing nasty, then I'm satisfied.'

'Nothing nasty, I assure you.'

'Thank you, Mr Hallam. I won't take up any more of your time.'

He could see that she was upset about something. She was not the kind of woman to come for a trivial reason.

Gina hesitated. She longed to confide in someone and to have her fears allayed.

'Could one ... could one look into a mirror and not see what one might expect to see?' she asked. She saw Mr Hallam's expression change fractionally. 'For instance, and I know this sounds silly ... supposing one expected to see your own brown eyes ... and you saw instead green eyes. Someone else's eyes. I mean, would that be possible?'

It took a superhuman effort to actually say what had happened in the car and again in her bedroom. Her manner and confidence had slipped; she was raw nerves. She could not look anywhere, afraid that the green eyes might materialize from reflective surfaces, windows, lamps, shiny equipment.

'You're talking about hallucinations – the kind of thing that can happen under stress, lines of communication between brain and eye becoming tangled. I think your doctor could help you more than I can. Perhaps you ought to go and see him, Miss Conway.'

'Are you suggesting it might be a mental illness?'

'Hallucinations are not totally understood. Some are symptomatic of a serious mental condition, but I hardly think so in your case. You seem to me to be a normal, well balanced young woman. But have you been under any emotional stress lately?'

'Jilted at the altar, left in the lurch at the church,' said Gina, attempting a lightness. 'Is that stressful enough?'

'That could be traumatic enough to trigger off stress symptoms. It's highly complex. For instance, we know that a wrongly prescribed dose of a certain allergy drug can produce habit hallucinations. The patient sees letters on the mat – a habit reflex. He goes to pick them up but there's nothing there. He sees a cup of tea on the table and reaches out for it – again nothing. The brain is sending habit images to the eyes because it's out of step.'

'I'm not hallucinating things or people, but part of me ... this is so embarrassing. I'm seeing different eyes in my face. Mine are brown, quite dark and...' her voice trailed off as a wave of nausea swept over her. She held on to the back of a chair; the one stable thing in the room. The walls were closing in on her; Mr Hallam's face was peering down. He

124

poured out a glass of water.

'I do think you should see your doctor. He could put your mind at rest.'

'Perhaps I will.' She gulped down the water.

'Feel free to come back, anytime.'

'Thank you.'

The London street was the same, thronged with cars, buses, taxis, hurrying pedestrians. Gina was relieved that she was not harbouring some odious disease. She was overwrought. Who wouldn't be upset after Timothy's disappearance and his brother's relentless accusations?

It was nothing a week at a health farm wouldn't cure. She would take some leave, go wallow in a hot jacuzzi. Perhaps she had kept the hurt hidden too successfully and the distress was showing itself in a different guise.

She walked along the pavement with her gaze firmly ahead, holding her neck stiffly in case it should stray to a shop window. She was learning that reflections were not all that they seemed to be. She remembered the cat in the grocer's window and shuddered. The cat had green eyes.

The feeling that she was not herself persisted all evening. She dressed carefully in a dark velvet dress and throw-over wrap, making up her face by touch, lightly as if she was blind. She went to the ballet, sitting alone, trying to concentrate on the floating figures and letting the music soothe and refresh. She wouldn't go to the company doctor. She would find someone who did not know her.

As she sipped a glass of white wine in the interval, a feeling of optimism suddenly took over. She almost laughed. Perhaps she would ring Lindsie with a mock complaint.

'Your spooky castle!' she would say. 'It had me seeing things. You'd better come up to London for some shopping, a theatre or two, before you start seeing goblins.'

After the performance she followed the crowds on to the pavement, pushed by a surge of people overflowing into the road. She tried to get a taxi but it was impossible to find one. She phoned Howard to come and rescue her. She paced up and down, memories flooding her mind as she pulled the wrap closer, waiting for Howard to arrive.

Her parents had been a handsome, dream-like pair, travelling the world while their daughter was at a private school, then an expensive boarding school. They loved their skinny, tawny-haired daughter, but from a distance. When they discovered she had become a fiercely independent and outspoken teenager, it was almost too late. They were flying back to see her when the plane crashed.

She had cried. Then Grandfather died and she cried again.

Was it her mother's voice she sometimes heard? But there was a dominance, a latent cruelty in the voice. Not her mother at all.

'You should wear flowers in your hair and let your hair hang loose,' he said.

'My mother would not like it. She says I am a woman now and must wear my hair plaited and in a net.'

Will turned away and continued cutting the laurel hedge. It was a high hedge, silvery-green, weightless, but not high enough. There were eyes everywhere and he did not want to be seen talking to the master's daughter. It would be the end of his work at the manor house and the cottage that went with it.

'Don't turn away when I am speaking to you,' she said, stamping her small slippered feet.

'M'lady, please. I cannot be seen speaking to you.'

'But you have spoken to me. About flowers, about my hair. You can't now pretend that you haven't.'

Will's eyes were amused. She noticed that they were a twinkling hazel set under heavy brows and that his nose was straight, his mouth warm and generous. He said nothing but handed her a flower. It was a glowing marigold, its petals matching the glints in her imprisoned hair.

Eleven

Gina could not remember their faces clearly. Her parents had receded into a shadowy past. She had that lost feeling now, waiting for Howard, uncertain of herself.

'Miss Gina?' Howard had to speak to her twice.

'Thank God you're here,' she said, getting into the passenger seat beside him. He was surprised but said nothing. He could see she was not herself and needed perhaps the reassurance of his familiar bulk.

'Lot of crowds about, miss. Not very pleasant.'

'No. I suppose I'm used to being with friends. Going out alone is a bit alarming. There wasn't a taxi in sight. Did I disturb your favourite TV programme?'

'No, miss. Same old rubbish. A repeat.'

Once indoors she hurried upstairs to her room, refusing any refreshment. She was deadly tired and wanted to sleep and sleep. It had been a long day and she was chilled to the bone. A breeze hurried rainclouds across the darkened sky as she stood at the window. She knew she was a fool to be standing there, getting cold, her spirit falling like stones.

Timothy ... she wanted to talk to him, to sort it out. She found herself dialling the number of his flat. She hardly recognized Mark's voice when he answered.

'Timothy?'

'Mark Trenchard,' he said.

'Mark? What are you doing there?'

'I'm living here, remember? I'm using Timothy's flat until I get settled at Erddig. Look, is this important? It's after midnight.'

'I'm sorry ... I didn't realize it was so late. I've been to the ballet.'

'How delightful. Perhaps you'd like to tell me about it some other time. I'd like to get some sleep.'

'Mark. Was that you, walking in Cranbourne Square the night of my wedding? It was you, wasn't it?'

He cleared his throat like someone caught out. 'Yes, I was trying to make up my mind about something.'

'At least I wasn't dreaming. It wasn't another hallucination. I'm beginning to wonder how long this has been going on.' She was trying to sound cool and normal to this man, but he detected the distraction in her voice. He was alert to a nuance in her voice that was so unlike the angry young woman who had flounced out of his car in the driveway of Plas Glwydan castle. He instinctively felt and acknowledged the fear.

'Is something the matter, Gina? Do you want to tell me about it?' He thought that at last she was going to tell him the truth. 'Would you like me to come over?'

He heard a sharp intake of breath.

'Would you?'

'I can be with you in fifteen minutes.'

Gina put down the phone with relief. Her hands were damp. It had cost a slice of pride to admit to Mark that she needed him. She would feel safer if he was with her, even if they were fighting and arguing. She needed his strength, his stubbornness, that inner steel.

She shivered. Hot water next, and plenty of it. She turned on the hot water in the shower so that the mirrors steamed up. She slipped out of her clothes, stepped into the shower and let the blessed water run over her chilled skin, bending back her head so that it streamed against her closed eyelids, washing out the gremlins.

Betsy had put out a clean nightgown, demure Victorian frills, laid on the bed. There was a flask of coffee by her bed and a posy of flowers on the dressing table.

Gina smiled at her maid's devotion, sipping coffee, glancing at the flowers reflected in the mirror. It was her undoing, a terrible, terrible mistake. For a moment she was off guard. The pale green eyes stared at her, the arched eyebrows moved slowly, raised themselves questioningly...

She froze, not breathing.

'Go away! Go away!' Gina cried, her voice rasping. 'I'm not seeing you. You aren't there...'

The eyes mocked, their knowing look draining any courage Gina might have. With a desperate cry she lunged at the mirror, knocking over the posy, water spilling on the carpet. She put her hands over the eyes in the mirror, trying to block them from sight, but they followed her head. She felt a scream starting to spurt in her mouth and heard at the same time a ringing in her ears. It was the front doorbell.

She fled from the room, pulling a big towel round her, feet leaving damp marks on the carpet. The insistent noise rang in her ears like an alarm. She reached the door before the Howards woke.

He stood in the doorway, big, even though the stern look was uncompromisingly Mark. She went straight towards him, forgetting wet hair, damp towel. She leaned against him, breathing the animal smell from his sheepskin coat, shuddering as the cold night air touched her bare shoulders.

'Hey, what's the matter?' he said, his arms

hanging at his sides, not daring to put them round her. She was vulnerable, shaken. If he touched her now, she would hate him for taking advantage. He rubbed his chin on the top of her wet hair, like an affectionate cat.

'You'll catch cold,' he said, closing the door with his foot.

'I'm afraid,' she cried out.

'Tell me about it.'

He fastened the towel more securely round her body with a gaucheness that Gina would have found touching. He guided her towards the drawing room where a fire still burned in the grate, the embers glowing rosily behind the guard. She looked as white as alabaster despite the honey tan.

A sudden longing made Gina's heart ache for a more intimate closeness. He gave her an odd searching look as if the same feelings were lodged in him. Neither spoke.

A shiver ran along her spine even though the room was pleasantly warm. He lifted her into his arms and carried her across to a deep armchair. She curled on his lap like a child, her head against his shoulder, her hair tickling his nose. She could feel strong heart beats, marvelling that the muscle would beat steadfastly in that broad chest for three score years and ten, then at its allotted moment in time it would flutter, falter and stop. He would ebb away. The pain of death caught Gina unawares and she sobbed aloud, fingers clawing at him.

'Hey ... don't cry,' he whispered, amazed by her intense emotion. His arms closed round her slowly so that she would not be frightened, unsure if she would push him away. Her distress was genuine and he was at a loss. The confident Miss Conway had become incoherent and helpless. But the perfume from her hair was intoxicating, her skin clean and moist and he longed to bury his face in such perfection.

'I'm sorry,' she said, shaken. 'I'm sorry.'

'What's the matter?'

'I had a terrible thought ... of the future.'

'Don't think of the future, only today.'

'I can't!' Her voice rose, almost hysterical. 'Today is unbearable. Today is a nightmare.'

It was impossible to tell him but his presence was reassuring. Everything about him was normal, earthy, even his annoyance at being brought out in the middle of the night.

'Something is happening to me. It's probably that old castle giving me the creeps. I've never been anywhere so old before. There's something weird about it.'

None of it made any sense. Mark waited patiently. His glance swept over her bare toes, the nails glossy with silvery pink varnish. He bent down and removed a tiny wet marigold petal stuck to the skin of her foot.

'Barefoot in the garden?' he asked quizzically, holding up the fragile petal on the tip of his finger.

'I knocked over some flowers ... in my room. I had to. She was there. In the mirror.'

'She?'

She began shaking, panic setting in. He was appalled at her state of mind.

'You need a drink,' he said.

'C ... coffee will be fine,' she said, saying the words automatically. The words echoed, echoed, echoed. She knew she drank a lot of coffee. But the words seemed like a warning, a forgotten phrase from the past.

Mark made her drink brandy. The fire helped to steady the trembling in her hands. He kept his fingers over hers as she lifted the glass to her mouth.

'Do you want to go upstairs and get dressed? Would you feel more comfortable with clothes on?'

'No!' She jerked out the word.

'What's the matter? Is there someone in your room?'

Gina closed her eyes. She could still see those other eyes imprinted on her memory. But was it a delusion? Her hair fell around her face, drying in tendrils from the heat of the dying fire.

'What colour are my eyes?' she asked suddenly, turning to him. 'Tell me. Go on, tell me.'

He tipped her chin, looking deeply into

her face.

'What an odd soul you are. Don't you know? They are brown. Very dark, beautiful. I can't be poetic.'

'I'm seeing green,' she moaned. 'I'm seeing green eyes, every time I look, they are green.'

'Look where?'

'In the mirror, any mirror,' she gasped. 'Wherever I look, they are there, staring at me. A pair of green eyes, pale like water in a pond, with thin, arched brows. Mark, they are not my eyes. What am I seeing?'

'It could be a trick of the light,' he said, not helping. 'Light can do funny things. I've seen light in the mountains that looks like something else. Or perhaps the mirror is distorted.'

'In different mirrors. I've seen them in different mirrors,' said Gina, almost dangerously. 'I knew you wouldn't believe me. Now you'll go about saying that Gina Conway is going mad, going off her rocker, that your brother had a lucky escape. Burning the candle at both ends, drinking too much, drugs. I can imagine you'll get a great kick out of that.'

She began to cry again, tears spilling down her cheeks. The strain of the day had shattered her. She wanted to sleep and never wake up.

'I'm doing my best,' said Mark patiently. 'I am trying to understand. This illusion, call it what you will. I want to see these green eyes for myself.'

But she was hardly listening. Without thinking, he bent and kissed the back of her neck, a kiss so light and gentle that she could not be sure that his lips had touched her skin. It took her completely by surprise, so different from that other brutal kiss. She had not expected gentleness from Mark, only strength and resolution. But she had felt his breath on her neck as he parted the tangle of wet hair.

It was a sensation exquisite and her breath escaped, leaning on a long sigh. She wanted him to touch her and she tried to tell him without words. But she did not know how.

'You must sleep,' he said. 'You've had a bad dream.'

'It wasn't a dream. You don't believe me,' she wept.

He was dead tired. He had been asleep when she phoned. A smouldering coal fell from the fire, hissing and spluttering in the grate, a small shower of sparks following its trail. He moved the coal with the poker.

'Upstairs,' he said firmly.

Gina took comfort from his calmness. Even if he did not understand, he would not let that influence him. She forced herself to trust him as she had never trusted anyone before. Not even Timothy.

'That would be sensible, wouldn't it?' she

said in a small voice. She tripped over the trailing towel and he steered her towards the stairs. She smelled of meadow sweetness. The door to her bedroom was open and he saw the scattered flowers on the floor.

'Do you have to go?' she whispered.

'Do you want me to stay?'

'Please.'

He thought longingly of the comfortable bed that he had left. Suppressing a sigh, he pulled a duvet and some blankets off a bed in another room. He made a makeshift heap on the floor of Gina's room. He could sleep anywhere.

Before putting the light out he went over to Gina. She was already asleep, in her Victorian nightgown, her long lashes like dark fans on her cheeks. Her mouth was open slightly and she was breathing softly.

Mark did not kiss her. But he wanted to.

The shrill ringing of a distant telephone disturbed the silence. A quick look confirmed that Gina's extension was not switched on.

Mark hurried downstairs and whipped off the receiver.

'Yes?' he snapped.

'Miss Conway?'

'Miss Conway's asleep. It's very late.'

'I'm sorry but I must get some comments from Miss Conway for the last edition.'

'Your last edition can go to hell.'

'Haven't you heard? Her fiancé, Timothy Trenchard, he's been found. I must speak to Miss Conway.'

Mark breathed deeply through his nostrils, the relief like an inhalation of high-proof alcohol.

'Found. Timothy's been found? Thank goodness. Where is he?' he managed to say.

'In a mortuary. He was washed up on the South Coast, near Pevensey Bay. Drowned. Very dead. Now, can I speak to her?'

Twelve

Gina knew when she awoke that the world had changed. In the last few days she had become increasingly sensitive, picking up vibes from the air, from people. It was not the sight of Mark asleep on her bedroom floor in an ungainly heap that alerted her to the difference. He looked crampingly uncomfortable. Gina felt guilty for making him sleep like that.

His face told her that something had happened. He looked gaunt and drawn, a skin change that was not simply the result of a poor night's sleep. She crept silently out of bed and knelt down beside him, trying to cover his bare shoulders with the duvet. The mother instinct.

He stirred, aware of her warmth, her closeness, the scent of her skin. His arm went round her and he pulled her down to him without a word. Nothing motherly now.

Gina lay against him, wondering what had made him need her so suddenly. He was holding her in a vice-like grip. She could hardly breathe. She shifted so that her nose was clear to breathe and was surprised to find that Mark's cheek was damp, yet his skin was unexpectedly cold.

He opened his eyes and Gina saw the pain deep in their blueness, and she knew.

'Timothy?' she asked.

He nodded slowly, daylight returning to his eyes, the knowledge carved within. 'They've found him. He's dead, Gina. Drowned. He drowned himself.'

Gina did not recognize her own cry. It was a small, strangled sound of despair. Bile rose into her throat and she choked on it, brain numb with disbelief.

In that instant she remembered her parents' death, her grandfather's death, and knew that grief was in store for her again. Timothy, cold, lifeless, gone. She turned away from Mark.

'No, no ... oh no ... it can't be,' she whispered as Mark wrapped her in the duvet and held her, rocking her like a swaddled child. Her distress was so obvious, he could no longer doubt her feelings for his brother. This was no Oscar-winning performance. The tears were genuine, running down her face, scalding and blotching her skin.

'When? Where?' she sobbed when the first, shocked wave of crying subsided through exhaustion, trying to adjust her mind. 'How do you k-know?'

'A newspaper reporter phoned last night, one of the tabloids. The police will be round this morning. Perhaps they'll be able to tell us more. All I know is that his body was found near Pevensey Bay, on the South Coast.'

'His body ... I don't understand. We were so happy. We wanted to get married. We hadn't had a row or anything. You've got to believe me, Mark.'

Gina imagined his body in the water, floating, his fair hair clinging wetly, his face white and cold. Timothy, who had always been so vital, full of fun and laughter.

'I'm trying to believe you, Gina. But why should he kill himself? It doesn't make sense.'

'It must have been an accident. He fell in or someone mugged him on a ferry and pushed him in the sea. I won't believe that he killed himself. Never.'

'You'd better get dressed. The police will be here soon. Shall I ask Betsy to come up?

Bring you some tea?'

'Yes, p-please. I want to tell her myself. I'm so sorry, Mark,' she said, touching his face. 'He's your brother and I'd forgotten. Forgive me. You must be devastated.'

'I don't know what I feel,' he said grimly. 'I want to know the truth, I suppose. He wouldn't have killed himself for nothing...'

'He had no reason to kill himself.' Gina heard her voice creeping towards hysteria. 'Where is he? I want to see him. I want to know what happened.' She wrenched herself out of Mark's arms and rushed to the phone. He stopped her.

'Don't be silly, Gina. Seeing Timothy won't help. Wait until the police come and tell us what they can. You'd better get dressed, have some breakfast.'

Gina took deep breaths and, suddenly aware of her nightdress, reached for her wrap with untouchable dignity.

'Another bathroom?' he asked, rubbing stubble.

'The guest bathroom is off to the right.'

Mark disappeared, gathering clothes with him. Gina rang for Betsy, gulping several glasses of water to assuage her thirst, her mind sinking under the terrible news. Betsy came in and Gina turned to her.

'I have some news, Betsy,' she said, very low. 'It's about Timothy.'

* * *

Somehow Gina got through the next few hours. A bleakness settled on her shoulders, weighing her down, making every step heavy, every movement an effort. Betsy chose clothes and Gina put them on, navy trousers, beige silk shirt, cashmere pullover. She was frozen and sat shivering in front of the fire Mrs Howard had lit in the sitting room.

She sat with her head in her hands. She could not believe it. Timothy was dead. Cold as she was, only colder. Blood at a standstill. Lungs inflated with water. Limbs stiff. No more dancing, no more loving.

Two plain clothes police officers came, faces respectful. It was difficult to take in all they were saying. Timothy had been found off the coast. They estimated he had been in the water about three days. They said something about tides and currents.

'Three days?' Gina repeated. 'But he vanished over a month ago. We reported it. You must be wrong.'

'There will have to be a post-mortem, Miss Conway. It's necessary in all such cases. We have to be sure of the cause of death.'

'I understand that,' she said. 'But three days ... are you sure? Where has he been all this time?'

'Someone will have to identify Dr Trenchard's body. Perhaps you, sir? Or would you prefer we use dental records?'

'No, I'll come,' said Mark.

'I'm coming too.'

'No, you're not, Gina. You're staying here. There's no need for you to see him. Remember him as he was.'

Gina did not know what she wanted. But she needed to hurt herself, to twist the knife deeper, to feel the very worst pain that was possible.

'I want to see him,' she breathed, her nostrils pinched. The bones of her fingers showed white through the skin. But Mark was already leaving, buttoning his coat, speaking to Betsy. They were talking about her as if she were a child, making arrangements over her head.

'I don't have a mental age of nine,' she protested, but no one was listening. Someone put a brandy glass in her hand. Later Betsy brought in some coffee and Gina was able to drink a cup, asked for it to be sweetened.

'Honey, mead, nectar, sweetmeats...' She ignored words floating in her head and her longing for them.

She hardly remembered what day of the week it was. Later she went outside and walked round Cranbourne Square, her legs moving automatically, her arms listless, not seeing, only aware of the cool air on her face.

So he's dead, a voice said in her head but she did not know where the voice came from. She phoned through to Mavis.

143

'How did you get on at the Eye Hospital, Miss Conway? There's a pile of faxes from New York for you.'

'I'm not coming in,' Gina said. Was it only yesterday she saw Mr Hallam? It could have been a year ago. 'It's really bad news ... Timothy, my fiancé ... he's dead.'

'Oh, Miss Conway, how awful. I'm so sorry. Of course, stay at home. But can I do anything, anything at all?' Mavis was shocked and upset.

'Send me those new figures about cargo loads, displacement and transport arrangements. I need my mind occupied.' Gina had to hang on to some reality.

'Surely someone else can look at them? Mr Burroughs?'

'No, I want to do it,' Gina said. 'Send a messenger round with the files. And the New York faxes.'

The police came again the next morning. It was very formal. They asked her the same questions, but she knew nothing. They asked her about the day before her wedding, but she could hardly remember it at all.

'It was the last time Mr Trenchard was seen,' said the inspector. 'He was seen by a neighbour, going out.'

She got through the next few days in a mechanical daze, picking at what was put in front of her, wearing whatever Betsy chose.

She walked for miles through the London streets, hardly seeing the new leaves unfurling, the canopies of pink and white blossom in the parks and squares, beds of stiff tulips, velvety wallflowers. She ended up lost in a dingy suburb, streets of bedsitters and stray cats, and had to phone for Howard to come and find her. Sleep was evasive as her mind tormented itself with going over the days before her wedding and before Timothy's disappearance.

Had she really been so terrible? What had she done to send him away, into hiding for a whole month? Where had he been all the time while she endured the humiliation and despair of being abandoned by the groom on her wedding day?

'Miss Gina,' Betsy came into the shadowed room. 'Would you like the lights on? Mr Mark Trenchard is here to see you. Shall I show him in?'

'Yes, Betsy. Please bring in some coffee.'

She had not seen Mark since the news of Timothy's death. He was like a stranger. His features were haggard, his brows drawn close. He flung off his coat and pulled up a chair. He took both her hands.

'I've come from the police,' he said. 'The post-mortem report is disturbing. Do you want to hear it?'

'Yes,' she nodded. Another knife.

'Timothy didn't simply drown. He was

already dead when he was put in the sea.'

'Already dead?' Gina whispered. 'Put in the sea? I don't understand. He didn't drown then?'

'No, there was no inhaled seawater in the lungs. He died from an overdose. Not a single overdose, but a build up taken over time. He died of lithium intoxication, severe poisoning. He could have got the lithium salts at the hospital. It's a very strong anti-manic drug.'

'I don't believe it. Timothy overdosing? Holed up somewhere on drugs? That's not Timothy at all.'

'I agree. It's totally inconsistent with his character and lifestyle. No way was he taking drugs.'

'So how did he get in the sea? He sure didn't walk there if he was already dead,' she said bitterly.

Mark gripped her hands tighter. 'The person who found him dead perhaps, who thought it was a way of getting rid of his body. Someone who didn't want to get mixed up in his death. A dealer, perhaps.'

Gina shook her head in disbelief. 'No, that's all wrong. It doesn't ring true. I don't believe any of it.'

'They are going to bring in a verdict of accidental death. He had access to the drugs at the hospital.'

'I'll fight it,' she said vehemently. 'Someone

killed him. He didn't take drugs.'

'There's no point, Gina,' said Mark, trying to calm her. 'You've no evidence. We've nothing to go on. An odd thing, they found pond algae in his nostrils and throat.'

'Algae? From a pond? Where?'

'I'm a farmer, not a bloody private detective,' Mark said, his eyes glinting. 'But I do want to know the truth and who is going to tell us? Timothy can't. The police won't waste their time on a drug addict's death. They get a dozen a day. Timothy had access to barbiturates every working day of his life. Sometimes doctors do take drugs to keep themselves going – to help them face failures, deaths, long hours.'

'But Timothy wasn't like that. He didn't need a prop. He was always cheerful, lively, full of fun. He had his own way of dealing with the negative aspect of his work, and that was to live life to the full.' Her voice broke.

'Perhaps you only saw one side of him. Maybe there was another, a dark side. Perhaps we didn't know him at all.'

Gina could have shaken Mark but at that moment Betsy came in with coffee on a silver tray which she put on a small table beside Gina's chair. There was a dish of Mrs Howard's home-made shortbread, but neither felt like eating. Gina poured the coffee carefully, determined that Mark would not see how much she was trembling.

Betsy went back to the kitchen, shaking her head. 'She's not eating. Not even your short-bread.'

Mrs Howard stirred a big pot of meat and bones. 'I'm making a proper consommé. Full of goodness.'

Gina wanted Mark to react. He was un-emotional and it made her feel frustrated and suspicious. Did he know more and wasn't going to tell her?

'Have you told me everything?' she said, spooning in sugar without thinking. She was spooning it fast. Suddenly there was a taste of honey in her mouth and she reeled. 'I can find out, you know. I'll ask for a copy of the police report.'

'They won't give it to you. I'm the next of kin. A jilted bride doesn't count.'

Gina gasped at his cruelty. This was the same man who had berated her at the reception, who blamed her for his brother's disappearance and now for his death. She thought that unpleasant character had gone away but he hadn't. He was still here, drink-ing her coffee. The warm grip of his hands on hers was fresh in her memory. 'I'll pre-tend you didn't say that,' she said.

'I'll pretend I'm sorry.'

'Will there be a funeral? It is allowed now?'

'I'm making arrangements for next Tuesday afternoon. You don't have to come.'

'You're always telling me what to do and

148

what not to do. I can make up my own mind. Of course, I'm going to Timothy's funeral. Jilted brides have to see it through to the bitter end, don't they?' She was determined not to let Mark see how much he had hurt her.

'You don't have to,' he said, finishing his coffee. 'I've asked the police to leave the case open. They might discover something. I'll pick you up at two thirty on Tuesday.'

'No, thank you,' she said with a lift of her head. 'Howard will drive me. Betsy and Mrs Howard will come too.'

He stood up to leave, a physical barrier to physical pain. Yet she did not want him to go, ever. She only felt safe when he was near.

'There was something else,' he added. 'When they found Timothy, his feet were tied together with a scarf. A silk scarf with a pattern of small blue anchors.'

For a moment Gina did not know if it was day or night, morning or afternoon. The room swam, coloured misty.

'Small blue anchors, you say?' she croaked.

'Does that mean anything to you?'

She nodded. 'It's the Conway Line. Something I brought in recently. All the female counter staff wear the scarf as a cravat with their uniform. And female crew members too. They wear a blue suit and the scarf.'

She had one tucked away in a drawer. She never wore it because she didn't meet the public. She had chosen the design, given the go-ahead for the production order. Trendy.

'That's strange, isn't it?' said Mark coldly, eyes narrowing. 'A Conway Line scarf securing his feet.'

'How should I know?' Gina snapped. 'It's a mystery to me. Do you think I tied up his feet, fed him drugs and then dumped him in the sea?'

She could see his mistrust. He thought she was lying, that she knew more about Timothy's disappearance than she would say. That she had engineered his death, that it was on her agenda...

Thirteen

The sky was slate grey with tattered clouds racing like lost souls. She worked the morning of the funeral, hoping normal activity would help to occupy her mind. May was turning into another cold month and reservations were busy with cruise bookings. They needed a new system to speed things up. She changed into a black velvet suit in her private bathroom. Her skin was magnolia pale against the mole-like darkness of the suit. Her tan had faded in the last few weeks.

'I'm glad you're coming,' she said to Mavis. 'I shan't feel so lonely. Friendly face and all that.'

'There's mud on the sleeve of your suit,' said Mavis. 'Hold a moment and I'll brush it off.'

The funeral was unreal. The varnished wooden coffin meant nothing. She couldn't believe Timothy was inside. It didn't look long enough. Timothy had been tall. She sent flowers, masses of them, but couldn't remember what she ordered. What could flowers do? He couldn't see them.

There were a lot of people at the crematorium, more than Gina expected: doctors and nurses from Timothy's hospital that she didn't know, even some patients; Betsy, both the Howards. Mark was withdrawn and sombre in a dark suit. He came and stood by her side, his face unreadable. The curtains drew across the coffin with theatrical slowness accompanied by organ music. Gina hated it all. Mark took her outside quickly and they looked at some of the floral tributes, but Gina saw nothing but a mountain of colour on the ground. Her lenses felt scratchy and uncomfortable and it was difficult to focus. She could hear though. She could hear a bird singing, throwing his heart at the world. The bursts of song were joyful, telling her that life went on.

'There's a bird singing,' she said.

Gina asked everyone to come back to Cranbourne Square for tea. She knew Mrs Howard had made cakes and small savouries and they would be ready to serve. Betsy and Mrs Howard had gone back ahead in a taxi.

'Your cousins didn't come,' said Mark.

'I wouldn't expect them all the way from Wales.'

Gina supposed the ritual helped. The use of familiar china and silver, the lace cloth on the fine Sheraton library table. Small silver vases which had been used for flowers since her childhood. She remembered once filling them with daisies and dandelions and her mother had set them on the table as if they were the best arrangements from a florist's shop. If only she could wake up and find this was a bad dream.

She wore the same black velvet suit to the next monthly board meeting of the Conway Line. It had become a uniform, put on without thinking. The directors made their apologies for not being at the funeral. They were sympathetic, wondering if Gina Conway was going to be strong enough to cope with the stress and still run the company.

'It's all right,' she said. 'You didn't have to be there. You're let off the hook. There's no need to feel awkward. The wedding was special. I wanted all my friends around. Funerals are different. They're more private.

I don't know why we have to go to them.'

'They say it helps with the grieving.'

'It isn't helping me.'

'Gina ... we're all so sorry.'

'Thank you, gentlemen. Now, let's get down to business. I haven't had a chance to look at the agenda.'

Mr Burroughs, the company secretary, passed her a copy. 'Slipping,' he murmured. Gina smiled back. Edward Burroughs was allowed to say such things. She had known him most of her life.

Gina took her place at the head of the board table, feeling as at home there as at Cranbourne Square. She put on her glasses.

'Having trouble with my contacts,' she explained. 'Item one. Minutes of the last meeting. Mr Burroughs, please.'

She had almost given up wearing contact lenses. It was impossible for her to put them in without using a mirror. Mirrors were out of her life. Eye make-up was a problem but now she was becoming expert at applying grey and brown on a brush without actually looking. It was like being blind only without a stick. Touch and instinct guided her hand.

The business of the meeting went through without argument. She brought up the subject of screen strain under any other business.

'I think we ought to have an expert come in and talk to the operators of VDUs,' she said. 'There's a right way and a wrong way of using these screens.'

'I suggest we leave this one to you, Gina. You seem to know all about it.'

'I'll get someone in personnel to arrange for a couple of talks. Any further business? Very well, gentlemen. Thank you for coming. Meeting closed.'

'Does the next meeting have to be a Saturday?' Edward Burroughs said. 'My wife hates me coming in on a Saturday.'

'I'm sorry, Edward. It suits everyone else.'

'I suppose I'm the only member who does their own gardening.'

'Why don't you have an extra week's holiday? Call it overtime. Surprise your wife. George Barker will find you a discounted cruise or a last minute cancellation.' Gina grinned. She doubted if Edward Burroughs would take advantage of her offer. She'd never known him to go on one of the company's ships.

'My wife doesn't travel well. Sea-sickness.'

She let herself out of the building. She loved coming in when it was empty, rooms unlit and quiet, knowing it was hers, that she gave employment to so many people, and enjoyment to their passengers. The cargo side was less exciting but was an essential part of the business. Her grandfather had been a wise old man, and clever. He had built up Conway Lines as trade was expanding, had ships and tankers built when the yards were desperate for work.

Saturday ... she had got into the habit of seeing Timothy every Saturday, unless he was on weekend duty. Now she had nothing to do. Not even a funeral to go to.

She could shop. She chose a microwave for Lindsie's monstrosity of a kitchen. An electric tin-opener, a heated hostess tray and a yogurt maker.

Gina arranged to have the goods delivered, spelling Plas Glwydan with care. 'Thank you for your help,' she said to the assistant, hoping the commission was good.

She walked back to Cranbourne Square, facing the bleak sunshine, glad to have done something positive to make Lindsie's life easier, though not quite sure about the yogurt maker. It might be too complicated. A Range Rover was parked outside her house. It was Mark. Her spirits lifted.

He opened the door to her, tall and casual in slacks and a black leather jacket, his hair spiky on his forehead as if he had been swimming.

'Come in,' he said, waving her in.

'How kind,' she said, stepping past him. 'I will. I think I live here.'

'Betsy's day off.'

'And Wednesdays, if I can make her take it.'

'I was in London to see my lawyers. I

155

thought you might like to go out. Weddings and funerals are not good times for getting to know people.'

Gina was surprised by the unexpected kindling in his blue eyes. Had she for once done something right? 'Why should you want to take me out? I thought I was the very worst type of woman, a bad influence, a bitch, someone to steer clear of.'

'Sometimes a little danger can be exciting.'

'I wouldn't know,' said Gina. 'I'm too busy at work. Feet in the drawer stuff.'

He raised his eyebrows. 'Must be a strain.'

'It's nearly ten years since my parents died. I needed to fill my time, so I learned my grandfather's business, starting as a clerk and working up.'

'I seem to be confused by seeing two Ginas. You might want to get changed. That suit's too smart for where we're going.'

Why did he say there were two Ginas? Sometimes she felt she was becoming two people. 'Where are we going?'

'I thought you'd enjoy going out on a small boat. A trip down the river.'

Gina had never been on a Thames pleasure steamer but had always wanted to. People looked happy on them, waving to anyone on shore who cared to wave back.

'Give me five minutes,' she said, running upstairs.

'You can have ten,' he said. 'Mrs Howard is

feeding me fabulous walnut cake in the kitchen.'

It was a wonderful trip down to Greenwich. The steamer was called the *Pearl of Pleasure*. The afternoon air took on a promise of summer and a rinsed sun beamed on them. They sat on deck, braced against the fresh breeze and choppy river.

It was a totally different view of London. Gina had not realized how many new high-rise blocks, church spires and giant cranes stabbed the skyline. The dock development was fascinating – some good, some gross – sites dominated by cranes. Despite being away four years, Mark knew what was happening and kept up a commentary. This was a London skyline unseen from taxis and cars.

They got off at Greenwich to have a look round. There were crowds visiting the National Maritime Museum.

'Henry VIII had a magnificent palace here, his favourite, and a tiltyard,' said Mark, strolling across the green, hands deep in his pockets.

'Where's it all gone?'

'Burnt down or pulled down. I think the Queen's House is the only original building left.'

'It feels old,' said Gina. 'In a nice way, like Erddig. But not like Plas Glwydan, which doesn't feel nice at all. I wonder what happened there in the past, to give it such a creepy feeling.'

'I didn't know old could feel nice or not nice,' he said. 'One of these special instincts that women are supposed to have.'

'Don't you ever feel something about a place or a building?'

'Not a building, but I feel things about land. I know if it's good for sheep, cattle, whether it'll grow crops or whether it's done for, cropped out by greedy farmers.'

'It's the same kind of thing,' said Gina. 'Knowing something that you can't see.'

'Too deep for me,' he grinned. 'Let's take a look at the Queen's House. It's beautiful.'

For the first time in weeks, Gina began to feel a twinge of hunger and when Mark suggested having a meal, she was pleased. It raised good calorie cravings.

'But I'm not dressed to go anywhere,' she said reluctantly, glancing at her fawn cords and pale fleece top. Her hair was caught back with a silver clip.

'I wasn't thinking of taking you to the Ritz,' said Mark. 'I had in mind somewhere quite different. But first we have to cross the river. We'll take the river bus. No ferrymen these days.'

Gina had never been to a Pizza Hut before. At first she was dismayed when they had to wait for a table. But once they were seated and the glossy menu was in her hands, she began to enjoy herself. Filling a salad bowl to the brim was obviously an art and she was amazed how much some of the diners managed to pile on.

'You don't put bulky salad at the bottom of the bowl,' Mark explained. 'Start with small stuff like coleslaw and shredded carrot. Build the sides with cucumber or celery. Leave the lettuce, tomato and new potatoes for the top.'

'There speaks an expert. You've obviously been here before,' said Gina, following him round the salad counter, apprentice style.

'It was the only place I could afford to eat in my student days. I became an expert at piling salad.'

'Student days?'

'Agricultural college. There's more to sheep dipping than dipping sheep.'

The pizza arrived on a piping hot brown platter, glistening with cheese, pepperoni, peppers and mushrooms. The young waiter served a huge slice on to Gina's plate.

'This is gorgeous,' said Gina, taking a big mouthful. 'It's like Yorkshire pudding with a savoury topping.'

'Haven't you had a pizza before? You're kidding me?'

She shook her head. 'Only those little triangles they serve up at parties and you eat with your fingers. Not a huge, crispy, fatty plateful like this. I must ask Mrs Howard to make one.'

They walked the darkened streets back to Cranbourne Square. Gina felt completely safe. Mark was a big man beside her. No one would dare approach them. He could cope with any situation that might arise. There were hooded youths, football fans and drunks about on a Saturday night.

'I've been to my lawyers today,' he said, looking down at her even though she was tall. 'They were Timothy's lawyers as well.' He glimpsed the apprehension in her eyes and was quick to reassure her. 'Don't worry, Gina. No more bad news. In fact, I think you'll be pleased.'

'Pleased? That's a funny word to use.'

'Timothy didn't leave much money,' he said. 'I think he was having too much fun spending it. But there was his salary and he'd been trying to save, perhaps for your future together. He made a will recently. Maybe he thought he ought to make a will as he was getting married.'

'I don't want to know any more,' she said quickly.

'He left his money to medical research,' he went on. 'And as things are, that seems the right and proper place for it to go. I don't want it and you don't need it. However, there was a codicil to his will which I think you should hear.'

Gina stopped on a corner and her hair was bathed in the yellow light from the street lamp. Her clothes were clothed in the unnatural light too, and she looked as if she had been turned to a statue of alabaster. She did not move.

'He sent you all his love. He said you had made him the happiest man on earth and he was proud to be marrying you.'

Gina took in a deep, shuddering breath of cold air. It was Timothy's voice from the grave that she heard saying those words.

'There,' she said. 'All his love. He loved me.'

'Yes, he loved you,' said Mark. 'Now the hard part. I want you to come to Timothy's flat with me and go through everything. You might know if anything is missing, what he took with him, spot a clue.'

'I can't do that.'

His face hardened. 'Yes, you can and you will.'

Will had gathered wild strawberries in his cap and as they lay by the stream, he fed them to her, one at a time. They were well out of sight of the manor house by a meandering stream that ran free-flowing over silvery pebbles and made music as it ran. Kingfishers darted among the weeds and rushes, flashing a brilliant blue.

She had brought a flagon of wine from the

cellar. Her mother had made it from elder-flowers and flavoured it with raspberries. Its colour was pale and pink like a young jewel.

Will fed her the tiny sweet strawberries, placing them between her small white teeth. She had loosened her hair and it fell around her shoulders in soft strands. The haze of sunshine blinded them and they could hardly see.

Juice oozed from the corner of her mouth and he kissed it away, then bent to her lips, dewy and fresh and untouched before. She liked Will kissing her, and lying on the soft grass bank by the cool, green stream, he did not seem so short.

The sun poured through the leaves and the heat of the summer was intoxicating. His hand went to the lacing on her bodice. She stiffened as his fingers brushed her skin. The dappled canopy of leaves stirred in a tantalizing breeze.

'Will?' she said tentatively.

His hand went elsewhere and she shot up, cheeks crimson. She scrambled to her feet, rumpled skirts cascading to her ankles, and ran as fast as she could towards the turreted gatehouse, her heart pounding.

Fourteen

They were on their way to Erddig Manor Farm. Mark kept the Range Rover in the fast lane, glancing occasionally at the passenger huddled beside him. Her face was drained of colour and the amber lighting from the overhead motorway lights cast an unnatural stain on her skin.

'We've got to put an end to this fear, whatever you think you see. If you think it started at my farm, then that's the place to find out what it is.'

'Yes,' she breathed. 'I want to sort it out, find out why it's me, find out what's happening.'

'I realize that you are longing to return to parties and the social round. It must be a handicap not to be able to fix your face properly.'

'The parties don't mean anything,' she said. 'It's my peace of mind and I want that back. It's a terrifying thing to look into a mirror and see someone else's reflection.'

'Get some sleep,' he said. 'It's a long drive.'

Gina shivered. It had been a devastating

end to Basil's party. Bring a friend, Basil said, so she had taken Mark as brotherly insurance. But those eyes were in a mirror again, mocking and cruel. Mark had steered her from the party, out in the cool air of the street, away from stares and people's insatiable curiosity.

He reached into the back and pulled over his sheepskin coat. 'Put this on,' he said. 'Where's your coat?'

'I've left it behind. And my bag.'

'Do you need your bag?'

'No, it doesn't matter.'

She tugged the sheepskin over her shoulders, absorbing its heaviness and the warmth, knowing that she was lost. It was madness to be driving through the night to Wales, but she could not wait to get there. Every hour was an hour nearer oblivion. Mark glimpsed the disaster on her face and reacted instantly in the only way he knew.

'When we get to the farm, you'll find everything normal. A few days in the country will calm you down.'

'I don't need calming down,' Gina said.

She closed her eyes to the flashing lights. She knew she would not be able to sleep. She could see the lights through the thinness of her eyelids, like a necklace swooping over her. She was left with thoughts and they were not comfortable. Those green eyes terrified her and they knew it, gloating in the knowledge.

Maybe she was going mad, deranged, to be locked in a care home. Where would they put her, the men in white coats? Some expensive private clinic where no one would know her and it would be kept a secret? Would they clamp electrodes to her brain and shock the delusions? What would happen to her fortune, to the control of Conway Lines? Aunt Stasi had gone mad, at the end.

An eerie dawn light streaked cold fingers through the end of the night as they neared the Severn Bridge. Ground mist swirled about Gina's feet as she climbed stiffly down from the sturdy vehicle. The all night café was faded and dingy.

Gina watched the wash of crimson tinting the clouds, growing from a vague streak into the glorious rays of pink and orange of a new day. She had never seen anything so beautiful. Had other dawns been like this? She could not remember, though there had been many eggs and bacon, champagne breakfasts at after-dawn parties. Somewhere, very far away, she heard a rooster crowing a brave clear sound.

'I didn't realize there were so many people about this early in the morning,' she said as huge container lorries moved in and out of the parking lot. 'I thought it was only postmen and milkmen.'

'How about farmers?'

'Farmers, too. I'd forgotten. Brain slip.'

'I suppose this is the first time you have ever had a serious worry, a major problem in your entire life. Such a sheltered and protected existence.'

'Don't you count Timothy's death and disappearance as a serious worry?' she said. 'And I hated going through his flat. We didn't find anything amiss. Nothing.'

Gina swung away from him. She did not want Mark to see her face. She had lost more than her fiancé. She had lost her peace of mind, gone like dropped litter in a gutter. And she hated Mark, a man never remotely or ever possibly a friend. How could she have ever thought there might be something between them? He couldn't stand the sight of her.

'Someone may have had time to remove anything incriminating. Who's to know?'

'Men think everything is cut and dried, especially feelings, emotions. So many points for this and so many for that. Start on square one, move forward five paces, collect a forfeit. Everything in black and white.' She hardly knew what she was saying. It sounded rubbish.

'Are we having this coffee? Or are we going to stand out here arguing? If not, I'd rather move on to Erddig.'

'Whatever you please.'

'Coffee first,' he growled.

'I'd like a cup of hot chocolate,' she said, being awkward. She wanted to be awkward.

He marched into the café, Gina following. She fumed. No man had ever treated her in this brusque manner. It was unpleasant. Retaliation time.

She looked an odd figure, red taffeta skirt trailing, satin slippers, sheepskin coat, totally out of place in a café.

'I don't think the tone of this conversation is going to improve our relationship,' she said, eyes blazing. 'I lost both my parents in a flying accident. Isn't that traumatic enough? My grandfather was very special and I lost him too. Running Conway Lines is not a hobby. Work has saved my sanity over the years.'

He snarled. 'A token board meeting every quarter?'

'Every month.' Gina was furious at Mark's insensitivity. 'Why don't you sit in at a meeting? Come and see exactly what happens.'

'Who would be speaking? Which face, which mouth? Your supernatural phenomena might start talking for you.'

Gina gasped. What did he know? Why did he say that? A new fear gripped her and she tried to read his face.

'Or is it all a trick? A whim on your part? Attention seeking. Women do weird things,' he went on.

It was cruel. Mark did not know why he

said it, only that he wanted to hurt her for what she had done to Timothy and what she could do to him, if he allowed her to get under his skin. Gina could collect men like moths to a flame. He was not going to become another of her victims.

After sitting and drinking in the garishly lit café, they went back to the Range Rover. He did not help her into the high vehicle. She scrambled up herself, tucking her skirt between her legs. He threw it into reverse, angry with himself for frightening her, but his determination had not lessened with time. There were moments when she was enchanting and those were moments to beware. She would use him as she had used his brother, for her own purpose.

They travelled in silence.

The warmth of the sheepskin coat kept her from shaking. Gina was afraid of the power of the portrait at the foot of the stairs at Erddig, but she was determined to face it. She had to find out what was behind this terrifying phenomena. She had not given up hope of finding out why she was being haunted. There was no other word. She was being haunted. The impending pain set her apart from the man sitting sternly beside her.

Mark slowed down to pay the toll at the Severn Bridge. White horses, laced with froth, rippled the surface of the Severn, whipped by a gale from the Atlantic. The wide estuary was dramatically misted, unpredictable, dangerous, a muddy line of earth and water. Opposite the Forest of Dean loomed, hiding its Celtic temples, silting into medieval mines.

They drove into the morning light, through half-awake villages into Wales. The signposts were in Welsh and English. He took the road towards Chepstow and Newport. The cultivated countryside encompassed all shades of green, its freshness a visual tonic, soft and muted, trees blending with hills, valleys dipping dramatically into dense woodland, streams merging with banks of rushes and weeping willows, straggling hedges. Horses stood in groups, sheltering their foals.

'We're near Plas Glwydan castle,' she said, suddenly alert. 'Isn't that the turning, over there?'

'Yes, that's the castle. It's about six miles from my farm. It depends which route one takes. There's a quick way and a long way round.'

'What do you mean?'

'It's very Welsh.' He sounded boyish, but only for a second. 'The lane through the woods is quicker. It's a long way round by road. We came that way the other day. A companionable drive, you'll recall.'

'But we aren't compatible,' said Gina, dismayed by the tone of his voice. 'We fight all the time.'

'I'm beginning to understand the meaning of the word. It was invented for people like us.' He was nearing Erddig and he knew that he had been right to return to Wales after years in America. His roots were here, ready to spring to life after being dormant in the heat of another continent. 'Catch the weather forecast,' he said, switching on the radio.

Gina stiffened. Her apprehension was swamping her. She was drowning. She could hardly hear the announcer, her heart hammering loudly in her breast and her body encased in a clammy straitjacket despite the warm coat. The journey stretched. She was being borne relentlessly towards the unknown. The man beside her was the journey man, but not the Dark Ferryman.

She cast a quick, sideways glance at her driver, terrified that he might disappear and some sinister black hood take his place. Her imagination was berserk. She could not rely on anything remaining normal. She tried to imprint Timothy's fresh young face, fair-haired, clean-shaven, on her mind but the image kept wavering.

'Lover, lover,' she breathed silently. 'Be kind to me even if you do not love me.'

A lurch told her as they headed into the unmade lane that led to the farm. She was cold, her arms locked across her body, fingers like ice. There was a hair caught across her mouth but she was unable to brush it away. She heard the engine die as Mark switched off. The stillness hummed.

'Are you asleep? We're here.'

'I know,' she said.

'Let's go in. Let's get it over with.'

'I can't move,' she whispered. She couldn't. Her legs were not her own.

He rubbed her hands. They were icy cold. The old farmhouse looked on, mellow and waiting; the unusual mix like a young girl who could not make up her mind what to wear. It had an endearing face that had weathered centuries.

'There's nothing to be frightened of here at Erddig,' he said. 'This house has always been peaceful, a loving home.'

Gina forced herself out of the seat, limbs creaking like an old tree. Mark helped her along the path to the ornate porch, jangling his keys. It was an odd sound. This difficult man was happy. He was coming home, but it was no fun trip for her. She followed him into the hallway, the Elizabethan hunting lodge, inching along, overcome with panic. She could not face the moment.

'Mark,' she croaked. 'Mark ... I can't do it.'

He dug his hands into her flesh. 'Look at it now. Look now, Gina.'

She put her hand out seeking the old wood panelling, conscious of its smoothness, of the craftsmen who had crafted it, the faint warmth and fragrance of apple oak. There was nothing hostile about the hall. Its aura was genteel and homely, like an old mistress, tired but kindly.

She walked past him and he caught the coat as it fell from her shoulders. Her hand slid along the carved balustrade till she stopped at the foot of the stairs.

The gilt of the ornate frame gleamed in the light, the entwined roses and leaves were the work of some long-ago craftsman. Gina looked closely at the frame, seeing knife nicks and minute variations in the leaf veins where the primitive blade had slipped.

'Hold my hand,' she whispered.

His grip was firm. Gina was aware of him standing beside her as she looked up, her breathing shallow, halting.

She was there.

The young girl regarded her innocently, the grey-green eyes like deep pools of mossy water. The look was penetratingly clear and not at all hostile. All of a sudden, Gina felt strangely close to the girl in the portrait, drawn to her as if an invisible thread was spinning between them over the centuries. They were entwined by some strange alchemy.

Gina took in every detail of the girl's dress, her hair, the pearls braiding the cap. It was all as she had seen once before. Nothing had changed.

But it was changing now. Gina became aware of a knowledge, a hint of terrible sorrow in the depths of the girl's eyes. What had happened to her?

Gina shivered. 'Who is she?' she asked.

'I don't know.'

'But you must know. It's your house. Is she an ancestor? It's a very old portrait. Early Tudor? You must tell me what you know about her.'

Mark recognized Gina's desperate need to know about the girl in the ornate frame. 'Tell me exactly what you see,' he said quietly.

'She's young, about thirteen or fourteen years old, but it's difficult to pinpoint her age because her clothes are grown-up. She looks dressed up for some event. Something special ... perhaps her birthday or a visitor.'

'Her birthday or a visitor.'

'She has a plain face by today's idea of beauty, round and evenly featured, with frizzy pale hair. Thin pale eyebrows, arched, as if they had been shaved off. A longish nose, pretty curved mouth. A smile is hovering somewhere in the corners of her mouth. And she's looking straight at me, Mark, with those grey-green eyes that I keep seeing. This is a sweet expression. Can't you see her expression, Mark? What does it mean? What is she trying to say to me?'

'What is she wearing?'

Gina tried to concentrate. 'A sort-of head-dress sitting well back on her hair. The cap is gold and grey, edged with rows of pearls. The bodice is brown, with elaborate gold brocade sleeves. It's tight and elaborate, too stiff for a young girl, with a square neckline. She's wearing a chain necklace with a drop. Her family must be rich.'

Mark turned her away, making her face him. Her brow was dewed with perspiration. 'I think that's enough for now. I'm steering you straight towards a comfortable sofa while I rustle up some food. Are you going to argue with me?'

'No arguments.' She was exhausted.

'*Georgina...*' she heard a voice echo faintly.

She fell asleep almost immediately, hardly aware that Mark had taken off her red slippers and covered her with a tartan rug. She slept through the morning. He did not wake her for breakfast. He ate alone and went out on the farm.

The oak beams above her came into focus first. The sun shone through the old tapestry curtains with a pleasant rosiness. She moved her stiff limbs gingerly, the taffeta dress creased and clinging. She wanted a hot bath and a drink and a change of clothes. She was sure she could find all three items for herself.

The modern kitchen was a haven away from the portrait. She searched through the cupboards and found everything she needed, choosing blue china for her tea. There was fresh farm milk in the big refrigerator.

She leaned on the windowsill, drinking her tea and looking out into the garden. It was an old-fashioned garden with roses and lupins growing freely among the more sedate summer plants in the herbaceous border. Flowering shrubs were laden with blossom and in the distance a silver birch waved its feathery leaves.

She found the back staircase leading to the rooms above the modern part of the house. A housekeeper would have had her room here with stairs to the kitchen. Upstairs were two bedrooms, a small sitting room and a basic white bathroom. It reminded her of boarding school; she hoped she would be able to find a less scratchy towel than school had provided.

Gina was in luck. She found a linen cupboard full of thick towels and sheets stored in lavender. They were old but beautifully laundered and someone had repaired fraying hems with tiny stitches. She wondered if Mark's grandmother had left clothes anywhere. Mark's gear would be too big.

There was plenty of hot water and Gina was glad to step out of her evening dress and kick it away. She never wanted to wear it again.

When Mark returned to the farmhouse, he

was surprised to find Gina busy in the kitchen, dressed, a tea towel tied round her waist, hair in a plait. She was whisking eggs in a glass bowl but there were broken eggs on the working top.

'This is an omelette. Have you got any more eggs? These aren't breaking very well. I keep getting bits of shell in the bowl.'

Mark cleaned up the mess and swept the broken egg shells into the waste bin. 'I don't think you've got the knack of breaking them on the side of the bowl. This way.'

'I'm impressed. I'll do it.' She was not quick enough. The egg broke, the yolk oozing messily on to her hand. 'I can't believe that such a simple thing like breaking an egg is so difficult. I must get Mrs Howard to show me.'

'Why don't I cook and you lay the table?' Mark removed another broken egg and turned on the hot tap so that she could wash her hands. Gina gave in. Show her a cutlery drawer and she'd lay a decent table.

She curled up on a kitchen stool, watching Mark. The bold line of his jaw told her nothing. She could not tell if he was annoyed at her inefficiency or resigned to it.

'Resigned,' he said, reading her thoughts.

Fifteen

She watched him cooking a big fluffy omelette. A bachelor in action, a man who knew how to look after himself. He slipped the omelette on to a hot plate and cut it in half. The melting cheese oozed out in an aromatic creamy river.

'You cook a mean meal,' said Gina.

'You lay a mean table,' he said, regarding the two forks, two knives and a cruet. She could not tell if he was mocking her. 'Sit down and eat.'

It was then he noticed what Gina was wearing. She had found a mulberry-coloured dress, a bit on the long side, loosely cut, the bodice finely tucked, the long sleeves gathered into neat cuffs with tiny pearl buttons.

'Where did you find that?'

'There's a wardrobe full of old clothes,' she said. 'I hope you don't mind. It's practically the Thirties. I love it. Is it one of your grandmother's?'

He nodded. 'She never threw anything away. One day I'll have a good clear out.'

'Please don't do that. They are beautiful clothes and would cost a fortune in a sale room. I once paid four hundred pounds for a genuine beaded Twenties dress.'

'Four hundred pounds for a second-hand dress?'

'I accept your criticism of my lifestyle,' said Gina, controlling her temper, new for her. 'But I don't accept that I have any less right to do what I like with my money. I am helping to circulate money. It goes into someone else's pocket.'

There was a spark in her dark eyes as she challenged him to argue with her. She shook back her heavy plait, a forkful of egg halfway to her mouth.

'You eat my food, sleep on my sofa, wear my grandmother's dress and still argue with me,' he said.

'Great fun, isn't it?' she grinned.

He helped himself to some bread. 'Confusing. I never know which is the real you.'

He saw a flash of fear dim the sparkle and could have kicked himself. He had reminded her of the hallucinations that seemed to be taking over her life. It was the last thing he intended, even if she did irritate him.

'I'm sorry,' he said. 'Monster feet again.'

She lifted her face to the sunshine coming through the kitchen window. 'This reminds me of when I was a little girl. I used to eat in the kitchen with Mrs Howard. My parents were always away and it was silly to eat upstairs in the big dining room, all by myself. She used to let me read or we'd have the radio on. It was nice.'

'Poor little rich girl.'

'Don't be patronizing. The only way I could talk to my father was to ring him up. They were lovely people but wrapped up in their own lives. I was an embarrassment.'

'Lonely little rich girl. Is that better?'

'That's why meeting Timothy and falling in love with him was so special. He was fun and such good company. I didn't feel lonely any more.'

'Is that why you were getting married, so that you wouldn't be lonely any more?'

His words touched her heart like the damp wings of some small bird. She digested the suggestion, feeling a wintery sun thawing some of her inner frost.

'Maybe. The events of the last few days have turned my life upside down. I'm on the edge of something I don't understand. I'm shrivelling inside.'

'No,' he said, none too gently. 'You're being over-emotional but I don't blame you. You've had several nasty shocks and you're not going to be the same person again.'

'Thank goodness, I expect you're thinking. You made it quite clear from the beginning that you didn't like Gina Conway. She's not exactly your flavour of the month.'

'I like this new woman in an old pink frock, though. How am I to know that the other classy dame doesn't lurk somewhere, flashing her jewels and furs?'

'Can I keep the frock?'

'I think Grandmother would have liked you to have it. You look great.' Mark was smiling now.

They finished the simple meal. Mark stood up to clear the dishes. It was then that Gina knew she wanted him. Guilt flooded her veins. She followed him mutely to the bowl of suds, carrying dishes, helplessly ensnared.

There was a tightness, a tingling in her breasts, a weakness in her loins. She stood close to Mark, wanting to smell the musky scent of his body, watching the muscles moving within the plaid shirt. She put her hand tentatively on his forearm. She could not stop herself.

He turned and looked down at her. 'Hey, what's this? I need my muscles for forking hay.'

'Are you going to fork hay today?'

'No.'

'Then I could borrow them.' She slid her hand along his arm. She hardly knew what she was doing, but it felt good. Her heart soared with the recklessness of her actions. This was not the power-dressed Gina Conway, cool, contained. This was some other woman, wild, wanton, longing to drink of this man. If he touched her in return, she would not be able to stop him. Desire was taking possession of her senses. She moved her fingers softly, feeling the hard, unyielding solidness of his muscles through the material.

'Don't do that, Gina,' he said huskily.

'You feel so good.'

'I'm warning you. I won't feel too good in a moment. This kind of attention is driving me off balance. I may have to do something about it.'

His eyes were smouldering. He had forgotten that she was his brother's fiancée. He could only think how lovely she looked. How soft and feminine and with a light glowing in her eyes that spelled magic. He wanted to carry her upstairs, to lay her on the big bed, to undo all those tiny pearl buttons and peel away Grandmother's dress.

She laughed softly. 'So the strong, silent Mark Trenchard is human after all. Not a robot without feelings.'

She heard an echo of common sense warning her to be careful but she did not heed it. The time for common sense had gone. She felt intoxicated with her need for this man; yet she knew that she had lost him. She fought down anguish, trying to believe that it did not matter whether he loved her or not. She wanted him and he could have her.

He was dangerously close; he pushed up

her chin and looked into her eyes with steely intensity. She could feel his warm breath on her skin.

'Do you know what you are doing?'

Gina's hand crept up his shoulder, feeling the flesh of his brown neck, into the cropped silver hair. It felt gorgeous, made the tips of her fingers tingle. She wanted him to kiss her, but he wouldn't move. Damn his honour, damn his integrity. It was Mark she wanted. She pulled his head down to hers and kissed his mouth until she was dizzy and gasping for breath. Mark tried to disentangle her slim arms, but she clung to him with a vice-like grip, triumphantly. That kiss told her a lot. He was not made of stone.

'Don't, don't,' he groaned. 'This is no answer. You'll hate yourself for this tomorrow.'

'I don't care about tomorrow. It's today and that's all that matters.'

He pushed her away and held her at arm's length, pinning her arms to her side. He was strong, she couldn't move. She tried to pull herself together, to gather her pride. It had been a stupid, foolish thing to do, but the impulse had been so strong. She had been unable to resist his nearness, the magnetism of his masculinity.

'Fooling around,' she said lightly. 'Don't worry, a touch of Welsh fever. We didn't anticipate the marriage bed. It was the way

I'd been brought up. I'll go into the garden to cool down.'

She felt his grip slacken and she was able to move away, breaking the tension. Without thinking she went out of the kitchen, walking through the door towards the hall. She didn't care where she went, her mouth still burning from that kiss, her body still on fire and tingling.

Her mind was totally absorbed with thoughts of Mark and her own weakness. She had forgotten the portrait at the foot of the stairs. Gina swung into the dark, panelled hall, intent on finding a way into the garden.

The ornate gilt frame caught some light from the open door behind her. She stopped, fear rising in her throat. It exploded into a howl, the sound echoing and slapping into the walls. She was trembling violently, drenched in a wash of cold sweat, her brain bursting with terror.

'Mark ... Mark...' She did not recognize her own voice. She heard him running.

He was at her side in moments, his arms swiftly round her, crushing her against his chest, cradling her head, his hands deep in a mane of soft hair. There was no holding back now. He held her close, trying to calm her trembling, rocking her, mouthing words of comfort.

'Gina, Gina, I'm here. Hush darling, don't

cry. Nothing will hurt you.'

She was incoherent, unable to focus properly. She clawed at him. Old doubts swept through her. Madness, illness, being alone. It was a piercing pain, an agony clamping her pounding heart, a dreadful desperation that took away all her new courage.

'Mark, look, look,' she wept. 'Where has she gone? The young girl in the portrait. There's no portrait here. I don't understand. It's a mirror, an ordinary mirror. I'm looking into a mirror and seeing myself.'

'I know. I know, Gina,' he said quietly. 'It's always been a mirror. There never was a painting, no girl, no Tudor portrait. I've never seen anything. It has always been an old mirror in an ornate gilt frame.'

Gina raised her dark eyes, brimming, awash with tears, her lashes stuck together, wet and spiky.

'So, when I've looked into this mirror, I've been seeing myself?'

The words hung on the air. Mark did not know how to answer. He was lost for words.

'Which one is me, then?' Her voice trailed away. 'A fourteen-year-old girl from another century with frizzy hair in a pearl-edged cap? Is that the real me? Or is this the real me, now, in your grandmother's mulberry frock?'

Mark did not have to answer. Gina passed out, sinking to the floor, unable to take any more.

Sixteen

'Lindsie will look after you,' said Mark as they turned into the driveway of Plas Glwydan castle. 'You need someone with you all the time.'

'I'd rather go home. That castle gives me the creeps. I'd feel happier with Mrs Howard and Betsy.'

'They're worried about you, too. They'd be relieved if you stayed with your cousins.'

Gina felt exhausted as if brain was coming out of the side of her head. The tension was an elastic band twisting tightly, crushing hair into her skull. 'Why do I have to do what other people want me to do? I'm being bullied.'

'It's for your own good.'

'I don't understand,' she said for the tenth time. 'I know I saw a portrait the first time I visited your farm. You say it's really a mirror.'

'It's always been a mirror.'

Gina was hardly listening. Her mind was doing an instant replay of all the times she had seen the green eyes. 'In my car mirror, on my way home from Plas Glwydan, on the

185

motorway. That was the first time I saw the green eyes instead of my own. Then I've seen them in mirrors in my bedroom, in my bathroom, the drawing room.'

'Every single time?'

'No,' she said thoughtfully. 'It's not consistent. Let me think. There was one time I didn't see them and I was pleased, excited. I thought they had gone.'

'Slow down, Gina. Try to remember when it was.'

'I know when it was all right. I was having a bath before going to Basil's party. Betsy brought me a sherry, a schooner. I guess she thought it was time for a lift. When I looked into the mirror there was my own face, complete. I was happy on my way to Basil's party. You were with me and I felt safe with you. A sort of insurance.'

'Yes, I remember. You were a different person, sparkling.' He wanted to say she had been gorgeous, vivacious, enchanting, translucent with happiness, but he thought she might misunderstand him. 'So their appearance is not consistent. There are times when you see your own normal brown eyes?'

Gina nodded, her hair swinging with a life of its own, darkened corn in a tormented wind. She didn't like the way he said normal. 'So you think I'm going mad. Tact a foreign language? I'm afraid of being alone, afraid of what might happen, what I might see, but

I'm not going mad.'

'That's why it's best that you stay with your cousin and her husband. They are relatives and will take care of you.' Mark switched off the engine and turned to her. She looked pale under her tan, fragile as a doll. Her fear was visible. He could almost touch it.

'Lindsie and I have been friends since we were little. She lived with us for some years after her mother died. That was awful. She studied art. But then she met Barry, got married and he whisked her away, mostly abroad. It wasn't till they moved back to St John's Wood that Lindsie and I met up again. But I was working all hours.'

'Then we're doing the right thing.' Mark leaned forward and tied the empty sleeves of his sheepskin coat across her chest. 'A chance for you to catch up. A few days in the peace and quiet of the Welsh countryside and you'll feel a different woman.'

'I've never been sure about Barry. He's kind and serious, yet sometimes he looks at me in the oddest way.'

'You're imagining it.'

'Again, you don't believe me. You don't understand anything,' she moaned. 'Patronizing me.'

'Gina, I'm trying to be sensible and reasonable, but you won't listen. Getting through to you is like breaking concrete with bare hands.'

'I don't want to feel a different woman,' she said emphatically. 'But I'm afraid I might become one if this goes on. I'm changing into a different Gina Conway.'

'I think you ought to see someone, a consultant for nervous diseases. A specialist could come and see you.'

Gina shuddered. No shrinks for her. 'No, thank you. I don't want any white coats. I'll cope in my own way. I shan't tell Lindsie, and you're not to either. I don't want anyone to think I'm going off my rocker.'

They were brave words, but Gina had no idea of what she meant. No one was going to convince her that she was going mad; she would not allow it. She would fight with every drop of Conway blood. Those green eyes were not going to win.

She wanted to stay with Mark at Erddig, but he had work to do, things to buy for the farm, a vet inspection of livestock. He was not the kind of man to be tied to a nervous, sick, breakdown type of woman. Gina was too proud to ask. She might be at the head of a big shipping line, but today she was a shredded, hallucinating eggshell-thin no-body woman.

'I'll be back at the farm,' said Mark. 'And I'll phone you every evening.'

It would have to do, this promise of a phone call. 'That would be nice. Please phone. I need a lifeline.'

Mark shot her a look of concern. He did not want to be involved, especially with a woman like Gina. She was the kind of woman he resisted: bold, rich, beautiful. Timothy had succumbed and he had died for no reason. But she was still a human being, vulnerable, trouble and in trouble.

'I have to go,' he said, resisting the urge to touch her hand.

'I'm not asking you to stay,' she said. 'I'll be fine with Lindsie and Barry. You do what you have to do, buy your Speckled Face sheep and whatever food sheep have to eat. I'm sorry to have taken up so much of your time.'

'It may pass, whatever it is, this hallucination.'

'It's not a hallucination.'

'It's never happened at the castle, so you may be safe here.'

'Of course, I'm safe here.' She struggled with the handle of the door and pushed it open with her foot. She was still wearing the red silk slippers. Hardly the right footwear for a gravel drive. She could feel the sharp, flinty stones through wafer thin soles.

The Virginia creeper had crept with skinny fingers even further along the sandstone walls of the castle in the time that she had been away. The blackened oak door swung open and Lindsie rushed out. Her arms were full of clean towels piled like a soft mountain, blown dry that morning in unpolluted green Welsh air.

'Gina darling, how lovely to have you back. Are you all right? You look a bit peaky. You need feeding up.'

Gina shuddered at visions of endless trays of Lindsie's hospitality. If she stayed, then she must take a hand in the domestic arrangements. She could learn to cook. The thought was alarming.

'I'm not an invalid,' said Gina lightly. 'I feel jaded. A change of scene will do the trick.'

'That's not what Mark said on the phone. He sounded worried about you.'

'Quite unnecessary.'

'Thank you for bringing Gina,' said Lindsie to Mark. Her homely face was full of kindness, curls bouncing in disarray, a streak of ash on her cheek, a silver birch seedpod in her hair. She pushed back her hair and dropped several of the towels. 'We'll take good care of her.'

Gina felt smothered by Lindsie's promised administrations. She tried a hopeful smile, her face stiff.

Lindsie fastened on to the smile. 'It's going to be lovely having you here, Gina. I've got masses planned for us. We'll have such fun.'

Gina could see herself walking back to London with bleeding feet. She'd give it two days at the most.

'Let me help,' said Gina, picking up the

190

towels. 'Don't you have a washing machine and tumble drier?'

'Heavens no. We had a laundry that delivered at St John's Wood. I never did my own washing.'

Gina would have to let Mavis know that she was taking a few days off. Excellent memory on the blink; she simply couldn't remember if she had any appointments. What was happening to her? She wanted to hibernate like an animal, preferably at Cranbourne Square, or lead a normal life as the trouble-free days before her wedding. Surely her dear Timothy hadn't anything to do with this strange phenomenon? She leaned on a sigh and longed for peace.

'What's the matter?'

'I've remembered something I have to do,' she said. 'But I can fix it.'

'An invitation to cancel?' Mark said. 'This must be throwing your social life into disorder.'

'It's a commitment. You wouldn't understand.'

Scorn fell across his face which hurt Gina more than anything he might have said. He still thought she was nothing more than a party girl. Her years of independence had not prepared her for this ache. Her eyes flashed back, taut and angry with fire in them. He had no right to assume that she was without feelings.

She stood helplessly in the porch, knowing he was about to drive away. Her mind fermented, torn with a longing to make him stay, wanting him to go, keep out of her life.

'You'd better go,' she said. 'You've obviously got seriously important things to do, feeding millions of pigs and cows. Planting enough corn to feed Egypt, fields to dig up.' She turned her back on him, her spine unrelenting.

She heard him chuckle and the sound drenched her with splinters of broken glass. She was going to explode from tension if he did not go soon.

'You need a washing machine, Lindsie.'

'Nowhere to plug it in. Where there's water there is no electricity, and where there's power, no water supply. And the wiring is appalling; half the insulation is off.'

'Sounds dangerous.'

'Not really. Barry's going to get it seen to.'

'I leave you to enjoy the simple pleasures of country life,' said Mark, switching on the ignition. He looked at Gina, but she willed herself not to move. She wanted to go to him, to thank him, but his eyes were dark and unapproachable. He raised his hand in a salute, drove away, spurts of gravel kicked up by the wide wheels.

Gina watched him go, heart sliced in two. He said he would telephone. She hung on to that promise.

The outline of his powerful shoulders was etched on her memory, always in focus. But physically he had gone.

'Come inside and have some coffee,' said Lindsie, tucking her arm in Gina's. 'Take your mind off things.'

'My mind is not on anything,' said Gina. 'Except what to wear. I can't exist with only a taffeta evening dress and Grandmother's old frock. I'll have to get something practical.'

'I'll drive you into the village this afternoon. It's not Bond Street, but you'll get a pair of jeans and a shirt. You left your gorgeous suede boots behind, so your feet will be shod. You must have known you were coming back. I'll put you in the turret room again. Is that all right?'

'Do I have a choice?'

'No. It's the only room fit for a visitor.'

'It's a nice little room. But I'll feel more comfortable when I've a few necessities of life.'

'I understand. Coffee first, then we'll go shopping. I said this was going to be fun.'

They made coffee together, took the tray out on to the terrace at the back of the castle wall. It was a suntrap and the old red stones were warm to the touch. Gina sat on a low parapet and gazed down at the rolling green hills and gentle woodlands. Tracks cobwebbed the landscape, dotted with stiles and walls of rocks. Ancient ruins lay under the grass, bones of bones, streams that once ran with blood. The distant sea glinted its message of morse on the horizon.

'It's beautiful,' she said. 'I love Wales.'

'Very nice if you like views,' said Lindsie.

'Will Barry mind my staying here?'

'Of course not,' said Lindsie quickly. 'He'll be glad for me to have company. He's busy and the castle is so big. He's got amazing ideas. We've got to get everything shipshape and ready to open for the public. It's the only way we'll be able to keep going. Overheads and everything. You should see the paperwork. It's as well I can type.'

'I'm sure you're a great help.'

'I get through pints of Tippex. Slosh the stuff like paint on my typing. Stay here and finish your coffee. I'll get the car out.'

Gina ran her hand over the rough stone, loving the texture, feeling the softness of the moss in the crevices. Her fingers touched a scrap of paper caught in a crack, and she pulled it out. It was a page torn from a shorthand notebook. She read the words without comprehension: 'Dear Gina, Dear Gina, Dear Gina...' The two words wandered along every line.

She blinked. 'Dear Gina...' It looked like the beginning of a letter to her, but who would be writing such nonsense? She screwed up the fragment and threw it over the side of the castle wall, not giving it another thought.

As they drove to the nearest village, Gina realized she had no money. She could hardly ask the insolvent Lindsie to lend her any when they were obviously so short. She hoped there was a bank where she could use her bank card. Her spirits fell even further when she saw the size of the village. It was a tiny hamlet clustered round a chapel and green, a few stone cottages and a timbered coaching inn that claimed a long and gruesome past.

There was a general store next to a newsagents, selling everything from pins to polish. A doorbell tinkled and a woman came through from the back.

'Hello,' said Gina. 'Do you sell any clothes? I only have what I am wearing.'

The woman looked dubious. She took in Gina's natural elegance even in an old dress and a sheepskin coat many sizes too large.

'I doubt if I've anything to suit you, miss. I only carry a few working togs for the farmers around here. Nothing smart or dressy.'

'Working togs. That's exactly what I want. Will you show me what you have?'

She came back with a pile of garments. They were made of cheap material and stiff with starch, quite unlike the jeans Gina usually wore. She put aside the least awful of the blue jeans. She chose two bright plaid shirts and a huge T-shirt to wear in bed.

'Haven't you got anything else?' she asked, her voice tinged with desperation.

'Don't really stock clothes, miss. I've this padded waistcoat that Di Evans ordered and they sent the wrong size. I'd be glad to get rid of it.'

'I'll take the waistcoat. How about bras and pants?'

'You'll have to go into town for those.'

It was turning into a survival course. 'I'm staying at Plas Glwydan Castle. My name's Gina Conway. I don't actually have any money. How shall I pay?'

'The castle has an account. I'll make out a bill. But if you could remind Mrs Wykeham about paying the account.' The woman's voice trailed off hopefully. 'Is there anything else you might need?' The woman indicated a shelf of basic toiletries. Gina had forgotten about washing. She took down a toothbrush, toothpaste and green herb shampoo. It looked like pond sludge. It made her shudder. Gina added a jar of Pond's face cream and a packet of good coffee grounds.

'Would you let me use your phone? I'd be really grateful. Add it to the bill.'

'Out the back, miss.' Di Evans would be pleased.

Gina came out of the shop with her purchases in a carrier bag. A duck was swimming across the pond, her babies streaming behind her in arrow formation, their little webbed feet paddling furiously to keep up with their mother. Gina looked at her reflection in the mirrored surface, but it muddied over, ripples breaking up the outline. She saw nothing here to mock her. The portrait did not exist at Erddig but those eyes were real. She had not imagined that face, the period clothes, the elaborate pearl-encrusted headdress, the soft frizzled hair. It was like stepping into a painting.

'*Mine. You're mine,*' a voice hissed through her brain. Gina stepped back, startled, looking around for the speaker.

Lindsie waved from the car, distracting her. She had been to a farm shop and had a box of earthy, misshapen vegetables. 'Irish stew tonight,' she called out. 'I've some nice lamb.'

Gina smiled. She doubted if Lindsie's Irish stew would be anything like Mrs Howard's recipe for cooking lamb with rosemary.

'We could go out to eat,' said Gina hopefully.

'Good home cooking, that's what you need.'

'My treat tomorrow,' said Gina. 'We'll have a meal at that nice inn we went to before.'

'No way,' said Lindsie. 'They've closed.'

No money, no working plastic, no car. Her mobile needed recharging. Gina wondered how long she would last.

* ★ ★ ★

Her father had given her a horse for her birthday, a great cumbrous creature, for mounts were still bred to carry a soldier into battle. The day of the slim racer and eastern thoroughbred hunters had not yet arrived at English country houses.

It was a big snorting grey animal with hoofs like dinner plates and a wicked glint. She was not sure if she could control it, but she was not going to let anyone see her fear. Especially that Will Brigges, heaving logs the size of tree trunks for chopping for the fires. Georgina knew he was watching her from the corner of his eye. The enormous fireplaces in the kitchen would need wood all day because of the visitors coming.

'I shall call him Prince,' she said.

Her father grinned. She was a young minx and the sooner she was married off the better. He wanted no trouble at home. A neighbouring lord was bringing his son that day to arrange a betrothal.

The hawk, the bow and the crossbow had been busy fowling for the banquet and the kitchen hung with birds and beasts of all sorts. Her mother rushed about, scolding the cooks and maids, seeing that elaborate dishes were prepared to perfection, the rooms sweetened with fresh rushes and herbs.

When the young Lord Eustace arrived, the

girl could not believe her eyes. He was a weedy, pasty-faced nine-year-old done up in velvets, nodding feathers and ribbons.

'Ribbons,' she hissed into Prince's ear. 'I would rather Will's muddy boots, homespun shirt and breeches.'

Seventeen

No one knew she was at the isolated castle except Mark and the Howards. Doubts assailed her mind about Mark. Why did he hate her so? Surely he didn't think that she was responsible for Timothy's death?

She was homesick as they drove back to Plas Glwydan, the bulky bag on her lap. She wanted to see Mark's tall figure coming towards her, could see his shape everywhere. In a microsecond she had come to depend on him more than anyone she had ever met.

Mark, she thought silently, willing him to phone. She wanted to put things right. There was a lot she wanted to say.

'You're very quiet, Gina,' said Lindsie, driving slowly round some sheep wandering across the lane. 'Penny for your thoughts.'

'Thinking about Timothy,' Gina lied, hating herself.

'You must stop blaming yourself,' said Lindsie. 'It wasn't your fault he died. That young man can't have been right in the head if he was on drugs.'

'He wasn't taking drugs, I know that. He was as clean as you or me,' said Gina, wondering what she meant. She had doubts about herself. These weird hallucinations. The fine line. She had reached a dangerous level, tipping on a tightrope of sanity.

'Mine ... you're mine...' Nobody was there.

'Never mind,' said Lindsie. 'We'll get out while you're here. I haven't even unpacked my paints yet, but I have done some sketching. The castle is all lovely angles and shadows.'

'I'd like to see them,' said Gina.

'Would you? Really?' Lindsie's voice brightened considerably. 'I'll show you. Barry is always too busy.'

The castle was not lit. It loomed gloomy and forbidding, etched against a darkening sky. There had been a power cut. Lindsie rushed about finding candles. Eventually she found some torches and a small stub.

'You have the candle, Gina. I'm sure the lights will be back on soon. Barry is probably seeing to it now. Take this flask of coffee. It's still hot.'

Gina shivered. 'Thanks. I'd better put on something warmer than Grandmother's garden frock.'

The mood was oppressive, not only the dark wood, but the musky air which seemed to seep from the stones themselves. Gina coughed, the dampness invading her chest. She wondered if Lindsie had herbal cough mixture in a medieval cupboard.

She went upstairs to the room in the turret, walking uneasily along the gloomy corridors, the candle flickering. She put the candlestick carefully on a chest of drawers and tipped her purchases on to the poppy duvet. The gay flowers cheered her momentarily, though she grimaced at her new wardrobe as she tried it on. The coffee was still hot.

Everything was big and baggy. She felt like Charlie Chaplin flapping about in an outsize suit. She could pinch in four inches round the waist and hips. She stabbed a safety pin into the harsh fabric. She had learned to sew at boarding school, brilliant scholar.

Gina pulled on Di Evans' unwanted padded waistcoat, cheaply made, but the castle was cold and every layer of warmth was necessary. Gina glanced at the mirror, grinning at the gawky farm worker in the shadows. All she needed was a bit of mud and straw.

Suddenly the electricity came on, flooding the room with light.

The green eyes were riveted on her. Their gaze piercing and intense. They were boring into her skull, their power penetrating and lethal, grinding through bone.

She gasped. The impact had the sting of ice. She was suddenly deathly cold. She moistened her lips and forced herself to go nearer to the mirror.

'I can see you,' she breathed, misting the glass. 'What are you doing here? What do you want? Who are you?'

A fleeting expression of cynical amusement flashed across the eyes. They swivelled upwards. Gina drew back, a cry strangled in her throat. The eyes had movement and a life of their own, separate from her feelings. They had responded to her questions, her distress. She sensed cruelty in their sharp, emerald depths. But it was not that girl child. Not that sweet girl.

'What do you want?' she demanded more loudly. 'Who are you? Are you afraid of me? You don't really exist. I'm going to get rid of you. You're a monster.'

She spat the words at the green eyes, fear turning into sudden anger. The energy generated by her anger seemed to flow out of her into the mirror. Gina forced herself to watch, horrified, as like a blind slowly unrolling, the reflection began to change, her own familiar face dissolving centimetre by centimetre into a pale oval, long-nosed, thin-mouthed woman. It was like trick television, the image changing before her eyes. An older Tudor woman was taking over who had the power to superimpose her entire face over Gina's reflection.

The internal structure of the mirror shuddered. The molecules which existed in two opposing mirror images began to disintegrate, and a polarized light splintered, fragmenting in all directions.

The reflection was of a woman in her mid-thirties, dressed in black. A tight black cap covered her hair. A huge sleeved black surcoat hung over a black gown. A heavy fur collar touched the scrap of lace at her throat. The face was powder white, eyes narrowed and glinting.

With a stifled scream, Gina ran from the turret room, lost for a moment along an unfamiliar corridor. She ran down narrow back stairs to a grimy servants' hall she had never seen before. Rows of brass bells hung from the wall, each labelled with a room number. Her sleeve caught one of the looped handles and the bell began to jangle with a loud, discordant noise. She pushed open doors, finding pantries, storerooms, meat and poultry galleys, scullery, dairy, the below-stairs workrooms of a big household. At last she came out at the foot of the main staircase and hung on to the carved newel post, gasping for breath.

She tugged at the front door, her hands fumbling with the heavy bolts. She stumbled out into the porch, the evening air hitting her face with slaps. She ran down the gravel drive, slipping and stumbling, her breathing laboured.

She had no idea where she was going. The tangled trees and undergrowth were somewhere to hide; there were no mirrors in the garden. She ran onwards, her hand pressed hard against a sharp stitch in her side.

Iron gates stood ahead, high, heavy Victorian barriers. She had never seen them before. Perhaps they were fastened back during the daytime and the shrubbery hid them. They were locked with rusty chains that hung between the elaborate heraldic scrollwork.

Suddenly she heard rustling in the undergrowth and Jake and Jasper bounded out, growling and snarling, their big teeth bared in hostility.

Gina backed against the gates. She had never seen such a change in two dogs. They had seemed docile and friendly, now they looked as if they would tear her to pieces.

'Jake ... Jasper ... good dogs,' she said, trying to sound confident and masterful. 'Quiet now. Nice dogs, you remember me, don't you?'

They began to shuffle near, low growls rumbling, their front legs ramrod stiff, powerful shoulders moving, lips curled back in ferocious snarls. Gina was terrified. They were going to attack her.

She began unbuttoning the waistcoat, wrenching it off. She held it in front of her like a matador, distracting the dogs' attention, shaking it enticingly. Their yellowed eyes followed the garment, fangs dripping with saliva.

She sidled back against the gates, her trembling legs hardly supporting her, each step carefully planned. Any sudden movement would have the dogs on her. Old Dai, the gardener, he would have gone by now; there was no one to help her.

The gates were high. Could she possibly climb them? She didn't hear footsteps hurrying along the drive. Her ears were full of the slobbering of the dogs, their snarling, their sharp claws pawing the stones on the ground.

'Jasper! Jake! Off-guard. Off-guard. Down. Down.' Barry's cool command carried even from a distance.

The two dogs backed reluctantly, the growls dying in their throats. They sank on to their haunches, never taking their eyes off Gina.

'I'm so sorry,' Barry said, hurrying into view. 'Are you all right? We always let the dogs loose in the grounds at dusk. You can't be too careful these days, you know.'

'I didn't know they could be so fierce,' said Gina, dazed. 'They seemed such nice dogs.'

Barry smirked. 'They suffer from split personalities. Schizophrenia.'

'I'll try to remember that when I'm feeding them my last digestive,' said Gina, trying to dredge up a joke. She was shaking. 'They look pretty mean and dangerous.'

'Harmless as kittens,' said Barry, stroking the powerful heads. 'There, old fellows. How could you frighten our special guest? You've given her a nasty fright. Come along, Gina, and have a glass of sherry. Lindsie says supper is ready so that'll mean another half-hour.'

Gina tried to laugh, feeling a glimmer of communication with this dour man. Barry had endured Lindsie's cooking for years. The dogs followed, docile enough now, their big paws padding almost silently.

'It's your sherry,' Barry went on. 'Did we thank you for the crate? Lindsie was pleased. She loves a decent sherry. And the micro-wave is terrific, though Lindsie hasn't quite mastered it yet. All those digital dials.'

Gina was glad her gifts had arrived. Suddenly there was a taste of honey in her mouth, strong, scent like nectar. 'She'll get the hang of it,' she said, her spirit returning.

'Sorry about the dogs.'

'They were going to tear me to pieces.'

'Nonsense. They are perfectly harmless. Let's get that sherry. Come along, boys.'

They ate in front of the fire in the long sitting room. It was awkward and uncomfortable, but at least warm. The Irish stew was served hot from the hostess tray in a thin gravy. How could Lindsie go so wrong with fresh vegetables and farm lamb? It was salty as if she had thrown in a packet of beef cubes at the last minute, and the meat tough. Gina picked, chasing peas to the edge of the plate and spearing them with her fork, trying to find carrot that was cooked.

Dessert was tinned peaches and a whirl of instant raspberry whip. Gina thought of Mrs Howard's deliciously light soufflés and sorbets, an endless succession of perfect meals. She never really appreciated the skill that went into the preparation. Gina remembered how she had cancelled meals without a moment's thought; then brought home a bunch of friends, expecting food to materialize.

She would change. She would say something, be more considerate, learn from Mrs Howard.

'I must learn to cook,' said Gina aloud.

'I've never had time,' said Lindsie, eating quickly without chewing. 'I always meant to go to classes but every time I signed on, we went abroad. Now there's Plas Glwydan. We'll never get it finished. Time is running out.'

The sherry had loosened her tongue. It was the first doubt that Lindsie had voiced. Gina looked at her cousin sharply, wondering what she meant, not enough time. Time running out. Lindsie was staring at the fire, hands clasped tightly, a long stricken look to her face.

Lindsie went on talking, but Gina was not listening. She was gazing into the hearth, watching the spit and roar of logs catching fire and crumbling, the sparks eating along the bark like tiny, glowing animals. The flames wove pictures in her mind, pictures that were strange and evocative.

She was seeing Mark in the flames and it frightened her. She remembered the way he hesitated before he spoke; the short hair laced with silver, a helmet of steel. That voice, deep and growly, a voice one could listen to forever.

Why hadn't she met him first? How she would have loved this elder brother, fallen helplessly in love with him, loved him as she could love no other man. Timothy had been different. But there was no chance for her now. Mark hated her for what he thought she had done to his brother. And the green eyes were devouring her face and and perhaps she was sick, mad. She was sleepy, eyelids weighted from the heat of the fire. She was drifting.

'I think I'll turn in early. It's been a long day. I hope you don't mind.'

'Of course not,' said Lindsie. 'Shall I bring you some coffee when you are in bed?'

'No, thank you. It'll keep me awake and I do need to sleep. I feel as if I haven't slept for weeks.'

'Some hot milk, then?'

'Thank you. That would be nice.'

Lindsie slipped in with a mug of warm milk and biscuits while Gina was cleaning her teeth. It was such a long way from the kitchen that the milk had cooled down, skinned over the top.

Gina switched on the electric blanket, but when she climbed into the bed, it was still cold. The blanket must have a fault. She pulled the blanket out from under the lower sheet. Electric blankets were dangerous; people got electrocuted.

She couldn't understand why she was so cold. The castle was damp but she was a healthy young woman. Gina recalled shaking off icy winds during skiing holidays in the Austrian Alps; never normally worrying about gloves or scarves during English winters.

Now she was permanently cold. Perhaps it was part of this strange disturbing illness. It must be an illness. They had been cold, too, people who lived long ago. The heavy black surcoat, the fur collar, designed for cold rooms. She stared at the boarded ceiling above her; how tall and narrow the original turret room must have been. She wondered who else had slept within its stone walls, huddled in furs, washed from a basin. Had they felt the same fear?

She tried to keep her mind off the green eyes, but they dominated her thoughts. Those terrifying moments when her entire face dissolved into the features of that Tudor woman. Mark had told her it was a mirror at Erddig, but she did not believe him. It was a portrait, even if only she could see it.

She turned, restlessly, unable to sleep. Who would care if she was ill? Mark might be sympathetic, but only for a limited time and then his farm and farming would draw him back. The changing seasons would take the edge off his feelings. Besides, Timothy would always come between them. One day Mark would meet a robust, jam-making young woman, a healthy helpmate in Wellington boots, to breed fine children.

Tears gathered in Gina's eyes and she turned-ed her face into the pillow, unable to bear the thought. Some other woman would come into Mark's life, someone sane and sensible, slide into his arms, their bodies closely entwined with intimate loving and giving. Why couldn't she be that woman? Why couldn't she change herself into a wonderful farmer's wife capable of helping with the lambing, whatever helping meant? She groaned, knowing it to be hopeless.

She curled her knees up to her chin, trying to get warm. She was wearing the bright T-shirt and at least it was big enough to pull down and wrap round her knees. There was little chance of going to sleep when she was so cold. She rubbed her legs, trying to improve the circulation.

Eventually she could stand it no longer. She crawled out of bed, shivering, praying for hot water in the shower, wrenching the shirt over her head. The water ran lukewarm for minutes as it coursed a motorway of plumbing. Then came hot water and Gina stood under it, feeling life returning to her frozen body as the heat splashed off her skin. She reached for the bottle of green shampoo, hoping the water would last until she had rinsed out the suds.

As soon as the water began to cool, Gina hopped out of the stone-walled bathroom, wrapping her head in a towel and another round her body. She rolled herself into the duvet and fell on to the bed, trapping all the heat from the shower. It was foolish to sleep with wet hair, but it was too late to worry about that. There was a light knock on the door.

'Gina, it's me, Lindsie. Are you still awake? Are you absolutely frozen? The electrics have gone wrong again. We must get the place rewired. I've made you a hot water bottle. At least my calor gas stove is working.'

'Say no more, you're an angel.'

Lindsie stood in the doorway in a winceyette nightgown and carrying a flashlamp. She was carrying a red rubber bottle close to her chest. Gina tucked it inside the duvet, close to her knees. The heat flooded through her skin like a miraculous and saintly blessing.

'That's wonderful,' she whispered gratefully.

'Goodnight Gina. It's lovely having you here again. Sleep well.'

Lindsie closed the door quietly behind her. Gina was on the verge of sleep, the heat surging through her, making her limbs relax and her mind drowsy.

Her brain was functioning on autopilot. Thoughts drifted across her consciousness like small puffs of cloud. It was something to do with Lindsie. She could see her cousin bending towards her, holding out the bottle, her coppery curls bright and bobbing, her newly washed cheeks damp and rosy. Her nightgown was plain ... her neck, plump, faintly shining.

Gina was drifting away to sleep. She knew there was something she ought to have noticed about Lindsie. Something that was important, but it escaped her. She needed sleep desperately. She could not fight this battle for her sanity if she was weakened by lack of sleep.

If Mark were here, he would know. He would instantly spot what she had missed.

The elusive fragment of knowledge stayed like a moth hovering on the edge of her mind. She ought to wake up and pin it down, but she was too tired.

The girl rode wild in the forest, her anger boiling over into pales of despair.

'Never, never, never,' she shouted. 'I'll never marry that undersized brat! Stupid, whimpering baby face, throwing food on the floor, wailing for his mother. I refuse. I will not be bound.'

She was so incensed in her tirade to the trees that she did not see the overhanging branch and Prince had no skill to avoid it. The branch caught her square across the shoulders and plucked her easily from the back of the horse. She fell clumsily, skirts flying, but the leaves on the forest floor were inches deep and she was no more than winded. Prince galloped on, enjoying his freedom.

She sat up, momentarily scared. She was not sure where she was now and the forest looked dense everywhere from this angle. A long walk was daunting, especially when she was not sure which way to go. Suddenly she froze.

A steady crunching through the under-growth sent her near fainting with fear. She had heard tales of bears in the forest and there were wolves and other wild beasts. When Will Brigges strolled into sight, freshly caught fish hanging from his belt, she was relieved, but angry with him for the fright.

'How dare you come upon me in that manner,' she glared. 'I thought you were a bear. What have you been doing? Poaching, I see. My father's fish?'

'I did not know your father owned all the fish in the river too,' he said mildly. 'Come, I will walk you to your father's house. Every path is my friend.'

Eighteen

Gina sat on the windowseat of the sitting room the next morning ferociously trying to push a blunt needle through the thick denim of the jeans. Lindsie found a sewing kit and Gina began the task of taking the jeans in a few inches.

'Damn, damn,' she swore.

It was hard going and the tips of her fingers were punctured. Embroidery, drawn thread work, and schoolgirl hemming had not prepared Gina for punching denim. These tough jeans were an assault course.

Gina threw down the jeans in exasperation. Jake and Jasper looked up from their sentry post by the fireplace, as if smelling blood. She drew back, drawing up her legs, not trusting them an inch. She had the feeling that if she moved towards the door, they would pounce on her. She looked out of the window at the rising Welsh mist that seemed to wall her in. A fine rain blew across the treetops on the hills, invisible, penetrating every crack in the stone.

Lindsie came in with two mugs of coffee. The dogs sniffed at the wet hem of her jeans, smelling the damp turf and leaf mould.

'Elevenses,' she said. 'Don't say no. You ate hardly any breakfast.'

'I wasn't hungry,' said Gina. Burnt bacon, soggy fried bread, egg soaked in fat. Fodder for the fearless.

'Nonsense,' said Lindsie, curling up the other end of the windowseat. She plumped a cushion behind her back and pushed damp curls off her forehead. 'No wonder you're feeling ill. You never eat. All this slimming.'

'I'm not ill and I don't diet,' said Gina, cupping her fingers round the hot mug. At least it was heat for her hands and good coffee. Lindsie had not lit the big fire yet. 'Why does everyone keep saying I'm ill? I'm not. I'm only cold and tired.' She felt pity for Lindsie trapped in this crumbling castle. She was sure it was not her cousin's choice of residence. Lindsie was happy in their St John's Wood flat.

'As soon as there's some logs I'll light a fire,' said Lindsie. 'It needs chopping.'

'I could do it,' said Gina, with a spurt of energy. 'The exercise will do me good.'

'You? Chop wood? You couldn't chop wood, Gina.'

The pungent coffee had gone to her head like a shot of adrenaline. Gina sipped it with appreciation. 'What did Mark say when he phoned you?' she asked.

'He didn't exactly say you were ill. He said you were under a lot of strain, that you'd had a nasty shock. I suppose he meant the shock of Timothy's death. It must have been awful for you, that and the wedding.'

'It's more than the wedding and Timothy's death, Lindsie. I'm trying to accept that Timothy killed himself, perhaps with a drugs overdose, that he couldn't face our wedding. But that doesn't explain how he got into the sea.'

Gina could not bring herself to tell her cousin about the eyes. There was something wholesome and simple about Lindsie that made Gina hold back. Lindsie wouldn't understand any more than Mark did. Gina's words trailed off. She wanted to tell Mark how the face had changed now. Plas Glwydan gave her no feeling of safety, only the cramp of unscalable walls. She had the phone numbers of Erddig and Timothy's flat.

'You know, I haven't found where you keep your phone hidden,' said Gina lightly. 'It could be anywhere in this rambling mausoleum. I thought I'd order a hamper from Fortnum and Masons. We could go for a picnic.'

'What a gorgeous idea. Delicious duck paté and Dundee fruitcake. It makes my mouth water. Unfortunately there's something wrong with our phone. The line is down. The engineers are trying to trace the fault.'

'If they can find it.' Gina's hopes fell.

'The fault?'

'No, your telephone.'

'It's in the hall, silly,' said Lindsie. 'We put it in that ghastly old sedan chair. It's somewhere to sit out of the draught, if you're not allergic to cobwebs.'

Gina remembered the sedan chair in a gloomy corner of the hall. It was an ugly object, black lacquered wood and cracked leather, reeking of age, riddled with woodworm.

'That monstrous thing? Why don't you give it away? I'm sure some museum would be delighted to give it house room. You need light and graceful things, not that old stuff.'

'Try telling Barry that. This is his inheritance and he's sticking to it, every last broken bit of furniture too. We don't even know what's here yet. We're still making an inventory. Dead boring.'

'I could help you. One way to keep warm.'

'Oh would you? How lovely. You poor dear, are you so cold? I keep forgetting what a hothouse plant you are. I'll run upstairs and get a jersey for you.'

Lindsie hurried from the room, falling over the dogs who moved into her path. Moments later she returned with an armful of baggy jerseys. She tipped them on to Gina's lap.

'Take your pick. We can't have you freezing.'

Gina laughed. 'I'll wear them all.' She pulled on a chunky dark brown sweater. 'Show me the woodpile. We'll soon have a fire going.'

'Are you sure? Have you chopped wood before?'

'I can try.'

Gina did not feel as confident as she sounded, but she reckoned if she was careful with the axe, she could manage to chop small wood. She'd seen people do it on television. Put log steady on a flat surface, swing the axe down, keeping one's feet and fingers out of the way.

Wood was a harder substance than she thought, and her swings were badly aimed and erratic; splinters flew off in all directions. She was getting up a fine heat inside all the layers despite the drizzle, the warm rain feathering her face. She gathered every stick into the log basket as if there was a world shortage. Not a scrap escaped. Someone had not been so thrifty and bits lay gathered for a bonfire. Gina scratched among them for anything big enough to burn indoors.

Her fingers pulled out a rolled wedge of paper covered in small, jagged handwriting. She glanced at it. They seemed to be pages of notes of some kind: cardiovascular system, cardiac glycosides, diuretics, antiarrhythmic drugs, beta-adrenoceptor blocking drugs, anticoagulants ... controlling ventricular response in atrial fibrillation. What on earth was all this?

Gina's heart was shocked into stillness. She had seen this handwriting before. It was Timothy's writing. She knew it. The same writing as on that dreadful letter he had sent on her wedding day. These were medical notes. Medical notes? Why did that fact seem to ring a bell, and what were they doing here, waiting to be burnt?

Mark's words returned. Nothing was stolen except some medical notes. Had she imagined that? She shook her head, trying to remember, and the axe slipped. It fell in slow motion, blade flying low diagonally, glancing off the log basket and jabbing the ground an inch from her boot. She froze, living the expected pain, waiting for the blood to spout.

'Oh God,' she breathed.

Nothing happened. The axe was embedded in the earth. She moved her foot cautiously, unable to believe that she was all in one piece. She was not injured. It was her own crazy imagination going to pieces again.

Crazy. She shuddered. Suddenly she gathered up all the wood and piled it into the basket, tucked the notes into a space between logs, ran towards the door at the rear of the castle. She tried not to think as she wiped her feet and hurried with the basket towards the sitting room.

I've done it, I've got the wood, she kept saying to herself. Now fully qualified axe-woman. We will have fire.

'Well done,' said Lindsie, breezing in with a plate of biscuits. 'Let's have a bite before we start on the inventory.'

They spent the rest of the morning with paper and pen, listing rooms in the unused east wing. It could have been a depressing task in the dingy, untouched rooms, but they had plenty to talk about. Lindsie had an endless stream of chatter about the places they had lived abroad. But Gina could not stop thinking about finding Timothy's notes among the logs.

'We had such fun when we were kids,' said Lindsie, rubbing an old snuff box on her sleeve. 'Even though you were my rich cousin away at an expensive boarding school. I loved the holidays, especially cruising on one of your ships. I was sorry when we lost touch...'

'We met up again at a funeral,' said Gina.

'Oh Gina, I forgot. It was your parents' memorial service, wasn't it? I remember now. There wasn't a proper funeral was there? Couldn't be, could there?'

'I was glad you were at the service. It made me feel less alone. But you didn't stay.'

'No, we were due to fly off somewhere. I think it was Egypt or was it Bahrain?'

'There are only two Conways left.'

'I may be going to rectify that,' said Lindsie, her eyes bright. 'I have a head start in that department. Gina, I think I'm pregnant.'

'Really?' Gina hugged her cousin. 'Are you sure?'

Lindsie nodded. 'Nearly. I think so anyway. It must be the Welsh air.'

'Have you told Barry? Is he pleased?'

'I haven't told him yet. I must be quite sure first. You see, this isn't the first time that I've thought ... I don't want to disappoint him again. Barry would be upset. He wants an heir so much.' Her face had a troubled look as though there was also fear and anxiety.

'For Plas Glwydan,' said Gina. Not for Lindsie.

'That's right. For Plas Glwydan. And why not?'

Gina felt stirrings of envy. This baby would be family. It was exciting. She would make a brilliant aunt, a model aunt, a modern aunt, give it alibis for parties.

'Don't worry, Lindsie,' said Gina, dreaming. 'It'll be all right. I have a feeling. It's this magical Welsh air.' But she was thinking of Mark, working at Erddig.

'Heavens, how the time has flown. I must make lunch,' said Lindsie. 'Barry will be back soon. Thanks for helping. It's much more fun with company. I'd like to do some sketching this afternoon, if the rain clears.'

'I'll finish entering this bureau, then the room is done,' said Gina. 'It won't take me long.'

'Thanks.'

Gina explored the bureau, looking for marks which might identify the cabinet maker. She was interested in antiques, had always known exactly what was in her home in Cranbourne Square. Most of the furniture in the castle was Victorian or reproduction stuff of no value. She had not found a single collector's piece. Nothing they could sell. She cleared out a drawer of old papers and put them aside on the floor so Lindsie could look through them.

She felt a hand brush her shoulder and was aware of someone standing immediately behind her.

'You're doing fine, darling. Keep it up. Not long now,' said Barry in a low voice. 'Only a few more days.'

He was gone before Gina could point out his mistake. The room was shadowy and she was wearing Lindsie's brown jersey. She did not look her usual self, kneeling on the floor in bulky garments, her hair bunched back and tucked into the collar. It was not surprising that Barry fleetingly mistook her for his wife.

Not long now? Did he mean the baby? But he didn't know about the baby. And babies didn't arrive in days.

She drew a line under the last entry for the room and shut the door. It took some time to get back through the echoing corridors to the main landing above the staircase. The wing was a maze of corridors and unexpected stairways, each more musky and airless than the last, the bare floorboards covered with the undisturbed dust. The rooms had been tampered with, valuable panelling painted over, false ceilings added, ornate plasterwork destroyed.

Only the long sitting room, which had been built on by some Edwardian Wykeham, could be made into a comfortable room with decent central heating. The galleried dining room was too vast and draughty to eat in but it could be converted into a showplace for museum exhibits and the occasional string recital.

The dark baronial entrance hall might convert to a ticket office and cloakrooms. It would take money. Polished brass and flowers and inspiration galore.

Gina shuddered at the thought of living permanently in the castle. She felt a pang of homesickness for Cranbourne Square, longed to get home, go back to work, to sit at the boardroom table. She'd rather camp out in the grounds than spend another night in the turret room, despite Lindsie's efforts to civilize it with a poppy duvet and a plastic shower.

Camp out ... she smiled at the absurd thought. Gina Conway in a tent, all those insects. The grounds were tangled and overgrown, reverting further to wilderness with each season. The old gardener had given up the struggle and she didn't blame him. Where was he? She hadn't seen him lately.

This was the passageway that led to her turret room. Time for a quick tidy. It would give her the strength to face the next meal. It was the first time she had looked at the outside of her room in daylight. The door was carved oak, grained grey with age, shaped to a point at the top. She had not noticed that beside the latch was a heavy brass ring.

As she moved nearer she saw the glint of something recessed into the stonework of the wall. It was links of a chain, embedded firmly into a groove at the same level as the brass ring. It was clear that the two formed some kind of primitive lock, that a chain or rope put through the ring and fastened to the link would prevent anyone from leaving the turret room, ever. Her tiny room, gay with poppies and a carpet, had been used as a prison. It was a prison turret.

Gina recoiled from the thought. She knew she was right when she had felt something was wrong in the room. Its excessive coldness, a sense of pain. A sudden feeling flooded through her. A child shut in the room, crying. Her mouth went dry and she remembered the decanter of reasonable sherry from the village grocers. That is if Jake and Jasper would allow her to enter the sitting room.

But the dogs had gone. The fire had not been lit. Did Barry expect Lindsie to do everything? The vast grate was full of dead ashes, cold and grey. She looked around for a shovel and brush to clear the grate. She'd need matches. The jerseys were still scattered on the windowseat where she had left them. Gina could not bear the mess. She was used to Mrs Howard and Betsy clearing up. She picked up yesterday's newspapers, folded the jerseys, carried them upstairs to Lindsie's bedroom. She knew they slept on the second floor.

She found their room after peering into several unused rooms. The unmade bed was a shambles of sheets, blankets and a pink satin eiderdown. Lindsie didn't seem to have any domestic routine. Two armchairs were stacked with half-unpacked boxes and a collection of plans and blueprints were scattered on the floor.

It was trespassing, like catching the pair of them in bed. The door to the big mahogany wardrobe was swung open, witness to Lindsie's haste. Gina opened it further with her elbow, planning to dump the pile of jerseys anywhere inside. As she straightened up her eye was caught by a long black dress on a hanger. It was heavy and cumbersome.

She shut the door with a slam. Maybe she had seen Lindsie wearing it, maybe at her parents' memorial service when she had been vulnerable and impressions were stored away in her subconscious. She shook her head. It was too complicated.

It was more likely that Lindsie had worn the dress at their farewell party in St John's Wood. Gina had worn a flame silk crepe dress from Valentino. A clumsy fool had spilt red wine and mayonnaise down it. She had a dreadful headache and left the party early, despite Barry trying an Indian meditation technique to relieve the pain. He made her sit in his study. The technique was based on relaxation, he'd said.

'You're not giving it a chance,' he protested as she tried to leave the room. 'You were going off.'

'I don't want to go off,' she said, hunting for her bag. 'I want to take a couple of paracetamols and get out of this ruined dress.'

'But it really works,' Barry insisted. 'I've seen it happen many times. Just relax, Gina.'

Gina came out of their bedroom and closed the door. A stair window unrolled a panorama of high hills, fields of green and clumps of dense forest. It had a gentleness of altitude, nothing awesome, but an aura of height that was achieved without effort.

She wondered if she could ever be happy living in the country. Mark was happy. He loved it. She could not see herself enjoying the mud and the rain, the various horrid things one had to do to sheep; the practicalities of farming. She was a town girl. She liked shops and theatres and dining out, wearing lovely clothes.

Perhaps it was this closeness to the land that gave Mark his strength and calmness. Yet she knew instinctively that there was another side to him, a fierce passion that was waiting for the right woman. If only she could be that woman. How she longed to love one man, the only man, forever, to be in such a glorious partnership. Perhaps Timothy had not been that man. She was confused, her thoughts running away from her.

She went downstairs to the gloomy kitchen. Lindsie was chopping cabbage on the wooden table for coleslaw. Tomato soup was bubbling on the calor gas stove. Gina was drawn to the heat and gave it a stir. She could stir.

'Can I help?' she asked, turning her back on the roasting range with its turning spit, black with age, the crank rusted solid. The row of brass boilers were green with mildew, the brick ovens dust ridden. Turf the lot out.

'Hard boiled eggs in that saucepan. All done. Would you like to peel them?'

Gina was relieved that Lindsie had given her a simple task, but hard boiled eggs were not easy and peeling off the shell was a definite knack. She had crushed shell everywhere. Her eggs were pitted and misshapen by the time she had finished and she was glad when Lindsie gave her a jar of mayonnaise and told her to anoint the lot.

'Bash it all up together,' she said.

'What is it about eggs?' Gina groaned.

Barry came into the kitchen, his face like thunder. 'Who's been chopping wood?' he said. 'No one chops wood without my permission.'

Nineteen

'Who cares? We needed firewood.' Lindsie leaned forward to sweep broken shells off the table and into the wastebin.

Gina caught sight of a glint of gold. Lindsie was wearing a thin chain round her neck, half hidden by the cowl of her jersey.

'I don't like anyone touching the woodpile.'

Gina remembered elusive thoughts chasing about before she had gone to sleep, in the dim light from the flashlamp. She had seen a gold chain round Lindsie's neck, a chain with a single drop pearl. She stopped spooning mayonnaise and tried to think sensibly. There must be dozens of them in the cheap jewellers. A modern copy of a trinket which had been popular for centuries.

'Are you all right?' she heard Lindsie asking.

'I'm fine,' said Gina. 'This is hard labour.'

It was a funny sort of day. Sundays were longer in Wales. No telephone, no money, little to do. Lindsie found her sketching pad and settled down to commit the castle walls to paper. Gina finished taking in the waistband of the jeans, listening to an old collection of 78 rpm records.

'These old records are fabulous,' she said. 'They are probably valuable.'

'Barry wouldn't sell them. They're his favourites. You'd better not drop one. We don't want another telling off.'

Gina put the records back into tattered brown sleeves. Barry this, Barry that. It was like walking on broken glass. A bit like her wits against the eyes. She was determined not to be caught out again.

She took a walk round the grounds hoping the fresh air would make her sleep. She stumbled across wet rags, dark green and lumpy. It was Di Evans' unwanted waistcoat, torn to shreds. She moved the bits with the toe of her boot, her heart thudding, throat dry. Jake and Jasper; there could be no other explanation. Supposing she had been inside the waistcoat? Surely they weren't that dangerous? She looked about, half expecting the brutes to leap out of the shadows. She said nothing to Lindsie and Barry, keeping it to herself.

Gina wanted to tell Mark about the medical notes, about the piece of paper with 'Dear Gina' on it which now seemed relevant.

Barry came with the mail which the postman had delivered. He gave Gina a cream envelope from Coutts Bank.

'The post?' said Gina. 'Heavens, isn't Wales marvellous. Do they have postal deliveries on a Sunday?'

Barry looked at her blankly through his thick lenses. 'It's a perfectly normal Monday midday delivery.'

'What? What do you mean? This is Sunday, not Monday.'

Barry shook his head. 'No, Gina, this is Monday. You've been here three days.'

'Mark brought me to Plas Glwydan yesterday, Saturday, and in the afternoon, Lindsie and I went shopping. I bought jeans and shirts. I was sewing the jeans this morning before lunch. Then I helped get lunch ready. I did the eggs.'

Lindsie laughed. 'Eggs are today's lunch. Yesterday we only had time for sandwiches. Remember, we were doing the inventory? This is Monday, all day. You spent most of yesterday dozing in front of the fire while I was sketching.'

They were both looking at her as if inspecting her skin for spots. Gina tried to think clearly, sure in her own mind that it was still Sunday. She went over all the events of the morning: she had sewed in the morning, helped Lindsie with the inventory, peeled those damned eggs, served herself tinned tomato soup. Her glance went to the scratchy material on her legs. She was wearing the jeans.

Gina stared at the envelope in her hand. Where had Sunday gone? And the night. A whole day had vanished. She had a feeling of losing time, of it slipping away like those silvery grains of sand in an egg timer.

'Sandwiches yesterday?' she asked, numbly, counting days. 'What sandwiches?'

'Gina darling, you haven't been well. You are still very tired. Perhaps you ought to rest.'

'No,' said Gina with a supreme effort, tearing open the envelope. 'Great. A money order from the bank. I need to cash it. Can anyone give me a lift?'

Barry peered across the table. 'If it's a money order, you'll have to cash it through a bank. I'm going into town this afternoon so I could take it for you. You'll have to sign on the back. How did you get it sent here?'

'I phoned Mavis from the shop,' said Gina quickly. Anywhere that had a bank would have a public telephone. She could phone Mark. 'I'll come with you.'

'I was hoping you'd help me with the bedrooms in the east wing this afternoon,' said Lindsie offering toast, now diced and called croutons. 'You were marvellous yesterday. But if you'd rather go with Barry...'

'Yes, I would. I'm helpless without any ready money and want to cash that money order myself. After all, I haven't been on a spending spree for ages.' She forced herself to smile at Barry. 'I could spend a fortune on your kitchen.'

'You are a dear. I'd love a wall tin opener.'

Gina choked. She looked at Lindsie with astonishment. She had already bought a wall tin opener or had she imagined it? 'I'll get you one this afternoon.'

Gina did not want a helping of butterscotch instant whip, preferring an apple from the bowl. She took it upstairs, anxious to be ready when Barry left. She tucked the legs of the scratchy jeans into her boots and hurriedly buttoned up the sheepskin coat. She could not believe this was Monday.

It only took minutes to get ready. She was down in the hall in no time, waiting for Barry to finish his lunch.

She sat on a blackened oak linenfold chest that might have been made in the sixteenth century. Her interest was sharpened as she felt along the carving on the front for any date. This might be something they could sell.

To her surprise she heard the sound of the estate car coming straight from its garage in the stable block. She opened the front door and was in time to see the car going down the drive towards the gates.

'Barry,' she shouted. It was impossible for him to hear and pointless for her to run after him. He had left early on purpose, she thought angrily. Selfish beast. She wanted to phone Mark even more than she wanted to get hold of some money.

'Barry's gone without me,' said Gina, trying to keep the annoyance out of her voice. Lindsie looked up from clearing the table. 'How could he? He knew I wanted to go into town.'

'Oh Gina, what a shame. We thought you'd changed your mind. We thought you'd gone upstairs to lie down. You didn't have any dessert.'

'I went to tidy up and get a coat.'

'There's always tomorrow. The shop will probably send in an account. They are used to waiting. Don't worry, you won't need any money while you're staying with us. We don't charge our visitors,' she said grinning.

'That's not the point. I needed to get out,' said Gina. 'This castle is claustrophobic.'

'A place this size?' Lindsie was amused. 'You can't be serious. I haven't counted the rooms yet.'

Gina saw this as an opportunity to broach the subject of changing her room. It could not be that much of a problem. She would clean it herself, however much hard work that meant.

'I've noticed something strange about the turret room I'm in. Did you know it can be locked from the outside? There's a heavy brass ring and a link of chain aligned. It can be fastened with the chain. The room was obviously once used as a prison.'

'How fascinating. You're probably quite right.'

'Didn't you notice it when you were furnishing the room?'

'No, I can't say I did. I was far too busy.'

'Lindsie, I'd like to change my room. I'll sleep anywhere. A sleeping bag on the sofa would do.'

'Change your room?' Lindsie stopped stacking plates with a clatter. She looked upset. 'Whatever for? We got that turret room ready especially for you. We took a lot of time and trouble. The duvet's new.'

'I know and I appreciate it,' said Gina miserably. 'Please don't think I'm not grateful, but I don't like the fact that the door can be secured from the outside without the person inside knowing.'

Gina picked up the soup-stained mats. She knew she was being unreasonable, but even the simplest things seemed to unnerve her now. She held on to the back of a chair, her fingers clenched. She took a deep breath to steady herself. How could she upset Lindsie when she was being so kind?

'Forget it,' she said. 'I'm sorry.'

'Never mind. I've lit the fire in the sitting room. We'll have our coffee in there and then start on the other bedrooms. Is that

235

all right?'

Gina felt helpless. She was not in control of anything. She was being manipulated like a puppet. She tried to shake off a growing despair and uncertainty. Always a woman who was in command, now she was on a slippery slope, her feet sliding away from under her.

Could she have lost other days? If days could become blank, perhaps Mark was right and she did have something to do with Timothy's death. If it was Monday, she shouldn't be here, she should be at work. She ought to phone Edward Burroughs or George Barker, or Mavis. She had to phone someone.

Jake and Jasper growled softly, rose and stretched themselves, muscles rippling. They were watching her, yellow eyes foggy with carnality.

'Sit down, you stupid dogs. They haven't got used to you yet. Don't worry, they are perfectly harmless.'

Gina thought of the mangled waistcoat and went cold. 'About as harmless as were-wolves,' she said.

'That's the point of having them. We're remote here and people might think the castle is full of priceless and valuable antiques. Quite the reverse. I'd willingly pay someone to steal the lot. I'd rather have the insurance.'

Lindsie looked flushed and tired. Gina felt

sorry for her, coping with this draughty place and too much to do. If she was pregnant, she should not be working so hard. It was hard to imagine a pram in the hall. Lindsie would manage in her slapdash way, nappies and feeding bottles everywhere.

'You look tired, Lindsie. Why don't we give the bedrooms a miss? Let's go for a walk outside. It's not raining yet.'

'See those grey clouds gathering over the river? That's a sure sign of rain. No, we'll get on with the inventory.'

Gina suppressed a sigh. The smaller bedrooms were depressing with heavy Victorian pieces that could only be described as junk. Servants' rooms. There was no air. The oxygen had been used up decades ago. The beds were narrow with ancient horsehair mattresses, smelling of damp; big ugly wardrobes crowded against uglier dressing tables with protruding shelves and fat legs. Gina would have thrown out the whole lot. The inventory was a waste of time.

She had been avoiding any mirrors. It had been a good day, and she was congratulating herself on her skill. But a trap was lying in wait inside a scratched wardrobe door. A stained and tarnished mirror had been fixed to the door for eighty years, its metal coating peeled, a rim of green mould on its brass fittings. No one had looked in it for years. It had forgotten how to reflect. The daylight was disturbing, blindingly bright. Stress which had built up within it, suddenly fractured.

Gina stood rigid, her hand on the wardrobe door, her courage gone. Fear raced through her turning into a clamp that froze her blood. The green eyes narrowed, the colour staining their watery depths like a dye. They were boring into her head with a relentless intensity.

'No,' Gina cried. 'Go away!'

'No,' came the mocking answer. *'I'm not going away.'*

The words vibrated on the air, fibrillations that attacked the walls of Gina's heart. She clutched her chest as if she were having a heart attack. Was this a heart attack? She sank to the floor, a floor that rose up to her.

'Go away,' she moaned.

Instantly the expression in the eyes washed out and turned paler, clearing like bottle glass. The reflection rippled and features began to reappear in a downward flow, first the long nose, thin mouth and pointed jaw, long neck, a glint of gold on the throat. Gina's face disappeared in a curious myriad of disturbance. The reflection was another person, cold, full of calculating hatred, head black-capped.

Gina began to scream. The sound did not come from her throat. It came from some spot high in the ceiling. She could not move.

She was rooted to the wooden boards as surely as if chains bound her, her soul splintering.

Once inside the house, he did not know which way was her bedchamber. He had never been further than the great stone-flagged kitchen before. His apprehension was tangible, but it was she who had suggested her own room when all the family and servants were asleep.

'I am far in the south turret,' she said. 'There's only Old Moll who sleeps like a log. No one will know.'

The sweat broke out on Will's forehead as he stood in the narrow corridor, a tallow candle in his hand. But which way was south? This was a foolish escapade and if he had not been half out of his mind with love for his young mistress, he'd rather be flat out on his own bed, hard as it was.

But then she was there, like a white moth, beckoning him, her long, crinkly hair hanging to her waist. He followed her, lost now to all reason.

'Will,' she cautioned, her finger to her lips. He stooped to remove his clomping boots.

Her room was the most comfortable he had ever seen. A carved bedstead was hung with velvet curtains to keep out the draughts. There was an embroidered silk coverlet, an oak chest with linenfold panels for her clothes, a basin and ewer for her toilet, a rush mat on the floor.

Now he was truly tongue-tied as she laughed softly and drew him inside. She only wanted more and more of those tender kisses and her knowledge went no further.

The closed bed curtains made an even smaller, airless space and his sweating broke out worse till she untied his shirt and removed it. Only then could he kiss her and the sweetness of their kisses, so innocent and childlike, were like fresh dew on that sultry night. His hands were gentle and amazing on her silken skin, and light-headed with love, he cupped the small curve of her breasts. She twined her legs around him in her pleasure.

They were both lost to the world in each other's arms. A wondrous love was growing between them and it was like a miracle. They did not hear footsteps coming along the corridor.

Twenty

'Gina, heavens, what's the matter? What's happened?'

Gina was unable to speak. She was beyond coherent speech or thought. That face full of loathing ... was it herself? Did she have a split personality? Two faces? Spiders streaked across her mind, racing to dark corners.

Lindsie patted Gina's shoulder. She was at a loss to know what to do. She could only think of a time-old remedy.

'I think you'd better lie down,' said Lindsie, fussing. 'I'll bring you a cup of tea. You look pale. Oh dear, perhaps you ought to have a drop of brandy. We've got some left over from Christmas. Let's get you to bed.'

Gina nodded. Her face was pearled with perspiration, strands of hair sticking to her forehead. Lindsie hurried downstairs for the brandy.

Gina listened to the retreating footsteps, hating to be left alone. She was mentally ill with a disorder sweeping through her like a giant tidal wave. She was split off from reality, as if the divide from sanity had been

241

crossed. She was shuffling along a bare corridor in slippers, not knowing one day from another.

There was a point beyond normal fear and Gina had reached it. She was crushed. This new encounter with the eyes destroyed the last shreds. She did not feel hope any more, or belief in her sanity. The outside world was losing its clarity. It was shadowy, unfocused, fuzzing at the edges like a very bad photograph.

Had she once been chairman of Conway Lines, doing a responsible job behind a computer terminal? It did not seem possible. Even her wedding was dreamlike. Timothy ... who was he? Had she dreamed him, too? And she had lost a day, a whole day from her memory ... what had happened on that day? Could she have lost other days?

She was ill. That face had taken over her face completely. The well-known Gina Conway had disappeared into nothingness in the mirror as if she never existed.

And now the face had a voice, rusty, grating. *'I am here,'* she said, the eyes gleaming with triumph.

Gina's breath locked in her throat. She tried to call out, to deny it, but she had no command over her voice. The creature had taken her voice as well as her face.

Tears fell on her cheeks and she brushed them away. They were her own tears, wet and warm and salty, or were they? She buried her head in her arms, wanting to shut out the world. It was still Sunday, she could swear it, going over the events of the day, yet again. Barry and Lindsie said it was Monday. They were wrong.

Lindsie put a cup of tea and a glass of brandy by her bed. 'Was it a rat in the wardrobe? I've told Barry there are rats. I've seen quite a few mice, especially in the kitchen. I suppose they come in from the garden. Here, drink this. You look awful.'

Gina took a few drops of the amber liquid, hardly tasting it. It was cooking brandy. There was no glow, no alcoholic lift. Her head was throbbing as if she had a clamp of steel round her skull. It was no ordinary headache.

'I think we ought to get a doctor to see you,' said Lindsie. 'I'm really worried.'

Gina protested. She refused to see a local doctor at Plas Glwydan. He might say she could not leave, make her stay in the castle. She would get a hired car or a taxi to a station. Surely trains came to and from Wales? The nearest station was Newport. Her brain was working again. Howard.

'Lindsie ... I have to go home.'

'Yes, dear. When you're better.'

'No. Now, Lindsie, please. Will you phone Howard to come and fetch me immediately?'

'Drink your tea and have a sleep. It's going to rain. I said it would.'

Lindsie tipped the firewater into the tea. It was a comforting drink and Gina felt herself drifting off into a hazy, lazy sort of sleep. She was aware of Lindsie pulling off her boots and heard them fall on to the floor. The last thing she heard was the light patter of rain on the narrow windows.

When she awoke, it was pouring. Rain streamed down the glass as if her room stood in the middle of a waterfall. She could not see outside. Gina snuggled down into the bed, remembering how as a child she had loved to watch the rain from her bed. Her room at Cranbourne Square had been smaller then, the bed pulled close to the window, her toys on the windowsill in a row. She cuddled them each in turn. Night-night, teddy. She slept with the oldest teddy, one eye missing, one ear torn. They were her companions, her friends.

It had been a warm, secure feeling, to be out of the rain but able to watch it; seeing rivulets chasing each other and making new tracks down the glass. Two separate droplets raced, like wriggling tadpoles, each gathering more moisture and momentum on course till the heaviest suddenly ran to the bottom of the window in a glistening ribbon.

But there was no secure feeling now. She was not a child any more. She got up, shakily determined to phone Mark at all costs, hoping the phone in the hall had been repaired. She went soundlessly, the cold from the floors striking through the ten denier tights. Her hand paused on the carved balustrade. Everywhere was quiet. She prayed that the phone would work. She could hear her own breathing. It sounded desperately loud, even downstairs in the dark, gloomy hall. She was descending into a deep well, expecting to feel water swelling and rising round her, imagination going wild.

The sedan chair was early eighteenth century with red fringed curtains heavy with dust. It had been well used on the crowded, dirty streets of London, the varnish on the poles quite worn away. She climbed in gingerly, hating the smell of decay and dust and ancient body odours. The leather seat creaked as she sat on it, her knees bent in the small enclosure. The telephone was on a shelf opposite.

She picked up the receiver and listened. It was dead. Her heart fell like a stone. All her hopes had been pinned on reaching Mark. She sat back, aching with disappointment, coiling the cable, putting it tidily by the telephone. She stared at the end in her hand. The telephone had been disconnected from the wall socket.

She stayed in the darkened chair, trying to

sort out the implications of this odd discovery. Her brain was not working well and thoughts were muddled. Perhaps it had been disconnected by accident. Kicked out. She could replace it in the socket and dial Mark's number. The thought of speaking to him made her spirits rise...

She heard the front door creak open and footsteps coming into the hall. She was about to step out, phone in hand, and make a cheery remark about this being one way to save on the phone bill, but Barry spoke first. His voice was low-pitched, precise, urgent.

'For heaven's sake, calm down, Lindsie. It was your fault she found a phone outside. Bloody careless.'

'But it was awful, Barry. She was screaming and screaming. It was the most dreadful sound. I hardly knew what to do. She was so upset. I didn't expect her to be so upset.'

'You did the right thing. It was all you could do. Is she better now? Where is she?'

'I've left her sleeping. I gave her the last of the brandy. Was that all right?'

'Yes. You're doing fine. Stay with it.'

'Oh, Barry, I don't know if we should go on. I really don't know.' Lindsie's voice was shrill and agitated and yet underneath there was a kind of sublime indifference. 'You don't know what it was like.'

'You're not changing your mind, are you? We've talked and talked about this. You know how much it means to me. There's a lot at stake, especially for you, Lindsie, with the baby coming.'

'Yes, the baby.' Lindsie gave a little laugh. 'That'll make a difference, won't it? I mean, babies always have to come first, don't they?'

'Of course,' he soothed. 'Always come first.'

Gina heard them shaking the rain off their coats. They began to walk towards the sitting room, passing close to her. The dogs scampered ahead, barking and getting in the way. She was surprised that they had not come sniffing and growling round the sedan chair. The rain had affected their sense of smell.

She continued to hold her breath. An inner sense of caution made her keep her presence secret. Her nose began to tickle as dust rose, but she pinched it to control the sneeze which would have given her away.

'At first I didn't know what was happening. We were doing one of the bedrooms upstairs. She must have opened a wardrobe door and suddenly there was this awful shriek and Gina began screaming and screaming. Barry, it was terrible. I never want to hear anything like it again.'

'Did she say anything?'

'Nothing at all. She couldn't speak and her face was deathly white and staring. She collapsed and I had to drag her out of the room.'

'Perhaps you should have left her there.'

'Oh Barry, how could I? I had to get her out and into bed. I almost called a doctor.'

'No,' he said sharply. 'No doctor. It's too early for that. There'll be time enough later for the men in white coats. Lindsie, you handled it very well. Go and put your feet up. I'll make a pot of tea.'

Gina could not make sense of their conversation. Barry's reaction was odd. He did not seem surprised or alarmed. Didn't he want to go upstairs and investigate the cause of her screaming fit in the bedroom? A pot of tea? He was concerned about Lindsie's condition. He did know about the baby. Lindsie had lied to her about that.

And there had been something weird about Lindsie. She kept on about the awful sound and having to listen to it, but nothing about the cause of Gina's screaming. Neither of them seemed to be curious why she had screamed. Yet they couldn't possibly know. They had been talking about her in an analytical way, as one might discuss an object in an experiment, not their visitor, their cousin.

Gina moved the fringed curtain aside a fraction. Barry was standing with his arm round Lindsie, caressing the back of her neck like a snake.

'It won't be long now, Lindsie,' he went on. 'It was absolutely terrible.' There was a catch in her voice. 'You never told me what it would be like. I never imagined...'

'How could we know, dear? We can't tell what she's going through, how a mind becomes unhinged. Perhaps we ought to hurry things up, so that she doesn't suffer too much. Tomorrow would be a good time, tomorrow after lunch.'

'Will she die?'

Gina let out her breath in a long, silent sigh. She could not believe what she was hearing. Perhaps she had missed a change of subject. Were they still talking about her?

'Eventually, of course, this split from reality will affect her. She's hearing voices, having delusions and hallucinations ... textbook schizophrenic. She'll be heavily medicated, a walking zombie, but quite peaceful and calm in her own way. Then maybe, one day, it will become too much and she'll finish it off, do something irrational, take her own life. Or the drugs will damage her heart and...'

'You mean like Timothy?'

Every nerve in Gina's body stiffened. Timothy, drugs ... a walking zombie, schizophrenia. What were they saying about Timothy? She was in danger. The castle was not safe. It was a deadly trap, and she had walked straight into it. No, Mark had driven her back, insisted that she return.

The moment the door closed to the sitting

room, Gina slipped out of the sedan chair and ran across the hall, panicking, desperate to get away. As she opened the heavy front door, the rain blew in, lashing at her face. For a second she hesitated, then she remembered Lindsie's question: 'Will she die?'

Gina gritted her teeth. No, dammit ... she was not going to die. She ran out on to the gravelled driveway, avoiding the pale light from the sitting room windows. She had to get as far away as possible, find the road, find people, the police. Who would believe her? Eyes in a mirror driving her mad? She couldn't even see properly, half blinded by the rain and she had left her glasses by the bed. Her feet were soaked, the cheap jeans heavy and clinging.

The iron gates loomed ahead, tall and menacing, almost human in stance, cutting off the outside world. She tried opening them, but they were padlocked. She darted off into the undergrowth, slipping and stumbling, the wet leaves scratching her face as she pushed them aside. There must be another way out, fence, hedge, back gate. Surely it couldn't be this high stone wall all the way round?

Her breath was laboured, gasping. Her tights were torn, feet bleeding. She stumbled, crashed into a thorny shrub.

As she ran, her heart was crying silently. Her dear, bubbling, disorganized cousin.

She couldn't believe that Lindsie meant to harm her. It must be a mistake. But they knew that she was being driven mad. Did they know about the eyes, the dissolving face? Did they know what was happening?

'Will she die?' She heard Lindsie's words echoing through the trees. It was not her imagination. A walking zombie, a vegetable ... did they really say that or was the conversation also a fragment of her confusion?

She remembered the long black dress in Lindsie's wardrobe and the pearl on a chain round Lindsie's neck. They were real, important but she could not think why. She could not remember what they meant or how they fitted in.

Soon they would find out that she had gone and would be looking for her. This brought a rush of panic and she forced herself to move faster, even though her legs were weak and aching. She was bent double, a pounding tumult in her chest, her knuckles pressed hard against a piercing stitch in her side.

The ground was getting muddier; she was nearing the lake. She could smell the stagnant rain-spotted water, the wet trees and waving branches hiding it from view.

Old Dai watched her but did not move. He was sheltering in the underground passage, having a smoke out of the rain. This was not like the other one. A young woman running through the grounds meant nothing. He'd seen a lot of funny things lately, but he was too old to be curious. The castle was only half visible in the driving rain, curtained in mist and curling vapour from the ground, turrets lost in lowering cloud.

The wall was never ending. It had been built to keep out intruding enemies and it certainly worked at keeping Gina in. She would never get out at this rate. She imagined Barry bursting through the undergrowth, the two dogs snarling and snapping at his heels.

A big yew tree loomed ahead, ancient and gnarled. She saw that its main branch grew at an angle which reached across to the top of the wall. Desperation gave her courage. She had never climbed a tree in her life, but now her life depended on it. She hunted for footholds among the lower branches, but she could not reach any of them. She dragged a fallen log to the base of the tree, puncturing the soft palms of her hands with sodden splinters. She propped it against the trunk of the tree and scrambled up, slipping and grasping any slimy hold. She reached a sturdy branch and hauled herself over it, then kicked the log away.

For several seconds she hung there, exhausted, weak with fear. The Conway spirit deserted her. She hardly cared if she lived or died. It would be easy to give in, to let them find her, take her away, do whatever they were going to do, to submit. The Conway Line, Cranbourne Square, inherited wealth and possessions, meant nothing; they could not save her.

If Jake and Jasper found her they would soon have her for supper, claws ripping her legs, their jaws fastening on to her ankles, biting through to the bone.

She hung on, her arms and shoulders aching, knowing she only had minutes left. *Don't give in. I'm coming,* she heard the words clearly in her head. Once before she had cried out to her lover for help, on her wedding day, but there had been no answer. But now she heard words clearly in her head. She heard concern in the voice. Was it Timothy, sensing her distress? Answering...

Twenty-One

Mark had been working all day, the kind of hard manual labour that he enjoyed, clearing out a brook that was choked with weeds and debris. He needed free flowing water for his flocks. Even in a country as wet as Wales, there were signs of a summer drought. He had taken on some men that morning, a couple of good strong lads and an older, experienced shepherd.

'It's good, man, to see this farm coming alive again, Mr Trenchard,' said the older man. 'The old lady couldn't manage on her own.'

'Best grazing hills for miles,' said Mark. 'Erddig wool used to have a name for itself and it will again.'

He kept thinking of Timothy, remembering a letter full of meeting Gina, a cheerful phone call about their wedding. It began to rain, making the work more difficult. He threw his spade over his shoulder and tramped back to the farmhouse. He would try to phone Gina again this evening. What if she was right and the castle did have some evil effect on her?

He heard Gina's voice as clearly as if she was walking a few steps behind him, tone thin and weak.

'*Help me...*'

'Don't give in,' he said aloud. 'I'm coming.'

Her knees found a knot in the trunk where a branch had been sawn off. It took her weight momentarily and with that slight support, she found a way of grasping the branch with both arms. Those few inches of stability cleared her mind. The slanting rain was relentless but she was desperate for water, to make of it a friend. She opened her mouth to take rain on to her tongue. Somehow she pulled herself up, using the same knot to brace her foot, and lay along the branch, panting, smelling the odour of wet bark, its slimy roughness against her cheek. If the dogs came they couldn't reach her now. She was safe for a while. She could rest, but not for long, after climbing her first tree. Abseiling next.

When she had recovered her breath, she began to inch forward, crawling along the branch towards the wall. The shirt caught on sharp twigs and tore. She moved cautiously, nearing the wall. It would be disastrous if she fell now.

A surge of elation set her heart racing as the top of the wall appeared below the branch. She could actually touch the wet, mossy stone, crumbling bits with her hand. The branch was narrowing, beginning to sway under her weight. She had to get over the top of the wall, then she could drop.

The rain and wind were buffeting her, leaves and smaller branches getting in the way. It was not going to be a calculated drop. She would be lucky if the branch supported her long enough to cross the wall, but her weight was taking the branch down to lean on the stone. Ahead of her, dipping low was a screed of rustling leaves and blowing branches.

That moment's inattention was her downfall. She slithered forward, through the leaves and branches, arms flailing, tumbling over, clutching wildly at nothing. She fell into a waterlogged ditch, full of nettles and weeds. It was cold and painful, but broke her fall. She struggled out, stung, stumbling, muddy, bruised, eyes and mouth full of bits, wondering what she had broken.

She tried to spit out the mud and wipe her eyes clear, amazed that she was otherwise unhurt. The lane looked unfamiliar, what she could see of it. Supposing it merely went round the castle walls and back to the gates? They would be looking for her by now.

She ran across the lane and into the dense woods opposite. It would be safer under cover and not out in the open. Her feet were bleeding but wet moss and leaves were softer to walk on. She got into a rhythm, ran to a count of twenty, walked to a count of twenty, trying to keep in one direction and not taking any path that veered off.

One of the cuts under her foot was sore. It felt as if the flesh was splitting open. She shut her mind to the pain, not wanting to stop, but had to pause and wrap it with torn tights. She got a second wind as she realized that she had a chance of escaping. Plas Glwydan was behind her.

The woods were thinning and she glimpsed a road ahead. It was the secondary road that she had driven along, long, long ago when she had been a free, independent woman, driving her powerful Mercedes. She almost fell on her knees in relief. Joy. She knew where she was. The main road was a few miles further on. She could walk it, she could do anything. Competent walker.

But out in the open was not safe. She kept close to the verge, her ears pricked for the sound of any approaching vehicle, poised to leap back into the woods if she thought it was Barry's estate car. The light was fading fast from the rain filled skies. She welcomed the night. Darkness would be a friend.

Her teeth were chattering. I'll find a phone, she told herself, then realized she had no money, no card. I'll walk to Mark's farm. He said six miles. But six miles in which direction? Her heart fell. She might be walking in the opposite direction to Erddig. She was drenched, exhausted, deadened to the pain in her feet, accepting each racking step as the price of her escape.

Hitching a lift was too dangerous. She did not know who she could trust. She had trusted her cousins.

She slowed momentarily, appalled at a new thought. How was it that her kingfisher and wren were in Mark's possession, on show by his fireplace?

Panic gripped her again. Mark had a motive, a strong motive for wanting to see her suffer, revenge for the death of his brother, for the hurt he thought she had inflicted on Timothy. She remembered their first meeting, at the reception and the following morning. Mark had been incensed with anger. Oh yes, he had a motive.

Silly things crowded into her mind. He had appeared by chance at the inn and knocked over her coffee. She didn't believe in coincidences. Perhaps Barry had phoned him and told him where they were eating. His arrival as she was leaving for Basil's party. Another coincidence. Was Mark involved with her cousins? They only lived six miles apart and he said he used to explore the grounds of Plas Glwydan when he was a child. They could be boyhood friends.

She cried out aloud. The doubts began to

grow and magnify. She remembered the sweet moments, how she longed for him, how her body could melt with desire when he was near her. It was not fair, to find him at last, and now to know, that he was not for her, that he was her enemy.

She began to sob, racking sounds that tore at her chest. She did not care where she went now. Erddig was out of the question. She must find a police station or a hospital. Even an ordinary household was fraught with danger. They would think she was ill, mad, phone for Barry. She looked pretty mad with her torn and bloodied clothes, her hair plastered wetly to her head.

The noisy roar of an approaching motorbike broke the stillness, its single powerful headlight stabbing the darkness. Gina cowered in a thorny bush at the side of the road as it roared past.

Almost immediately twin headlamps appeared over a rise in the opposite direction. In the collision of lights, Gina saw the bulky square outline of a Range Rover. Gina flung herself back into the undergrowth, covering her face, heart thudding. She was sure she recognized it. To her horror, the vehicle was moving slowly, crawling along, as if searching for someone.

She scrambled on her knees, finding a gap in the thicket, stumbling back into the woods, starting to run. She heard the engine stop and the slam of a door. Someone was coming after her. There was a crunching of branches and leaves as a person ploughed through the undergrowth.

She paused only to swiftly grab a sturdy piece of fallen wood. It felt better to have a weapon in her hand. She was going to fight if she had the strength, but her breathing was already laboured. She could hardly run any more. The blood was pounding in her head, her ears ringing with noises, a fierce pain in her chest like a band of steel.

'Gina, Gina ... don't run away from me. Don't be frightened.'

It was Mark's voice. Urgent, concerned; an illusion. She was only hearing what she wanted to hear.

The crashing footsteps were nearing. She was trapped in a thicket of wood, trees growing close together, branches entwined, floundering in a wall of undergrowth, unable to see any way of escape. She faced him, gasping, the piece of wood raised in her hand. If she was going to die, then she would fight to the end.

The man towered over her, his face etched gauntly in the shadows, his blunt silver-grey hair plastered to his head. He held out his arms. She did not move, her rapid breathing a torture, her dark eyes mirroring her fear and terror.

'Gina, put it down. Come to me. Trust me.'

'I don't care,' she hissed. 'Kill me if you want. Nothing matters any more.'

'Gina darling, I'm not going to kill you. What a crazy idea.'

'Crazy, yes! You hoped I'd go crazy, didn't you? I know I can't trust you. Any of you. You, Lindsie, Barry, you're all in it together. God knows why ... Revenge, I suppose. Kill me, go on, kill me. I don't care.' She was overwhelmed, incoherent.

He moved a step closer, his arms at his side in non-threatening attitude, wondering how he could reassure her. She crouched like an animal, her eyes glaring.

'Gina, listen to me. I'm not going to harm you. Believe me, I could never hurt you in any way. You're very special to me; I know that now. I've thought about you so much in the last few days. I know why Timothy loved you. My brother chose his wife well.'

His words hung in the rain like jewels on a Christmas tree. Gina would have been so happy to hear them a few hours earlier, but now she was too distraught to care, her faith in Mark shattered. She wanted to believe him, but did not know what to believe.

'What day is it?' she trembled.

'Monday.'

'And you took me to Plas Glwydan on Saturday?'

'That's right. I drove you over to stay with your cousins on Saturday. Why?'

261

'It's still Sunday ... for me. God, it's still Sunday. Tell me it's Sunday. Somehow I've lost a whole day.'

'Gina, my darling...'

He strode across the few yards between them and took her into his arms. She clung to him, weeping, her face pressed against his chest. She didn't care what happened. He held her close, stroking her shaking shoulders, his hands deep into the tangle of wet hair.

'I'm here,' he breathed against her hair. 'You're safe with me. Sunday, Monday ... we'll find out about that lost day. Don't worry, I'll look after you now.'

She could not stop crying. She cried for loneliness, for Grandfather, for her parents, for needing them, for wanting them, for the last few terrifying weeks. There was a well of agony and anguish gushing to the surface, spilling over as never before.

'I'll take you home,' he said, lifting her into his arms.

They dragged him out, breechless, down the stairs on his knees, into the yard, his clothes flung after him. Will scrambled into his garments and limped home, for they had been rough with him. He was terrified. He resolved to leave as soon as it was light. And that was his mistake. He should have gone then.

Her father was furious. 'Lord Eustace will not marry shoddy goods,' he raged. 'Remember, he is promised attendance at the Royal Court at fifteen and his bride will be at his side. He has already sent a portrait of you to the Court.'

'That whelp,' she said haughtily. 'That snivelling brat. I won't have him as a husband.'

'You'll do as you are told, minx.'

Her mother was angry, too, but more gentle in her probing, her questions halting and confused.

'Mother, truly, we did no more than kiss and fondle. What is it done that is forbidden? Why won't you tell me?'

Twenty-Two

Mark helped her upstairs to the bathroom. He turned on the taps of the big Victorian bath, the dark mahogany wood surround glistening as the steam rose and eddied. Gina was too weary to protest, her frozen fingers fumbling with the buttons of her shirt. Her jeans were stiff with mud and blood, tights in shreds, blood congealed. Bits of leaves and bark clung to her hair. Textbook mess.

'Not exactly the glamorous Miss Conway,' he said, unfastening her shirt. His fingers brushed her skin by chance, but there was no sensation; her skin was numb.

'Mark, you have to answer some questions,' she said woodenly. 'You have to tell me the truth.'

'Later, you need thawing out before you turn to stone.'

'Please ... you must tell me.'

'The haughty Miss Conway begging?'

'I have to know the truth. Are you involved with Barry and Lindsie in any way? Did you already know them before I came down here? Is this some kind of gruesome revenge for Timothy's death?'

There was a deep scratch across one smooth shoulder. It looked swollen, bruised. The cheap jeans had shrunk and Mark had no idea how to get her out of them. Her feet were badly cut, one nail almost torn off; it looked nasty.

He took a pair of scissors out of his grandmother's cabinet and carefully removed the hanging nail. He looked at the bloodied, muddied jeans.

'Do these mean anything to you?' he asked.

She shook her head. 'I hate them.'

'You're always losing your clothes,' he said sternly as he began to cut them off, averting his eyes from glimpses of brief panties. 'If I didn't know how modest you are, I'd say you did it on purpose.'

'I can manage from here on,' said Gina, stirring.

'I'll get some antiseptic for those feet,' he said. 'I was wondering when I would become suspect Number One in this mystery. It was my mirror here at Erddig where it all began, and I have a motive for wreaking some kind of senseless revenge on the flighty Miss Conway. But I can't believe this haunting theory of yours. I'm a farmer, birth and death, the circle of the seasons, the weather, droughts and floods. There's no room in my life for anything mystical, ghostly or haunted. There must be a rational explanation and I'm glad that you have started to think that way too.'

'What do you mean?'

'You're thinking that I have something to do with the eyes in the mirror, so it follows that they are not supernatural. I'm not a ghost-hunter and I can't conjure ghosts up out of the air. If I'm flesh and blood, then so are those green eyes. And there must be a down-to-earth reason why you are seeing them.'

She saw the logic in the reasoning. It made sense.

'But Mark, they are so frightening. I was trying to phone you when I heard...' She was becoming hysterical again. 'You won't phone the castle and tell them that I'm here, will you?'

'There's plenty of time for you to tell me everything when you are cleaned up, patched up and rested. You've been through a lot, whatever happened, and you'll be able to tell me in a more rational way when you feel better. I won't go away and I won't phone the castle. I promise.'

Gina wanted to believe him. She had to trust someone and she wanted it to be Mark. The concerned expression on his gaunt face couldn't be false. The bathroom was warming up with clouds of steam. Her body was beginning to thaw. He took her hands and began examining each finger slowly, his eyes deep and penetrating. He looked directly into her eyes, avoiding the expanse of sweet curves already in the water.

'I'm going to take these splinters out of your hands with some tweezers. If you want to yell out, yell.'

She bit her lip as he probed the sore flesh with the tweezers. It hurt. 'Get it over with,' she said.

'That sounds more like your old self. I'll find you something to wear. You can lock the door if you want to, but I'd rather you didn't. I'd rather you trusted me.'

He left swiftly when Gina peeled off the rest of her clothes and sank into the hot water with a sigh. She had so much to think about, everything that had happened in the last few hours. Her body was aching; her feet were battered and sore as if she had run the London Marathon barefoot on broken glass.

The heat began to wash the tension from her mind. This had once been a bedroom and converted by Mark's grandmother. It was a comfortable bathroom. A deep floral carpet covered uneven floorboards, flowered curtains dressed the small dormer windows, louvred cupboards flanked one wall with a Vanitory unit and mirrors. An armchair was covered in the same material, and a low foot-stool spoke of lazy hours of hot drinks and reading. Gina thought she would have liked Mark's grandmother.

Mark came in with a mug of tea, a pile of clothes and some fluffy towels smelling of lavender.

'Get into these when you're ready,' he said. 'I'll come back later and fix your feet.'

Gina sipped the tea, wondering when she had last worn her own clothes. She, who always took such pride in her appearance, shopped at the best designers, now spent her days in borrowed handouts. She did not look in the steamed-up mirror as she dried her long legs and rubbed her wet hair. Mark's clothes, white cricket trousers and a cashmere sweater, were far too large for her. She held the fine wool close to her breasts, longing to feel his arms round her again and his body pressed against hers. But it was too soon. She felt she was still engaged to Timothy. She had accused Mark of being part of this torment.

She sat in the armchair, drinking tea, while Mark cleaned the last of the grit and dirt out of her cuts with a mild antiseptic. She winced. 'Will that cut need a stitch?'

'I don't think so. I'll pull the edges of the skin together with sticking plaster. We used to do that when we were out working and got cut. It makes a neater scar than stitches. Try not to walk on the ball of your foot, if that's possible. You may need an anti-tetanus injection.'

'I'm sure I've had a tetanus and it's up to date.'

She was still pale but had stopped shivering. She wanted to tell Mark everything that had happened, but did not know where to start. Load it all on to his shoulders.

'I found Timothy's notes,' she said. 'In the woodpile.'

'What notes? His notes?' He sat back on his haunches, plaster curling round his finger. He looked at her, puzzled. 'What are you talking about?'

'I was chopping wood and I found a bundle of his medical notes among the wood. I recognized the writing.'

'My God, chopping wood? With an axe?'

His blood ran cold. 'You're not safe to be let loose. Why were you doing that? You could have chopped off a finger.'

'Lindsie is overworked and the castle is so damned cold. We needed wood for a fire. If I had my way I'd burn the place down. It's a white elephant, but try telling Barry that. He's besotted with his heritage, as he calls it.'

'Timothy's notes were at the castle?'

'Yes. But Timothy's flat was broken into before our wedding, wasn't it? You told me.' Her voice faltered. 'I can't seem to remember properly these days. Didn't some notes go missing?'

'If these are the same notes, then why are they at Plas Glwydan? Are you sure this isn't another hallucination?'

'There you go again. I know you think I'm going mad, but why should I hallucinate notes? It doesn't make any sense but they are still there. Go and see for yourself. I put them back in the woodpile.'

'I might just do that,' said Mark as he finished patching up her feet. He pulled on a thick pair of ski-socks that would double for slippers. The heels of the socks wrinkled behind her ankles.

Mark had a fire burning in the inglenook, still missing American sunshine. He bent to put on more logs and Gina wanted to touch his hair as the strands caught the light from the fire. She needed reminding that life went on, though not for Timothy. Surely Mark wouldn't be caring this way if he thought she was directly responsible for Timothy's death.

It came to her suddenly. Someone had pumped drugs into Timothy to quieten him while keeping him a prisoner. Maybe the overdose had been an accident and then they had to get rid of his body. It was a chilling thought.

'There's something awfully strange going on,' Gina insisted. 'I have to tell you about Lindsie, about what I overheard, the writing I found on a piece of paper.' The reason came to her. 'As if someone was practising my name.'

'I'll fix some food and you can talk while I cook.'

'I'm not hungry,' she said as the heat of the fire and her bath began to make her drowsy.

'But I am. I've done a hard day's work.'

'Don't leave me,' she panicked, as if Barry might suddenly walk through the door. 'They might have followed me.'

'I'll leave the door open to the kitchen and if I pull the sofa round, like this, you'll be able to watch.' He picked up a curly black puppy, all floppy and yawning, and put it on her lap. 'A little company.'

'A puppy ... how lovely.'

'I've two. No names yet.'

'Were you coming to the castle when you

found me?' she asked, hardly able to keep her eyes open, stroking the tight black curls on the puppy's head.

He nodded. 'I'd been busy since noon, working on the farm, but I kept getting a feeling about you.' He didn't say that he kept hearing a voice. It was too uncanny. 'As if you were trying to contact me.'

'I was ... desperately. I kept trying to phone. The phone had been pulled out. Someone had pulled it out from the socket so it wouldn't work.'

'Then it was telepathy. It happens, doesn't it? When people are very close.'

'Are we very close?'

It was the kind of question she vowed she would never ask a man, especially a man like Mark. She could have bitten her tongue. Now he'd think she was after him.

'Yes, we are close,' he said hesitantly. 'It's too soon, I know, to know why. But something's there, Gina. Don't feel guilty. The living have to go on living.'

A second puppy reared unsteadily on its back paws, trying to clamber on to Gina's lap. She picked up the little creature and settled it beside its brother. They curled round each other and went instantly to sleep.

'They need names,' said Mark.

'Mack and Mabel,' she said.

'Perfect.'

Gina closed her eyes, listening to the

crackling fire, the beat of the rain on the windows. She could hear Mark moving about the kitchen, whistling under his breath, the faint clatter of a saucepan. She was about to tell him the saga of the telephone when she drifted off. She sailed into the shallows of sleep but without anyone at the helm.

The stewards took Will deep into the heart of the forest where the canopy of leaves was as black as night. They left him bound to a tree, and blindfolded, for the bears and wolves to find.

Twenty-Three

Mark brought through plates of steaming ravioli and set them on a low table before the fire. The puppies rolled off Gina's lap, instantly wide awake. Their noses wrinkled as they smelt food.

'Down,' said Mark, pushing away the inquisitive noses. 'Your supper is in the kitchen.'

He took the puppies with him while he went to fetch wine which had been chilling in the refrigerator. He came back with two glasses, the wine bottle tucked under his arm, balancing a basket of brown rolls, a dish of farm butter.

'I know an Italian place in Soho that makes this mouth-watering home-made ravioli. I've been dreaming about this meal for months, Erddig, a fire burning and you here to share it.'

He poured out the chilled hock and handed a glass to Gina. His deep-set eyes were more acutely blue, but their expression cautious. He was not sure he was ready to hear what Gina was going to tell him, afraid she was going to reveal something about Timothy that he did not want to hear.

'Still don't trust me, do you?' she said, pushing her fingers through her hair. 'I could say the same of you. How do I know you are not involved? You could be, hating me as you do ... blaming me for Timothy's death.'

'I'm not involved, Gina, and you have to believe it. And I don't hate you any more. Why should I want to hurt you? I like you, haven't I made that clear, idiot woman. Why should I go traipsing round the countryside in the pouring rain, looking for you, if I didn't care?'

He leaned forward to touch her hand. It was like electricity.

Kill him, kill him, the voice said.

'Let's eat,' he went on.

The ravioli was delicious, cooked in a wine

sauce with fresh tomatoes, basil and garlic, generously sprinkled with a dry, crumbly cheese. Gina ate hungrily.

Kill him, kill him, it said again.

Gina trembled. 'It's lovely.'

'Any more ravioli?' Gina shook her head. 'Fruit? Coffee?'

'I don't want to spoil the delicious ginger taste.'

Mark looked at her sharply, but she seemed unaware of what she had said. He poured out more wine, pushed the table away and moved next to Gina, careful not to alarm her.

'Now, you are going to tell me everything, from beginning to end. Why you were running along a country lane in the pouring rain with no shoes, your clothes torn, refusing lifts from strangers.' The question was light, but beneath the banter, Mark was serious. She put her hand against his shirt, feeling for the round button on the pocket flap. She did not know where to begin, how to reveal the fear and the panic.

'I am going out of my mind. Yet, I can't be. I don't feel any different. I'm a strong person and I work hard, although I know you find that difficult to believe. But it's getting worse, Mark, those green eyes ... This afternoon at the castle, there was a mirror in a wardrobe door ... she ... they began to take over my whole face. I could see my features dissolving and her nose, her mouth, her chin coming in their place. It wasn't only her eyes, it was all of her. And that black cap. A death cap. *My* death cap.'

Gina covered her eyes, not wanting to see the face that was haunting her, not even as a memory. Mark waited while she regained her composure.

'So the face, the Tudor girl's face is beginning to gain control, to gain strength,' he said carefully, not wanting to add to her alarm.

'No, not the same face. This is a woman's face. Then it happened again and it was almost as if she was creeping into my mind. I was terrified. She spoke. I heard words coming from her mouth, or was it me speaking and she was taking over my voice? I don't know...'

Gina tugged at Mark's shirt and his arm came round her. She lay against his shoulder, only able to relive those horrifying moments if he was very close. His strength and sense were reassuring. She knew nothing would happen while she was with him.

'I am going mad. That's why they said they would take me away and stuff me full of drugs ... a walking zombie, that's what they said I would become. Perhaps that's what will happen. I'll give up and let it happen.'

'Who said that?' Mark said.

'Lindsie and Barry. I heard them talking

when I was hiding in the sedan chair in the hall. I'd been trying to phone you but the phone had been disconnected, the cord pulled out of the socket. They didn't know I was there.'

'So that's what it was. I reported a fault but the engineers said that there was nothing wrong with the line. I had this strong feeling that you were trying to contact me.'

'I was, I was. I wanted to talk to you more than anything. Perhaps Barry and Lindsie were deliberately stopping me making any calls, or maybe it was accidental. They didn't know that you might call.'

'If Lindsie had answered the phone and said you were going on fine, I would probably have stayed at home, reasonably sure that you were sleeping or out walking.' He was keeping the anger in his voice under control.

'I'm not afraid here at Erddig farm. I seem to know that nothing and no one will hurt me here. Whereas at the castle, I am aware of all sorts of shifting feelings and undercurrents that I don't understand: the necklace and the dress that I found, what Barry said to me when he mistook me for Lindsie. I was wearing her brown jersey and the light was bad and my back was to the door.' Gina knew she was rambling.

'What did he say?'

'He said, "You're doing fine, darling. Keep

it up. Stay with it".'

'It doesn't make sense.'

Gina sighed. 'I know it doesn't. We'd been working on the inventory of the rooms in the unused east wing. It's a terrible old place, full of junk. He wasn't complimenting Lindsie on the inventory; he seemed to be referring to something else. I'm not telling this very well...'

Mark watched the distress pass across her face like a dark cloud. Her party face was beautiful but the last few days had fined down the contours and curves to hollows and shadows which dusted her with fragility.

'Don't go on if it's upsetting.'

'I must, while there's time. Time's running out for me. I must tell you all that I overheard in the hall. They were talking about me, in the oddest way, as if I wasn't a real person, as if I was a sort of thing that existed. Lindsie was upset. She had been there when I saw the green eyes in the wardrobe door. It's the first time that anyone has been with me when it's happened. Except that once, here with you, at Erddig when I saw the portrait.'

She felt the pressure of his hand and was reassured.

'Lindsie helped me to bed. But then she was telling Barry about it and she asked him if I was going to die? Why did she say that? She couldn't have known what I'd seen in the mirror. I never explained, never said a word.'

'What else did they say?'

'Barry kept saying the same kind of thing, about keeping it up and doing fine and she couldn't back out now. He seemed angry with Lindsie for being upset. Then he said, in a cold sort of voice, that they would take me away and give me drugs so that I wouldn't know what was happening. He said that I might feel so terrible that I would kill myself.'

Gina's voice dropped to a whisper and Mark had to lean closer to catch the words. 'I didn't understand, but I knew I was in great danger, but what kind I didn't know. I had to get away, immediately. I ran and ran, trying to find a way out. Somehow I climbed a tree and got over the wall, then ran through the woods.'

'And I took you back to the castle,' said Mark, clenching his fist. 'Damned fool. There's no doubt that you are in danger there. Are you quite sure you haven't mentioned the Tudor girl to either of your cousins?'

'I'm absolutely sure I haven't. I didn't think they would believe me, as you didn't.'

'But they're talking as if you have a serious mental illness, or are going to have a breakdown ... on the strength of you screaming once, witnessed only by Lindsie? They can't know about the girl in the mirror. It doesn't make sense.'

'All they know is what you told them. That I'd had a shock, that I was upset and could I stay with them for a few days? Remember? That's all they know.'

Mark tried to absorb all the possibilities. 'They can't be referring to your grief about Timothy or they would have said so. They don't know about the eyes. There must be more to it. Tell me about the necklace and the dress.'

The puppies were trying to climb up her legs and she gave them a helping hand, hauling them on to her lap. They were playful and inquisitive. She had never had a puppy. Boarding schools left few opportunities for pets.

'They're sweet,' she said, stroking them. 'Funny babies. Do you remember when you asked me to describe the portrait? I told you every detail of her appearance, the cap, the dress, her hair ... and round her neck was a fine chain with a single pearl drop. It was faint and I wasn't sure I could see it. Then when I was at the castle, I saw the same necklace, although at first I could not remember where. But then I saw it again, Mark. It was round Lindsie's neck. She was in the kitchen and she was wearing a gold chain with a single pearl, only...'

'Only how could it possibly be the same

necklace?' Mark finished for her. 'A necklace from a Tudor neck must be four hundred years old. Lindsie wouldn't be wearing something so old and valuable when they are desperately short of money.'

'That's what I thought. Then there's a dress in her wardrobe, a long black dress. It's a bit like what the older woman wears...'

'Fancy dress for a pageant.'

'More of my stupid imaginings?' said Gina bitterly.

'We have to go back to Plas Glwydan. The answer must be there. We've got to have a look round, find those notes.'

She gripped his arm. 'No, I'm not going back, never. Don't ask me to, please.'

But he did not seem to be listening. 'I don't understand why sometimes you see the eyes and then other times you don't. There must be a trigger.'

'Trigger? Mark, this is too much for me to take in. I want to sleep and sleep and never wake up.'

'Sorry, but we've got to do this. We've got to go through it again, make a chart, listing the times when you have seen the eyes, and the times that you haven't.'

Gina clapped her hands to her ears and shook her head. 'No, not now,' she cried. 'I don't want to remember. You can't make me go through it all again. It's too much to ask. I'll be able to think clearer in the morning.'

'All right. Sleep now. Everything will look brighter in the morning. We'll get to the bottom of this mystery. We'll find out what is happening to you and what happened to my brother.'

'Timothy ... is this also about Timothy?'

'I think so.' He searched her eyes. They were full of doubt. 'We're going to find out about Timothy, too.'

She was kept in her room until the staining of blood on her shift reassured her mother of at least one thing. The girl emerged, quiet and white-faced, but with her head held high, and she immediately began making enquiries about Will.

No one would say anything, nor could she find him. The servants shut their lips. Old Moll pretended to be even deafer.

She asked her father outright.

'I have sent him away,' he said, without looking up from his legal papers.

'Then you have also sent my heart away,' she said.

'I won't listen to such childish nonsense. Leave me to my work.'

Twenty-Four

The night hours came and went in a dreamless sleep. Gina awoke to gentle sunlight, filled with a sense of comfort and delight, her limbs heavy. She had slept, curled against his back like a loving spoon. He was breathing peacefully, bare shoulders smooth and brown.

Forgive me, Timothy, she breathed. And she knew that he did. They both knew it was too soon for more than sleep. A kind of warmth flowed over her as if Timothy was happy for her.

She crept down the stairs, wrapped in Mark's bathrobe, all fears of the mirror gone. She barely glanced at it, but when she did, she saw herself: her face glowing, hair tousled, her dark eyes languorous with love. She looked like a woman who really loved.

What was it that ruled the appearance of the evil green eyes? A trigger, Mark called it. If that was true and they could find out what it was, then she would have some means of controlling the haunting. Yes, it was a haunting. It was a relief to put a name to the phenomenon. She would start a website: hauntedwomen.co.uk. They could swop encounters.

Gina made a pot of tea in the kitchen, smiling to herself. How beautiful and fresh was the early morning garden, full of bird song and washed clean by the dew. She opened a window and leaned out on to the sill. She had never smelled such clean air. It was all things sweet, blossom on the wind, rain on leaves.

The kettle switched itself off and Gina made the tea. Everything was normal and soothing. She carefully carried the tray upstairs. She was not ready for full time domesticity, but she could cope with a minor role.

She nodded to her reflection in the mirror and saw the same face smiling back to her. It was one hundred per cent Gina Conway, tousled and happy.

She paused in the doorway of the bedroom. Mark was still sprawled across the bed, hunched shoulders brown and powerful. How would he greet her? It would break her heart if he was offhand and casual, giving her the fish eye. The wrong note could destroy all those lovely feelings, make something cheap out of their night together.

She put the tray down carefully on the table beside the bed, aware of her dependence on his first reaction to her on wakening. She bent and planted a tentative kiss at the nape of his neck, somewhere among the short silver hair.

'How now, my sweet love,' he whispered lazily, pulling her close down beside him. 'So we grew together, like a double cherry...'

'I didn't know Welsh farmers knew their Shakespeare,' said Gina, curling gratefully into his arms. His early morning skin was warm and soft, his arms strong. He ruffled her hair and kissed her bare shoulder.

'You have a lot to learn about farmers,' he said. 'We're not just a row of muddy boots.'

'I've made us a pot of tea,' Gina said.

'What a clever girl.' He glanced at the tray. 'No spoons and no sugar.'

'I'll go and get some.'

'You'll do nothing of the sort. We'll do without. You're sweet enough for me,' he grinned. He gazed deeply into her eyes, unhesitatingly. 'Good morning, Mrs Trenchard.'

She was startled. 'Mrs Trenchard? Hey, what do you mean?'

'I always mean what I say. We are going to get married. I don't intend to let you slip through my fingers. This was our first wedding night, Gina. There's only signing bits of paper to do now; the public part.'

Gina slid down into the cosy hollow against the curves of his body, nuzzling into his musky skin.

'But not yet, not yet. I have to wait. I want to be quite well, first,' she said. 'You can't be saddled with a mental cripple or a neurotic woman who imagines and sees things. I've got to get rid of this ghastly, gruesome thing in my head. If you really want to marry me.'

'How many times do I have to tell you?'

Gina turned her face free so that she could stare at the sun-dappled ceiling. 'A hundred million times, till I'm really sure.'

'Trust a Conway to talk in millions.'

'I need reassurance,' said Gina. 'These eyes have done more than scare the living daylights out of me. They've destroyed my confidence, my ability to think straight. I can't make simple decisions. I hardly know what I'm doing any more.'

'Don't talk like that. I'm here. We'll beat this together.'

Kill him. Kill him. It was a long way away but clear enough.

'I'm afraid of my thoughts,' she gasped, momentarily stunned. 'Sometimes I think she's got inside my head. It wouldn't matter if I never looked in a mirror again. Blind people manage to do without. But there's a voice now...'

Kill him. Kill him before it's too late.

Her body began to shudder but he held her until the spasm was over. Then he kissed her gently and their tea grew cold. Breakfast would be late.

Mark soon had to get up; there were chores to do around the farm. Gina did not linger in the bath. She was keen to make some sort of breakfast as a surprise for Mark. His grandmother's closet was rifled again for something to wear and Gina was delighted when she found an old rose coloured crepe-dechine dress that fitted. It was long and straight from the Thirties. She brushed her hair and tied it back with the rose sash. Her glowing face needed no cosmetics.

She poked around the kitchen, tied a tea towel round her waist. She wished she had taken more notice of Mrs Howard's skills. She got out a non-stick saucepan and an egg whisk. Scrambled egg was not going to beat her a second time. She found a basket of fresh mushrooms and washed them under running water. Mushrooms cook in butter, she remembered that from somewhere. This was gourmet standard. Move over, Nigella.

Mark came in the back door with a bowl of fresh brown eggs and a can of milk. His crew-necked sweater looked good on him, his cords splashed with mud but he had taken his boots off. Gina smiled at him, amazed how happy she felt. The butter began to melt in the saucepan.

'Gina, we have to talk. There isn't much time.'

'No time? You mean Barry and Lindsie are looking for me already? Are they hunting me down?' Gina's happiness glazed over with fear.

'They phoned while you were in the bath. I didn't tell them you were here. I made some suggestion about checking local hotels and pubs. They were, of course, very concerned for your whereabouts.'

'I bet,' said Gina bitterly. 'They'll want to track me down, bring me to heel.'

'This is what puzzles me. The eyes are not consistent. Sometimes you see them, then other times you don't. There's a reason. We must find out.'

'No, no ... I can't do it,' Gina groaned. 'It's impossible.' She stirred the mushrooms. Ace hand at stirring. 'Don't make me do this.'

Mark took her by the shoulders and turned her to face him. 'You want your life to get back to normal, don't you? You want a life with me? If you do, then we have got to find the truth, even if it's painful and it hurts.'

She nodded wearily. Mark removed the saucepan from the heat before the mushrooms burnt. Her face was drained of colour.

'The first time was in my car mirror as I was driving back from Plas Glwydan. That was the first time I saw the green eyes, after seeing the portrait here, or what I thought was a portrait. The portrait that was really a mirror. God, I know it's a mirror now. I stopped at a motorway service café and had the most ghastly cup of coffee. Then I saw the eyes in the driving mirror.'

'And the next time?'

'How can I possibly remember every incident?' Her voice rose hysterically. 'I've been doing my best to forget them. It's been a nightmare.'

'We've got to pin down what was different about the times when you see the eyes and when you don't.'

'I didn't this morning and I looked in the mirror at the foot of the stairs twice. Little old washed-out me.'

'Good for being brave and looking.' He switched on the kettle while Gina cut jagged slices of bread from a fresh loaf. 'Tea or coffee?'

'Coffee will be fine,' she said absently. The phrase echoed in her mind, surprisingly familiar, yet she had a feeling she had not said it herself. She really wanted another cup of tea.

'Gina ... what are you thinking?' Mark's voice intruded into her thoughts.

'I said I'd like some coffee, but I actually want a cup of tea. Isn't that weird? It was like some echo in my head. Coffee will be fine ... it wasn't even me saying it.' She shook her head, bewildered.

Mark did not look up from the eggs he was whisking in a bowl. The mountain of golden froth was rising against the glass sides in a tide of bubbles.

'You drink a lot of coffee, don't you?'

'Caffeine addict. Hot and strong.'

'I remember you saying something about a sherry in the bath that Betsy brought to you. Then you drank wine at Basil's party before a coffee, and last night we drank wine.'

'So what? What are you trying to say?'

He propped the whisk against the side of the bowl and turned Gina to face him. He was serious, searching into her dark eyes, willing her to be strong.

'Can you be even braver than you were earlier?' he asked. 'I want to try an experiment. Will you trust me? I'll be with you and I won't let you get hurt.'

'Experiment ... with me?'

Kill him. Use the knife. Quick, now.

She looked at the sharp knife in her hand. She looked at his strong pulsing throat. Her breathing was erratic.

He was stirring a cup of coffee and steering her through the sitting room into the dark panelled hall.

'Here's your coffee,' he said firmly.

A familiar horror swept through her. He stood her in front of the mirror and put the cup into her hand. She looked at the swirling brown liquid, the rich fumes rising into her nostrils and fuelling her veins.

'Drink it.'

'No, I can't.'

'You will.'

Her hand was trembling as she sipped the coffee. It could have been laced with poison. There was no taste in it, no pleasure. Her throat dried up, parched.

'Now, together.' He took the cup from her hand. 'We will both look into the mirror together.'

'Please, no.'

Gina fought down rising terror and panic. The green eyes were already staring at her from the mirror, their coolness full of hate and disdain. Those pale intense eyes were boring holes into her skull like emerald drills. She would have fallen if Mark had not been behind her, holding her. A scream began to form in her throat ... choking her.

You must kill him before it's too late.

Mark saw only Gina and the sheer terror on her gaunt face, with himself standing behind her.

'She's there,' Gina gasped.

'No one is there. Only Gina Conway and me.'

Mark pressed a glass into her hand and tried to lift her stiffened arm.

'Now drink this, quickly, Gina,' he said urgently. 'It's orange juice. Plain, ordinary orange juice.'

Gina looked unbelievingly at the glass of orange juice in his hand. It was ridiculous. Why start breakfast in the middle of this horror? Mark was asking her to drink orange juice when those eyes were terrifying her and her features were beginning to waver and dissolve like reflections in a pool. Her face was disappearing. She was going to lose her whole face.

'I'm going...' she moaned, clutching the frame. 'My face is dissolving.'

'Drink it!' he shouted at her. 'Gina! Don't let it happen. Drink the juice.'

He held the glass against her lips. She was drowning in the hatred that emanated from the Tudor woman. She was losing her identity. Gina Conway was no more. She had gone. The other face was triumphant, victorious. Gina was too tired to fight back.

Mark tilted her head and forced juice into her mouth, spilling some down her chin. She choked, but swallowed a few mouthfuls. He held her firmly, making her drink, hardly letting her breathe or twist out of his grasp.

She became aware of a tingling in her head, along her scalp, down her spine. It was pins and needles along every nerve in her body. She cried out with the pain.

'Look again in the mirror. What do you see...?'

The pain was excruciating. She thought her head was going to burst open. Events were happening with tachyonic speed. She forced her glued eyes to open and look into the mirror.

The cart rumbled and trundled through the turreted gatehouse entrance into the unevenly paved courtyard. There was a body lying on the rough wooden boards.

The stable boys rushed out, then the servants from the kitchen. Word spread through the house like a fire. They stood huddled in groups, too fearful to come near or look.

'A bear got him,' said the driver, getting down from his seat. 'A bear or wolves, I'd swear.'

Someone turned him over and his young face, bloodied, waxen, was caught in an expression of surprise. His clothes were torn, stiff with blood, a stout stick still clenched in his hand, his wrists red and skinned from tight bonds.

'Look, he fought. He fought bravely, did our Will.'

An older man moved aside the stained jerkin and the crowd gasped at the gaping wound deep in the youth's heart.

'That weren't no bear,' said the old man.

Twenty-Five

The telephone began to ring shrilly. Mark picked it up. 'Erddig Farm. Hello, Lindsie. Gina?'

Gina shook her head. Don't tell them I'm here, her eyes pleaded. Please don't tell them.

'I have spoken to her,' said Mark, not exactly lying. 'She put up somewhere for the night. She seems to have had a shock, was a bit upset. I think she's going back to Cranbourne Square, but she didn't say when. I'm sure she'll want to pick up her things. I could drive her over. Bye now.'

Mark put the phone down. 'Lindsie sends her love.'

Gina was shocked and hurt. Mark was going to take her back to Plas Glwydan; she could not trust him after all. Her old doubts flooded her mind.

'We have to go back, don't you see? We've got to find those notes of Timothy's. And the castle is the right starting place to search for explanations. We'll go together. And you'll do exactly as I say, promise me? Are you listening, Gina?' He shook her gently, his eyes holding her frightened gaze. 'You must do exactly as I say.'

'How do I know if I can trust you?' she breathed.

He tapped her nose. 'Feminine instinct.'

'Gina darling!' Lindsie threw her arms round Gina. It was an instant replay of previous arrivals. 'Barry and I have been worried stiff about you. We couldn't think where you had gone in that dreadful rain. Mark, how kind of you to bring Gina back. Gina, let me look at you. Yes, you're looking a lot better. It must be the dress. Such a pretty colour.'

'It's very old,' said Gina.

'You don't get workmanship like that these days. Look at those buttonholes ... a work of art. I feel an absolute mess beside you. Come in and have a drink.'

Lindsie was in her uniform jeans, flip-flops and ethnic smock, curls bouncing around her face. They went into the long sitting room. There had been a big tidy-up; for Mark's benefit, Gina supposed. The dogs had been banished and a tray was laid with a decanter and a bowl of nuts and crisps.

'Sherry?'

'Please,' said Gina and drank it like a drowning man.

'No, thank you,' said Mark, strolling over

to the window. 'I won't be able to stay long. Things to do.'

'But you will stay for lunch? I've defrosted the dining room in your honour.'

'I'm sorry. I'm tied up for the rest of the day. But I would like to have a look round the grounds. It'll remind me of when I used to come over here as a boy.'

'Of course,' said Lindsie. 'Why don't you take Mark round, Gina. A breath of air will do you good. I can manage lunch on my own.'

Mark draped his sweater round Gina's shoulders. Even he felt the chill of the castle. 'Let's get going on this guided tour. I hope you are word perfect.'

'I can't do this,' she said outside. It was too disturbing, back at the castle, a place she hated so much.

The salty air brought a whiff of the sea, the green of the landscape soft and muted like an old patchwork. A waft of herbs came unexpectedly to her on a breeze. Some memory stirred but escaped. They walked casually in case Lindsie was watching. A morning stroll.

Gina took the long way round to the store of wood. No one could see them from the castle, only from the kitchen windows, and they were placed so high it was not easy to see out of them. Someone had been chopping wood that morning for there were fresh chippings round the block. Gina shuddered.

She thought of facing the block at the Tower.

'They're here somewhere,' she said, her fingers going between the stacks of logs waiting to be split.

'Which of those two is really your cousin?' Mark asked. 'You're a Conway. He's a Wykeham.'

'Lindsie is my cousin. Her mother, Stasi, was my mother's younger sister. But somewhere back in the Dark Ages, a woman on my grandmother's side of the family, the Fairweathers, married a Wykeham and lost the inheritance along the female line.'

'You mean Plas Glwydan once belonged to the Fairweathers before the Wykehams?'

'Yes, way back, before it fell to pieces and the money disappeared. It's very complicated. No one has ever researched it properly. I don't suppose anyone remembers.'

Her fingers closed over a wodge of paper and she pulled it out. Timothy's notes lay in her hand, the edges wet and browned after last night's downpour. She had not been dreaming, hallucinating. This had been for real.

Mark turned them over carefully; his face grim.

'They are definitely Timothy's notes. Could be the ones that went in that burglary. But why take them? It doesn't make sense.'

'I know why,' said Gina. The words hung in the air. Part of a jigsaw fell into place. A piece of sky that fitted.

Mark waited until she regained her composure. He put the notes away in a pocket.

'Lindsie and I were having coffee on the terrace. I found a scrap of paper with my name written on it over and over again. It didn't mean anything at the time. Now it does. Someone was practising my name in a different handwriting, Timothy's writing, which they had copied from these notes.'

'But whatever for?' It was Mark's turn to be mystified.

'It was that letter. A terrible letter I got from Timothy on my wedding day. It was delivered to me at the reception, at my home. I couldn't believe what it said. It was full of poisonous accusations. None of which sounded like Timothy at all. And it wasn't him, of course. He didn't write it, poor darling. It was a forgery.'

'He was already a prisoner. Here.'

'Here? You think he was a prisoner here?'

'I'm sure. A gut feeling. That pond algae in his throat. It ought to be checked.' He took her hand.

They skirted the long wet edge of the lake. The height of the water had gone down in the last few years after poor summer rains. Mark knew his way round the grounds.

'Used to be good fishing in the lake. When it rained, we took shelter in the tunnel.'

'The tunnel? What tunnel?'

'There's a tunnel from the castle that comes out near the lake. A priest's passage. We used to scare each other silly, going further and further in, making noises. I've no idea where it comes out in the castle. A cellar perhaps.'

The entrance to the tunnel was half hidden by weeds and creeper, like woody cobwebs. Dai, the old gardener stood, leaning on his spade, his gnarled hands crossed over.

'Come to look for your young friend, have you?' he said, wiping his rheumy eyes with his sleeve. 'Reckon you're too late. There's no one in there now.'

Mark caught Gina as she stumbled.

'Our friend?' said Mark.

'Young chap. Not well, they said. Bad eyes, had to have complete darkness. I spoke to him a couple of times. Didn't seem natural, keeping him in a tunnel when they had all them rooms in the castle.'

'Did he say anything? What did he say?'

'Lot of mumbo-jumbo. Summit about a church. And gin ... gin? He were rambling a lot. He were on some strong medicine for his eyes, they said.'

'Why didn't you do something about it?' Gina said, a cold, hollow feeling in her stomach. 'You must have known it was wrong to keep a sick man hidden in a tunnel.'

'I'd lose my job, miss. I couldn't get another job at my age. No one would take me.'

He shambled off, disturbed by Gina's anger. She clenched her hands, nails biting into flesh. Mark turned abruptly and delved into the darkness of the tunnel. He came out with a damp sleeping bag, a plastic cup, a pair of trainers.

'Do you recognize them?'

Trainers look similar the world over, but Timothy had worn charity-week laces in his. The Fight Cancer motif was woven into these shoes, the laces still tied in double knots. The trainers had been wrenched off him.

She nodded, barely able to speak. 'They're Timothy's.'

Mark held her close. 'They are not going to get away with this. They killed Timothy. Can you go on? If you say no, I'll understand. It's almost too dangerous.'

Kill him. Kill him. She heard the voice again.

'Don't get in your Range Rover,' she said suddenly. 'Don't get in without checking the brakes, electrics.'

'But why? They wouldn't touch me.'

'Timothy was in their way. They got rid of him. They used my scarf to tie up his feet. A scarf they had stolen from my bedroom. The day before my wedding is a complete blank. What did I do on that day?'

'I'll be very careful, Gina. Anyway, I'm not going anywhere. Remember what we planned.' He leaned over the lake edge and took a sample in the plastic cup.

They went soberly back to Plas Glwydan, the great pitted walls looking sadly down at them as if they had nothing to relate, but centuries of bitterness and pain. It was not an easy walk. Gina was terrified. The cool and collected woman who chaired the board of the Conway Line, making decisions that cost millions of pounds, had gone.

They went into the castle, the door clanging behind them like a barricade.

'And stay put this time, young woman,' said Mark, as if continuing a lecture. 'I haven't time to keep chasing around the countryside after you.'

'I will,' said Gina meekly. 'It was claustrophobia, I'm sure. That tiny room in the turret. I had to get out.'

Lindsie laughed. 'Isn't the castle big enough for you? We'll find you another room. Any one you like.'

'There's no need,' said Gina. 'I phoned Howard this morning. He's driving down to pick me up late this afternoon. I feel I ought to go home. Betsy and Mrs Howard will look after me. They always have done, for years.'

'Oh dear.' Lindsie looked put out. 'You must do as you think best. But I like having you here. Why not stay on for a few more days? Are you planning to see a doctor?'

'No,' said Gina. 'I'm much better. I don't

think I need to see a doctor.'

'Is that wise? Perhaps you need a tonic.'

'I don't think so,' said Gina evenly. 'I feel perfectly all right now.'

'I'll make some fresh coffee before you go,' said Lindsie.

'I won't say no to a coffee,' said Mark.

'And I *never* say no to a coffee,' said Gina, forcing a brittle lightness.

'Right,' said Lindsie as if pulled by strings. 'Coffees coming up. That sounds like Barry now. I'll tell him you're both here.'

Gina joined Mark by the window. He smiled down at her with a special look. 'That's my girl,' he murmured.

'I can't do it. It's giving me the creeps.' She was edgy and apprehensive, shaken by finding Timothy's prison, and appalled at the way he had died. 'I'm scared.'

'Do it for Timothy,' said Mark.

They heard Barry coming through the hall, voices talking, then the door opened and he came in. Barry went straight over to Gina and put his arm round her.

'My dear Gina,' he said earnestly. 'We were so worried about you. Thank goodness you are safe.'

They could not stop her screaming. Her voice rent the air in agony. The dreadful sound echoed through the rooms. She ran

301

the long gallery in her bare feet, down the stairs and out into the courtyard. They tried to stop her going to the cart, but she fought like a wild cat, struggling against the restricting arms.

She threw herself on the body, willing life to return, but it had been long gone many hours. Even his soul had gone. There was nothing any more, only a bloodied shell.

She showered the dead face with kisses, cradled the heavy head, clutched the crumpled body with her small arms.

Her father came and carried her away, his heart heavy.

Twenty-Six

Gina remembered Mark's sheepskin coat and it was a heaven-sent excuse to extract herself.

'I'll get your coat before you go,' she said. 'I expect you'd like it back.'

She fled upstairs to the turret room and sat on the edge of the bed, the duvet's poppies dancing around her. She bowed her head in her hands and wept for Timothy, remembering the darkness and dampness of the tunnel and his cruel and lonely death. For his sake, she had to do this.

She was not used to having to think carefully before every move, every word she spoke, though she and Mark had gone over the plan thoroughly in the car. It was guess work, two people trying to fight an evil they didn't understand.

She splashed tepid water on her face and put moisturizer on her skin. She eased her feet into her boots, being careful not to crinkle the plasters on the cuts. She picked up Mark's coat and the other lawn dress. It still evoked a scent of tea roses. Mark could take both if she folded the dress inside the coat.

Lindsie was handing round coffee. There was a buzz of conversation and she made an effort to join in. Gina moved around the room, admiring the Atlantic view, looking at pictures, cup and saucer in her hand, raising the cup to her lips. It was like being in a play, acting.

She went over to the window and put her cup down on the oak sill. Mark joined her, placing his empty cup next to hers.

'There are wonderful waterfalls in the Neath Vale and the gorge is great walking. Sgwd Gwladys is a particularly spectacular waterfall. Perhaps you'd like to see it.'

'Yes, I would. The next time I come down but not in the rain, please.'

'I'll organize the weather. You'll need sensible shoes.'

Gina picked up Mark's empty cup. 'I'll dig out my walking boots.'

Mark drained her cup of coffee. No one noticed the switch. 'I must go.' He collected his coat and said his goodbyes. She gave him a casual wave and returned to the blazing fire.

'I'd better see what's happening to that chicken,' Lindsie said, hurrying down the corridor to the kitchen. 'Not a lot, I suspect.'

'More coffee?' Barry asked. 'We're in for a long wait.'

'Yes, please. Thanks.' She gave him the empty cup for a refill and sank into a deep saggy armchair by the fire. Her slim body was taut, scared of what might be going to happen. She could not look at Barry.

'You are a sleepy girl,' said Barry, going to the chair opposite her. 'I've never known such a sleepy girl. Always falling asleep in front of the fire. I've lost count of the number of times you've fallen asleep in that chair.'

That was news to her. She could not remember ever having fallen asleep downstairs at Plas Glwydan.

Barry sat forward, a glass of whisky rocking in his hand. She could see the firelight catching on the cut surfaces of the glass, shooting sparks of light. He twisted the glass, making a rainbow of rays. 'Take it easy. Close your eyes if you want to, Gina. We've plenty of time. Lindsie will be ages. Roasting a chicken is a major culinary exercise.'

She was aware that at some point Barry leaned forward and took the coffee cup from her inert hand. The room was very quiet. She was struggling to keep awake. The dogs had gone. She could hear the grandfather clock ticking heavily in the corner of the room, the hush-brush of creeper leaves against the windows asking to be let in, their sucker fingers inching a slow stampede across the glass. She was listening to these things, rather than to Barry's voice. Then she remembered nothing more as she fell into an uneasy doze.

'Listen carefully to what I have to say. Your eyes are heavy and closed. You are feeling comfortable, relaxed, thinking of nothing, nothing at all, but you are listening to me. You are relaxed and comfortable. Warm and content. Heavy and relaxed. Your arms are growing heavier, heavier ... soon they will fall to your side...'

Gina's arms fell from her lap.

'You are going backwards, further and further backwards into the darkness, a great void of nothing, feeling heavy and empty. Your mind is empty and you are travelling backwards through time, feeling more and more drowsy, thinking of nothing, absolutely nothing, remembering nothing ... going into a deep and sound sleep, a deep sound sleep, a lovely sleep, a deep sound sleep, a lovely sleep, deeper and deeper back into time, years and years ago, regressing, back into another time and as I count from one to ten your sleep will become even deeper. One deeper and deeper, two deeper and deeper, three deeper, four still deeper...'

His voice changed.

'Now you are asleep, soundly asleep, deeply asleep, breathing deeply and evenly. Sleep, sleep ... she's gone. You can come in, Lindsie.'

Barry moved towards Gina and lifted her arm. It fell like that of a rag doll and lay on her lap.

Lindsie had come quietly into the room in her flip-flops. She was standing in the doorway. 'Do we have to?'

'Yes, we do,' he said, almost fiercely. 'She's going back to London. Howard is coming down for her. We haven't much time left. We may never have another chance. And she's looking better, far stronger. She has too much resilience. This might be the final time. You'd like to be the Duchess of Milan again, wouldn't you? Put on the black robe. And the black cap. And don't forget to put in the contacts.'

'Do I have to dress up?' Lindsie sounded fed up. 'I don't want to do it. Must I?'

306

'You can't back out now,' he insisted, his voice so quiet it could hardly be heard. 'Think what it means. She's got everything and we've nothing. Our child deserves its inheritance, not a ruin round its neck. Lindsie, that money is yours, yours as much hers. Your mothers were sisters. It's a blood tie. Why should it all be hers? Gina is nothing but a selfish, spoilt woman.'

'I'm sure she'd give us some if we asked her,' Lindsie said, plucking at her skirt.

'We don't want some, we want it all.' Barry's voice became high and harsh. 'This is a reaction to yesterday, because you saw her, heard her. We don't know how much Mark Trenchard knows. Timothy is no longer a problem but this brother might be a tougher nut to crack. If she goes back to London, we will lose control and we won't know what's happening. She must have her final instructions now.'

'Why don't we make her forget a few more days? That seemed to work.'

'Too risky now. It's got to be my way. Then no more worries, no more cooking, no housework. Goodbye to draughts, damp and dry rot at Plas Glwydan. Now put on the black robe and cap. Think about what she did to you.'

'I don't want Gina to get hurt.'

'She won't get hurt. She's a perfectly willing subject. We were lucky to discover that right from the start. It couldn't have worked out better.'

'Supposing she remembers our farewell party and your hypnotic game?'

'She won't. I've erased them totally. She'll only remember that someone spilt red wine on her dress and she left in a temper.' He turned to Gina. 'Gina, are you asleep?'

'I am asleep,' said Gina. There was a long pause.

'Say, I do not want to leave Plas Glwydan.'

'I ... I do not want to leave Plas Glwydan.'

'I want to stay with Lindsie,' he prompted.

'I want to stay with Lindsie.'

'What was the last instruction to you?'

'Kill him. Kill him.'

'And did you?' He waited for her answer.

'No.'

'Why not?'

'Not yet.'

Barry let his breath out between clenched teeth. 'Now you can open your eyes. Open. What do you see?'

Gina opened her eyes. There was no expression in them. They were dull and opaque. She sat still and obedient, staring into the fire.

'Look towards the door, Gina. You'll see a woman in the doorway. She has your face. Can you see her eyes? They are a vivid green. You are seeing your previous self.'

Lindsie stood absolutely still in the

shadows wearing the long black robe edged with fur, her hair tucked into a close black cap. Her face was ashen and her eyes were full of smouldering hatred. She was remembering the terrible day when her mother jumped off Westminster Bridge and everything had changed.

She had not eaten for six days. She sat on a windowseat, ramrod stiff, staring as a violent thunderstorm raged across the sky and the rain poured in torrents. The little stream overflowed its banks and the gardens flooded, sweeping away young plants.

Her mother wrung her hands in the kitchen. 'She will not eat. She refuses everything. I don't know what to do with the girl.'

'I'll make her a honey-flavoured curd,' said Old Moll. 'That's her favourite, with ginger sprinkled on top. She'll eat that.'

But Georgina did not touch it.

Twenty-Seven

'Look at the woman in black, Gina. You can see those green eyes staring at you, full of hate. Full of hatred.'

'I can see green eyes ... staring at me ... full of hate,' said Gina.

'A long nose and thin unsmiling mouth.'

'A long nose,' she repeated. 'Thin, unsmiling mouth.'

'The black robe, the black cap of death.'

'The black robe, the black cap of death.'

'Your death cap.'

'My death cap. I'm seeing my death cap.'

Lindsie gasped and her hand flew to her mouth. Barry's eyes narrowed. Any noise could spoil the deep trance.

'The next time you look into a mirror you will see these green eyes, full of hatred. Your features will begin to dissolve and you will see the long nose and thin mouth. You will watch your face disappear and instead her face will be there. Then, slowly your body will disintegrate and in its place will be this black robed figure, waiting for you, waiting for your death.'

'Barry, don't...' Lindsie made to move.

'Quiet, woman,' he said through gritted teeth. 'We have to take it this far. There's no going back.'

The room was paralysed with tension. Lindsie breathed quickly, her fingers plucking at the material of the robe. There was a film of perspiration on Barry's receding hairline. He took off his pebble-glasses and wiped them.

'It's only a hallucination, to see the green eyes instead of her own. No permanent harm,' he said soothingly for Lindsie's benefit. 'I have simply hypnotized her perception of an object – herself in this case – to have a changed physical reality. I could as easily suggest that whenever she saw a banana, she thought it was an apple. She has a post-hypnotic signal and whenever this signal is properly given, she re-enters the hypnotic state.' His voice went cold. 'I've told you all this before. No need to make such a fuss.'

'But it wasn't like this the first time.'

Barry could barely contain his irritation. 'It's had to be a gradual progression. Stop worrying.'

He turned back to Gina, leaning forward, concentrating intensely. 'What have I said? Repeat to me.'

'No need to make a fuss.'

He snorted with annoyance that she had picked up an aside, but immediately changed to a even, smooth tone. 'About the green eyes, the face, the robe.'

'My body will disappear. I will become the woman in the black robe. I will see my death cap.'

'Yes, you will become the woman in the black robe. She will possess your body and your mind. You will lose your identity. You will no longer be Gina Conway. You will never see or be Gina Conway again. This woman will be the real you. But she is from the Tudor period, and you will be trapped in her body, living in the wrong century, in the wrong body. It will become a living hell, a living prison. Imagine your terror, your fear, your inability to escape.'

Gina began to shake as if she was already feeling these emotions coming over her in waves. Barry noted the signs and knew he must finish quickly.

'Coffee is lovely. You'll want more and more. It is your only comfort. Every time your brain is soaked in caffeine you will remember what I have told you and you will become the woman in the black robe. Say, coffee will be fine.'

'Coffee will be fine.'

Lindsie rushed away and tore at the velcro fastenings of the long black robe. She couldn't get out of it fast enough. She didn't like this game any more.

'Kill him,' he went on, changing tactics. 'You must kill him. He is a danger to you.

Mark Trenchard. As his brother was also a danger. Kill him, Gina. Repeat.'

'Kill him. I will kill him.'

'That's a good girl. In a minute I will awaken you. Your sleep is becoming much lighter and you are beginning to wake. But you will remember nothing of this, nothing at all. You will wake and you will feel happy and content, refreshed by your sleep. You are practically awake now. You are wide awake now. Wake up, Gina.'

Gina opened her eyes. She must have dozed off. The fire was scorching her legs through the thin material of the dress. Her pulse was strangely racing. She pushed a strand of hair behind her ear. She was sweating.

Barry laughed, lifting the glass to his lips and finishing off the whisky. 'Lindsie can't bake either. She made a cake once that even the birds wouldn't touch.'

'Perhaps a cookery course for Christmas?'

'I think a few take-away food shops close by would suit me better. Chinese or curry. I'm not fussy.'

'No need to make a fuss,' said Gina. Barry shot a look at her so fast that she missed it.

'I think lunch is ready,' said Lindsie from round the door. 'The skin is brown. It ought to be cooked by now. We're eating in the dining room. There are no minstrels playing in the gallery but I could put on a tape.'

'I'd like to wash my hands,' said Gina. In the bathroom she cupped her hands and drank copiously from the cold tap. She had no way of knowing if anything had happened, but she was taking no chances. She dried her mouth and wished she had some lipstick. She looked hollow and pale.

Lindsie had laid the long oak table with four places together at the end nearest the fire. She had taken some trouble with red linen place mats and matching napkins which looked as if they had been hastily unpacked. The silver cutlery did not gleam but it was an improvement on the cheap stainless steel used at other meals. She had obviously intended to impress Mark, but she could do nothing about the damp smell and the overall gloominess.

'This looks nice,' said Gina, hoping she would be seated near the fire.

'We've been eating like pigs,' said Lindsie. 'Today we're going to be civilized. I've put you by the fire, Gina. We're more used to the cold.'

Over the moulded and carved oak chimney was a gilded rococo mirror, tarnished with age. Gina's courage fled. She couldn't do it. Where was Mark? She wanted him near.

Lindsie brought in the roast chicken and put it on the table for Barry to carve. It was a free-range bird, glistening with fat. There were tureens of carrots and potatoes, a boat of instant gravy and a dish of ready-made herb stuffing which Lindsie forgot to put in the chicken. It was a valiant effort.

'My, you have been busy,' said Gina. 'It smells wonderful. Mark will be sorry he didn't stay.'

'It's only tinned fruit afterwards,' said Lindsie.

Gina went over to the blemished mirror to tighten the sash in her hair which was working loose. She would have to do it now. There might be wine with the lunch, but more coffee after lunch. So it had to be now. She scraped her hair back with her fingers, head down, knowing they were watching her.

A tremor of fear laid a chill hand on her spine. Supposing Mark was wrong. She had been careful not to drink any coffee, but she could not know for certain till she looked into the mirror above. If the green eyes of hatred were there, if the Tudor woman existed, then Mark was wrong and she was doomed.

She tossed up her head, clutching the mane of tawny hair in one hand, the sash in the other. The seconds hung in the air. Then she opened her mouth and screamed. It was an unearthly sound that shattered the stillness of the lofty dining room, high shrieks that bounced off the panelled walls and vibrated into the high rafters.

'Go away, go away,' she howled, trying to push something aside. She clawed at the mirror.

'Do nothing,' said Barry firmly. 'Pretend not to hear.'

Lindsie clutched the back of a chair, frozen with horror. 'Oh my God,' she cried. 'This is awful.' Barry was struck silent. He stroked his thin face uneasily.

Gina tore herself away from the mirror and threw herself on a chair, burying her face in her arms so that they would not see her expression of pure relief. She was dizzy and overwhelmed. The eyes in the mirror had been her own brown.

'Are you all right?' said Lindsie, far away.

The face was hers, her dark brown eyes, not a glimpse of the spectre, the alien eyes, the face of evil and hatred. She had remembered in a split second to pretend to see the eyes, to scream. It had been easy to recall the distress, to visualize how those eyes had been on other occasions, to bring back terrifying memories.

'Shall I carve?' said Barry.

'I hope it's done,' said Lindsie.

Gina could have cried aloud with joy. She had seen her cousins' shocked reflections in the mirror. She was free of that monster. Yet there was that voice...

Kill him, kill him.

Suddenly she was angry that Barry and

Lindsie could be so cruel. But she was strong now. She could do anything, fight anything that might happen. She would never see those evil green eyes again. It was a total release.

'Gina...?' began Lindsie in a strangled voice.

Gina did not know how to react. What should she do? Be the green-eyed woman or herself? They had engineered a drama and they were going to get it.

'Kill him. Kill him,' she cried, lunging for the carving knife.

The impact was immediate. Lindsie leaped up and backed away. Barry went white.

Gina rushed towards him. 'Kill him,' she shrieked, waving the knife.

They bled her till she passed out. Old Moll went to a wise woman in the village and came back with leaves of borage and basil to brew a healing tea which would prevent nausea and vomiting and make a merry heart; also rock parsley of Alexandria, the leaves, stem and root to be boiled to promote appetite.

'Make also a brandy by distilling the flowers of the lily of the valley and it will restore speech to those that are fallen into the appoplexie and melancholike,' the woman told Old Moll.

'She says nothing, nothing at all.'

The wise woman shook her head. 'Purgation of black hellebor for madness...'

Old Moll interrupted furiously. 'She is not mad.'

'Thyme infused well in vinegar then sodden and mingled with rosewater is a singular remedy for a girl's long phrensie or lethargie...'

But there were no lilies in the garden at that time of the year. They made the brews, but the girl's mouth closed on the liquid and it dribbled down her chin.

They had to keep moving her for her wasted body was covered in putrid sores which they treated with St John's Wort flowers in olive oil. They did not wash her for fear of the water robbing her frail strength. She began to stink and the room was odorous despite the bunches of fresh herbs brought in daily from the garden.

'My poor daughter,' the mother wept, neglecting her other duties.

Twenty-Eight

'Get a doctor. Get the phone. She's gone mad. She's flipped the bloody brink,' Barry shouted at Lindsie as he ran.

'That won't be necessary,' said a man's voice from the gallery. The words were clipped and cold. 'Gina is saner than either of you. There's no need to call a doctor.'

Mark was leaning over the richly carved balustrade of the gallery as casually as if he were at the theatre. He straightened up, his shoulders like armour making him look more powerful than ever. He came down the narrow spiral stairs, a black tape recorder in his hand.

Gina could not move. He took the carving knife from her hands and put it on the table.

'Now what shall we do with these two characters?' Mark went on, full of disgust. 'My brother died here at Plas Glwydan and now we have proof, not only the old gardener's evidence, but this tape. This tape is proof, Gina. It's criminal what they were planning to do to you. Fraud, mental cruelty, premeditated manslaughter, if that is how

319

you describe sending an innocent victim completely mad. I'm sure there is a good, long prison sentence to cover all their crimes.'

Lindsie moaned, swaying.

'We'll get a doctor unless Lindsie is still acting and we know she's a good actress. The woman in the black robe was convincing. She likes dressing up. Look at Lindsie closely and you'll see that her eyes are a vivid green, contact lenses, and under that fringe, you'll find she has shaved off her eyebrows.'

'This is all a terrible mistake,' said Barry, ashen-faced. 'Gina is very ill, mentally ill. You heard her screaming. She doesn't know who she is or what she's saying.'

'Nonsense,' rapped Mark. 'It's over. I have all the evidence that we need. I recorded the whole of that scene before lunch when you hypnotized Gina into thinking that she was losing her mind, her face and body changing. It was quite simple to put a tape recorder on the windowsill, a very sophisticated microphone that picks up sound at fifty yards. You came over, loud and clear, Mr Wykeham.'

'Mark, is this true?'

'You were hypnotized, Gina, as you sat in front of the fire. Barry has had you under his control for weeks, ever since their party. He was telling you to see those green eyes, he was putting their thoughts of hatred into your head.'

'That's cruel ... how cruel,' Gina breathed.

'Had Barry ever hypnotized you as a willing participant?'

'Yes,' said Gina, suddenly remembering. 'It was at St John's Wood, their farewell party. I had a headache and Barry said he had learned an old Indian technique, meditation and hypnotism. He tried it on me but it didn't work.'

'It worked all right, Gina. Only too well. He was testing to see if you could be hypnotized. He made you receptive to immediate re-entry into the hypnotic state at his command. That's when it began. That's when they set the trap. You were theirs from that moment onwards.'

'But that was months ago. When I was first engaged to Timothy.'

'Timothy was in their way.'

Kill him, kill him.

She had to kill someone. The feeling was very strong, dominating her thoughts, pulsing like a second heart. Someone was her enemy and she had to kill him. The voice had been telling her that for days.

Mark called the police, but it was hours before the formalities at the police station were over. It meant going through the circumstances of Timothy's death again, checking details on the main computer system.

'The algae they found in his lungs?' asked Gina.

'Probably from the lake at Plas Glwydan,' said Mark grimly. 'They held him down in the lake, then put him in the Severn Estuary and he washed out to sea. I've given the police the sample from the lake for checking.'

Gina was numbed. 'I'll never forgive them,' she said, shaking.

The tape was played in the presence of Gina, Mark, Barry and Lindsie, two CID detectives and two WPOs. It was rivetting. Gina went white as she listened to Barry's voice, and his insidious destruction of her sanity.

'I deny it all, deny it all,' Barry blustered.

'I think you had better telephone your solicitor, Mr Wykeham,' said Detective Inspector Carter, slapping shut the file. 'We have all the evidence we need to charge you for the murder of Timothy Trenchard and premeditated assault on Miss Conway.'

Gina stood security for the Wykehams' bail. The officers at the station were incredulous. Mark said nothing. He couldn't stop her. She felt she had to do it.

She was exhausted. She hardly knew what time of day it was, or where she was. The late evening was warmer than the chill of the castle, but she had Mark's sheepskin coat draped round her shoulders and that was comforting.

They got into the Range Rover and Mark drove her through the peaceful Welsh roads towards Chepstow. Howard was coming on the motorway to meet them there and the plan was that he should drive her back to Cranbourne Square.

'I've been commanded to kill someone,' said Gina. 'I could have killed you. That command is still implanted in my head. I still hear it. I've got to get it out. But why did they do this? Was it for my money?'

'Yes, they were after your fortune. Barry is paranoid about restoring Plas Glwydan to its former glory, but it desperately needs a huge infusion of money.'

'I would have willingly given it to them,' said Gina. 'They only had to ask.'

'It would never have been enough. They wanted it all, your holding in Conway Lines, too. No doubt they planned that once you were committed to a mental institution, Lindsie would apply for and get power of attorney over your considerable wealth. They would milk the accounts, sell your shares, sell Cranbourne Square, pretty certain that no one could object. Then along came Timothy and he was the first major obstacle to their plans.'

'So they got rid of him.'

'The ultimate end of their plan was your suicide. Then Lindsie, as your nearest relative, would have inherited everything that was left. But first they had to get rid of Timothy and they were not quite sure how to do that. Perhaps they thought that keeping him a prisoner at Plas Glwydan was enough, keeping him drugged till you were safely committed. Then one day they gave him too much.'

Gina saw the tunnel. 'I'll never forgive them for what they did to Timothy,' she said. 'But Lindsie didn't like doing it. You heard her on the tape.'

'I think Lindsie was an unwilling accomplice, only going along with it as long as she did not see any actual suffering. She was able to shut her mind to what they were doing, to dress up and play act, put her baby first, to do anything that kept Barry happy.'

'The turret room was waiting, ready for me.'

'Coming to Plas Glwydan was planted in your mind.'

She shuddered at the thought of being so out of control of her own actions.

'So what else has been planted?' Her voice began to shake. 'How do I know what will happen next? I've a time bomb ticking inside my body, a self-destruct mechanism which could activate any time, any day. I'm a danger. To everyone.'

Twenty-Nine

Mark noticed Gina's increasing restlessness in London. She went around with her arms clasped across her body as if she was holding herself together, afraid of something vital falling out. She stared out of windows, not seeing the view. She went to work, functioning on auto-pilot.

'Something is going to happen,' she said again and again. 'I can feel it but I don't know what it is. I won't let it happen, I won't.'

Mark found a professional hypnotist, Lucan Demitri, who was willing to put Gina under hypnosis and remove all previous instructions. Mark drove up from Wales and went with Gina to the consulting rooms.

'How shall I know if this works?' she asked.

'We shan't know but we have to have faith in someone. Fingers crossed.'

'Everything crossed.' She sipped water. 'They must have taken the blue Conway scarf from my bedroom. I can't find it anywhere.'

'Don't worry about it any more. It's too late.'

The de-hypnotization was a harrowing experience even under the considerate care of Mr Demitri. Gina found it difficult to relax even with Mark there. When it was over, she was exhausted. They could not make any tests because she refused to touch coffee.

'Hypnotherapy is often used for the treatment of mental and physical disorders,' said Mr Demitri.

'I'm not mental,' said Gina.

'I'm sorry, I didn't mean it like that. I was trying to say that this is a normal medical procedure.'

'I won't put it to the test,' she said later, back at Cranbourne Square. 'Supposing it hasn't worked and what Barry said will happen, that I will lose my identity, become this woman from Tudor times, living in the wrong body in the wrong century. I'm not prepared to risk it.'

'Gina, it's your choice,' said Mark.

It was a warm evening, muggy with a threat of thunder in the air. They were enjoying an unexpected mid-week evening together and an informal meal in the walled garden, produced by Mrs Howard at short notice. They ate poached salmon with fresh vegetables, then Gina's favourite honey curd tart served with lemon sorbet. They smiled at each other, at peace.

'Your appetite has recovered,' said Mark.

'I'm absolutely ravenous these days,' said Gina with a twinkle in her dark eyes. 'It's all the farmwork you force me to do at the weekends.'

'A weekend wife.'

'Sounds good to me.'

Work at Erddig was progressing well. The lambs were healthy and Mark was experimenting with a new crop, linseed oil. He had to drive back that night. The distance was nothing to him after living in America.

'The field looks like a pool of blue water,' he said, holding her close. 'It's a mirage. You'll love it.'

'I know I will. Take care.'

'The motorway will be clear.'

It was an unbearably hot night. Gina tossed every which way, unable to sleep. She slipped out of bed and pulled on thin cotton jeans and a T-shirt, pushed her feet into sandals. She thought she was going downstairs for a drink, but there was iced water beside her bed. The house was still, only the ticking of the grandfather clock disturbing the quietness.

For some reason she remembered being shut in the attic when she was a child. She remembered the fear. Could Lindsie have closed that door? Her art class could have been cancelled. She had been a secretive girl.

Gina's shoulder bag lay on the table in the hallway where she had left it. The keys to the

Mercedes were inside. She would not wake Howard. She got the car out herself.

Soon she was driving through the empty, neon lit streets, heading for Hammersmith Junction which was the beginning of the M4 to Wales. The motorway would be clear.

The big car took the fast lane and settled to an even eighty, by-passing Reading and Swindon without noticing the signs. She turned on the radio and a late night music station lulled her with sultry oldies, Sinatra and Crosby, Artie Shaw and Nat King Cole. The music eddied in soft waves.

Dawn was touching the sky as she paid the toll and drove across the Severn Bridge. She was the only car on the bridge, apart from a few lumbering lorries coming the other way. She could smell salt in the air from the Severn. It was a muddy sheet of metallic water, hardly moving. She drove deeper into South Wales, Newport and Cardiff barely awake.

Suddenly she had an overwhelming longing for coffee. Her mouth was dry and tasted of old rope. She ran her tongue over her lips, trying to produce saliva. For a moment she could hardly swallow. She must have a can of orange juice.

The all-night garage had a dispensing machine with the usual selection of tea, coffee, chocolate, soup, fizzy orange. She put in coins and selected the cold drink. A plastic beaker appeared, full of steaming brown coloured coffee. She put the drink on the top of the machine, her hand unsteady, and tried again. She watched the dispenser give her another coffee. Was she pressing the wrong buttons?

'This is ridiculous,' she said.

She was running out of coins. There was no one around to help. She began to panic. There was a hard lump in her throat. She was gasping for a drink. Then it was too late. She grasped the plastic cup and drank coffee. It burned her throat but she didn't care. Then she drank the second one and, more calmly, put in her last coins for a third.

The caffeine surged through her veins, giddily. A young man in overalls appeared from the back of the garage.

'Lovely coffee,' she said, giving him a shaky but beaming smile.

Adrenalin was pumping round her body. She drove the Mercedes at speed. Twice she scraped a kerb. She drove without thought. She had a feeling that she was escaping from the heat. That was all she could think about.

She reached the long drive to the castle. Plas Glwydan loomed ahead, a once palatial Tudor residence and fortress, now on the downward slide into obscurity. The curtain walls and towers pulled down by villagers for their stone, the postern gate and the gatehouse marked by heavy iron gates. The earthworks on which an earlier twelfth-century castle had been built had sunk into oblivion. But Gina knew it was still there. She felt acutely aware of the past as if she had once lived and breathed the same air.

The gates were half open. Barry kept them locked unless he was expecting someone. She drove in slowly, parked on the apron of gravel some distance from the front door.

It was a dream, unreal. Nothing she touched had any substance. She pushed open the creaking front door and went into the gloomy hall. Nothing had changed, the heavy furniture coated in more dust, the cracked sedan chair, the old carved chest. The air was stale as if it was a long time since a window was opened or anyone walked the corridors.

She did not feel afraid, but she didn't know why she was there. A feeling warned her to leave but she ignored it, with an aura of calmness that was difficult to dislodge.

'Hello...' she said.

They carried her out on a pallet, gently so that any jolting would not distress her sore body. Her head rested on a pillow filled with whole feathers. She was too weak to bear the heavy weight of a gown, so they had wrapped her in a light robe, careful not to touch the stick-thin arms that were wracked with pain.

The fading afternoon sun was warm to her

pale skin and she blinked against the rays that still streamed through the branches to the walled garden. Her mind drifted in and out of consciousness. She remembered another sunlit afternoon by a stream and wished she had not run away. She pulled other memories from the corners of her mind and tears gathered in her eyes.

Old Moll dabbed fragrant rosewater on the girl's mouth for her lips were dried up and split and acid tasting. She tried to thank the old woman but the effort was too much.

'Let the child sleep. Perhaps the peacefulness of the gardens will heal her.'

She slept for a while in the silence that Will had left behind. Then she was aware of someone looking down at her. It was a young boy of about eight or nine, someone new to work in the grounds. He held a marigold in his hand and hesitating, placed it between her bone-white fingers. Its fragile petals were already closing.

'Will,' she breathed...

Thirty

She went up the staircase, trailing her hand in the dust. The silence was a dying sound, the language of air, of echoes, of forgotten memories. She thought she heard light footsteps running the length of the long gallery, but there was no long gallery at Plas Glwydan. It had long gone.

She became aware of a rim of light from a bedroom at the end of the corridor. The thin beam pierced the darkness like a laser. She moved towards it cautiously.

The door was flung open and the light momentarily blinded her. Barry stood in silhouette, one arm resting on the door frame as if to stop her going further.

'Hello, Gina. I thought you'd be coming soon. It was a matter of waiting for the right time.'

'You're expecting me?'

'Oh yes,' he laughed, pleased with himself. 'I programmed you to come. I'm quite surprised at myself really. It was a clever move and, as it turns out, a sensible forethought in case things went wrong.'

'I don't understand.'

He smoothed back his hair. 'You and your friend, Mark Trenchard, ruined our plan with your interference, but did you really think we'd leave it at that? It would have been a bit stupid to put all our eggs in one basket, even cracked ones like you. Everyone realizes you're mentally ill now. Didn't you see what those police officers thought of your wild goose story? They weren't fooled.'

Gina shook her head. 'That's not true. It's a lie. They believed me.'

'They'll be very sure quite soon. No one knows what you'll do next. Come in, excuse the mess. I've been camping out in one room. Easier on my own.'

'Where's Lindsie?'

'Poor Lindsie. She's not at all well. All your fault if she loses the baby. I've sent her to the coast, rented a small cottage. The dogs have gone as well. She likes it by the sea. I've been waiting here for you.'

'How did you know I would come?' Her voice was thick, her throat parched. She was suffocating, longing desperately for a drink.

'Because I programmed you to come. Earlier I put the instruction in your mind to come down to Plas Glwydan, to be extremely thirsty, to do whatever I said, just for a drink. The trigger was easy to implant, perfect and so clever. If someone tried to tamper with your hypnotic state, to dehypnotize you in other words, then you would immediately follow these new instructions. You didn't know about that, did you?'

'The time bomb...' she whispered.

'That's it. A time bomb in your head and it's about to go off. I've been very busy recently. I've filled all these bedrooms with that dreadful Victorian furniture. The pieces are insured as valuable antiques. It should burn well and I'll collect a tidy sum. Enough money to disappear with before the trial. No one knows you're here. They'll find your pathetic remains among the burnt rubble.' He put a box of matches in her hand. 'You know how bad our electrics are. They could spark off a fire any time. The wiring is a disgrace. Would you like a drink, my dear?'

'Yes, please. A drink of water.'

'Of course. Light a match for me, Gina, and drop it on the bed. I was making coffee when you came in.'

The match flared as she struck it, burning her fingers. She dropped it awkwardly and it rolled away on the floor. She trod on it immediately.

'Now, now, Gina. That's not what I said. Here's a drink. Would you like this drink? Take it.'

She took the mug and gulped a mouthful then spat it out. It was strong black coffee. She choked in despair. Her throat was parched. The room was full of mirrors hanging from every wall. Barry had moved all the mirrors in the castle into that one room, ready for her.

'I won't give in to you,' said Gina, refusing to look at the mirrors. 'You'll go to prison when your trial comes up. You'll be convicted of killing Timothy. You're guilty. Guilty as hell.'

'What a little innocent you are,' Barry said with a malicious smile. 'Who brought Timothy down to Plas Glwydan in her car the day before the wedding? It was that Friday you can't remember. Who helped us carry the poor young man indoors when he passed out? I've still got your silver flask loaded with pills. And who gave us her blue scarf to tie up his feet when he became violent?'

Gina staggered back. The shock was unbearable. It couldn't be true. She wouldn't have done that.

'I don't believe you,' she said.

'Well, you'll never really know, will you?' said Barry. 'I should have taken photographs. But you did look very smart, as always. Lindsie particularly admired your velvet suit. Pity, it got some mud on the sleeve.'

Things began to spin round her as his words hit home. Her heart was fluttering like an injured bird. Surely she could not have been part of the plan to kill Timothy? She could never live with that knowledge.

'Ever checked the mileage on your Mercedes? It ought to be easy enough to see if there's three hundred plus miles unaccounted for on the clock.'

'I'm not listening to another word of these lies.'

'Such a willing accomplice. But you won't go, Gina, because you're too thirsty,' he said. 'Light a match and you can have this glass of water. You can see it's water. Clear mineral water. Drop a lighted match on the bed. Over here, good girl ... like this. Such pretty flames. You're always cold, you'll like the heat.'

She watched the tiny flames, her throat as dry as a desert. Gina went for the glass but Barry backed away, then threw it to the other side of the room.

The sound of the glass shattering seemed to jolt her senses. What was she doing here? The flames were licking like tongues, flickering, racing along the edge of the bedspread and down the valance towards the carpet. She watched in horror, turned and ran towards the door.

The synthetic carpet went up with a roar into a melting inferno. There was a back-draught of flame with Barry on the wrong side of it. The heat was intense. Through the haze she saw Barry shielding his face, making for the window. It was the wrong thing to do. He wrestled with the catch. The window had not been opened in years and the catch was rusted solid.

Gina took advantage of those extra seconds, began hurrying along the corridor away from the flames licking the dry furniture, catching alight, crackling and hissing. The fire spread. She heard Barry running after her, calling to her, but she didn't stop. She stumbled down the stairs, slipping and sliding, clinging to the balustrade.

She looked up and saw Barry standing at the top of the stairs, a mocking look on his face. He would never let her go. She stood between him and all he wanted.

A second figure appeared behind him. Gina caught her breath as she recognized the coppery curls. Lindsie was holding the heavy brass lamp which always stood at the top of the stairs. She looked like a statue.

Flames were racing along the wall, devouring tapestries and tattered flags which Gina had never noticed in the gloom. Lindsie was lit by the harsh, crackling light, sharpening the features of her face.

'No, Lindsie. Don't!' Gina shouted as she saw Lindsie lift the lamp high and bring it down on Barry's head. She heard the crack. For a second he looked astonished, then crumpled on to the banisters. With a slow, rolling motion, his body folded over the rail and came tumbling down into the hall. He fell, landing on the carved chest, sprawled like a puppet.

'Lindsie, come down. The fire's spreading. You've got to get out.'

Lindsie stood, frozen, staring at Barry's body. She seemed unaware of the flames licking round her. Gina ran up the stairs toward the wall of heat and grabbed her cousin's arm. She tugged and pulled her towards the stairs.

'Come on, Lindsie. We've got to get out. Think of the baby.'

Lindsie stumbled after her, moving like an automaton. She was distracted, incoherent, wild-eyed, grunting like a pig.

'I had to do it, don't you see? I couldn't let it go on. Barry was evil and I didn't know how to stop it. Supposing my baby is evil, too. What shall I do?'

Burning shreds were falling around them as they reached the hall. Lindsie stopped, unaware of the hot debris and the danger. She shook her head.

'I've always hated you, you know,' said Lindsie, looking at Gina with a curious expression. 'My mother killed herself because she loved your father, the famous Royce Quentin. It was his fault. He refused her because of you. He wouldn't leave you, spoilt little rich girl. You didn't even take his name. Grandfather was richer. You ruined my life and I swore one day I would ruin yours.'

'You've had a damned good try, now for heaven's sake, get outside before we both perish.' Gina pushed Lindsie out into the porch. 'I want to know one thing. Did you shut me in the attic when I was a little girl?'

Lindsie grinned. 'Sure, what a lark. That scared you all right, didn't it? You were looking through your mother's dresses. My mother was drowned and dead. I shut you in and went straight out. Served you right, you and your posh Conway name. Load of old rubbish.'

'And what else did you do? My sweet, smiling cousin Lindsie. Tell me.'

'Dozens of things. I took your diamond bracelet, your blue scarf, and years ago, some porcelain birds to sell. It was a doddle. You never noticed.'

'The little wren?'

'Charity girl, that's what I always was.'

'Get outside before I change my mind about saving you,' Gina coughed. The hall was filling with smoke.

The telephone was working. It had been reconnected. Gina dialled 999, her fingers trembling.

'Fire, fire,' she croaked, thick smoke drifting down the stairs like an invasion of black death. 'The castle ... Plas Glwydan. Come quickly.'

She pushed open the heavy door and staggered out, gulping in fresh air. Dawn was glowing in the sky like a second fire. By now the whole of the first floor of the castle was alight, each window glowing orange. Heat splintered the glass, explosion after explosion, and flames shot out from the broken windows. The tall Elizabethan chimneys stood darkly stark against the raging inferno.

Gina huddled under a sweeping oak tree, watching the fire. Lindsie had disappeared. She was too tired to care about looking for her. The last hours were becoming clear to her. She remembered leaving Cranbourne Square, consumed by thirst. She heard the sirens of the fire appliances arriving and skidding to a halt in the driveway. Soon their powerful hoses were directing lake water on to the blaze, but they were too late to save the east wing.

One of the firemen put his jacket round her. Someone gave her a mug of tea, and she drank it gratefully.

She didn't know how long it was before she heard the familiar throb of the Range Rover engine over the noise of the firemen and walkie-talkies and crashing timbers. A door slammed. Footsteps hurried over.

'I knew you had come here. There was only one person, Barry, who could make you do something so ridiculous in the middle of the night. Gina, are you all right?' Mark held her close and she felt his heart pounding. She clung to him, comforted by his familiar bulk.

'Barry tried to kill me. He'd planned for me to start a fire, die in it, then he'd collect the insurance. But Lindsie killed him. She hit him with a l-lamp and he fell down the stairs. He's still in there.' She began to cry.

'A fire is a clean end,' he said. 'You're rid of the castle and your cousin.'

'It doesn't seem finished,' she said, unable to explain her feelings. 'Lindsie is still around somewhere. She hates me, has always hated me. Perhaps she's waiting to kill me next.'

'Forget her. You're safe with me.'

Gina tried to calm herself. 'I'd like to walk round once more when it's light. Take a last look.'

The acrid air was full of the fumes of the dead fire. Plas Glwydan appeared before them, a shamble of blackened beams and fallen masonry. The windows were gaping holes where the heat had shattered the glass. The invasive creeper had withered in the flames and clung like a grey cobweb to the standing walls, a mourning drape.

The east wing was devastated. It was cooling enough for men to start pulling down dangerous flooring, piling debris up in the grounds in dismal heaps of burnt timber and furniture.

Mark and Gina walked the grounds, hand in hand, viewing the sad scene in silence.

'No question of repairing the castle now,' said Mark. 'One way of getting rid of the dry rot.'

'Will I be charged?'

'How do we know if it was your match or his that started the fire? You weren't responsible for your actions. It was Barry's idea, he was using you as the instrument. I don't think you'll be held responsible.'

'Do you think he can still control me, even if he is dead?'

'Most unlikely. The hypnotic control should vanish with his death. Do you want to test it out?'

'No way. Supposing there's another time bomb in my head? Supposing Barry planted more instructions? Maybe something will snap on my birthday, or at Christmas, and I'll suddenly grab a knife and try to stab you.'

'What a cracker,' said Mark. 'I shall have to watch you like a hawk. Massacre down on the farm.'

'It's not funny,' she wailed.

'I can't give you an answer. And you can't put yourself in a straitjacket. They would have won then.'

In time, the creeper would grow again and hide the ugly scars. The castle would become a picturesque ruin, a favourite spot for picnicking families and ramblers. A setting for local pageants, a camping site for cubs and scouts. But Gina would never be sure if she was free.

They wandered over to a growing pile of burnt timbers and debris from the castle, the grey and blackened rubble of household goods. Gina recognized a rag of brocade curtain, a sodden lump of pink eiderdown. Some of the wood was still smouldering.

A youth came over with a lumbering wheelbarrow of rubble and tipped it on to the pile. Ash flew in all directions, settling on the grass and bushes like second-hand snow.

Gina was about to turn away from the depressing sight when something caught her eye. She moved closer to the pile and looked carefully at the charred edge of a piece of canvas.

Suddenly her heart was racing, her throat constricted. She lifted off bits of wood and fragments of cloth with trembling fingers, bending as the canvas slithered down the pile. She picked off the last bits and gently blew at the film of ash.

It was a portrait of a girl. The frame was almost burnt to a cinder and the painting was badly scorched, the varnish cracked into a mosaic of a thousand veins. Sparks had pitted the canvas, eating the oil, giving the girl's skin pockmarks that had not been there in real life.

It was a young girl, gazing at her now from the ravages of the fire: a pale, gentle face with limpid pools of green eyes, a long nose and sweet, curving mouth that had not properly learned how to smile. Gina stared at the portrait, exploring the features, face to face with the origin of her nightmare.

Mark was beside her, looking down at the scorched canvas. He touched her arm, to show that he was there.

'Mark, look! This is the girl ... in the portrait,' said Gina, sitting back, her voice hushed with excitement. 'The girl that I saw in the mirror at Erddig. I know it is, everything is exactly the same as I saw her, in every detail. See the clothes as I described them. What does it mean? Did she really exist after all?'

'It was a mirror at Erddig. Perhaps you saw this portrait in the castle when you were wandering about and it made an impression.'

Gina looked deeply into the girl's face, blowing gently at the film of ash. There was a gold chain and pearl drop around the girl's throat, glimmering.

'I could never be afraid of this sweet girl,' she said at last. 'Look at her eyes, so young and innocent, a little haughty. I bet she had courage and spirit. I wonder what happened to her. I'd love to know.'

Gina brushed away some charred fragments of wood, part of the frame, and a tiny brass nameplate appeared beneath her fingers. She peered closer, the strangest feeling of discovery sweeping through her body, tingling.

'Georgina Fairweather,' she breathed, reading the engraved italic script. '1458–1472. My name. And she had my name, Mark. I can't believe it ... She has my name.'

Gina sat back on her heels, gazing at the girl who had borne the same name so many centuries before. It couldn't be a coincidence. She remembered a fleeting moment when she had felt so close to the girl in the mirror. She had not mentioned it to anyone because it seemed bizarre. Could it be that for one moment, amid all that fear and horror, this young and sweet-faced girl had tried to get through to her, spanning the barrier of time? Perhaps with a message, a warning, trying to save her?

'Georgina Fairweather is an ancestor of mine. She died when she was fourteen,' said Gina. 'It's so sad.'

'No more than a child.'

'I've nothing to fear from this Georgina. I think she was trying to help me. Sometimes I smelled herbs as if she was around. I think she liked honey and sweetmeats. I longed for honey, tasted it, as if she was here.'

'And ginger? Let's go now, Gina. There's nothing more we can do here. Do you want to look for Lindsie?'

'No, let her go back to her cottage by the sea. There's the baby to think about. Perhaps it isn't Barry's.'

He helped her to her feet, his eyes tender with concern. He ruffled her hair as she brushed the ash and charcoal splinters from the knees of her jeans. She could not go without the portrait. She could not leave Georgina Fairweather behind to be added to the bonfire of rubbish which the workmen would surely light soon.

'Do you think I could keep the picture?' she asked Mark. 'I don't want to leave her here. I want Georgina Fairweather's portrait. It seems unkind and uncaring to abandon her here, in all this mess.'

'But she would remind you of the horror, something you want to forget.'

'No, I don't think so. She would never hurt me.'

They heard a crash as another load of debris was tipped on to the pile. A charred newel post slipped and fell on to the painting and in an instant it disintegrated into flying fragments, a small cloud of ash and charred canvas blurring a last fleeting view of the young girl's face. Gina felt a stab of pain as the portrait fell apart.

The youth from the village grinned at them as he reversed the barrow. 'What a mess.'

The sun slid through a break in the clouds and its rays bathed the sandstone in a kind, softening light. Gina caught sight of glitter at her feet. She bent down swiftly and picked it up. It was the small brass nameplate from the portrait. She held it in the palm of her hand, pressing the edge into her flesh. It was still warm as if Georgina had breathed on it.

'At least I'll have this nameplate. A remembrance of a young girl who hardly lived at all. Bright treasure from a child. Georgina will watch out for me. There's no need now to be afraid of time bombs in my head. I've a guardian angel.'

'And you will have me. Are you ready to go?' asked Mark, holding out his hand. Gina lost her place in the conversation. It was a heady feeling.

'Ready to go,' she said.